AUTUMN

BOOK ONE: THE GUARDIANS OF MAGIC SERIES

MELISSA NASH

RIVERSONG BOOKS

An Imprint of Sulis International Press
Los Angeles | London

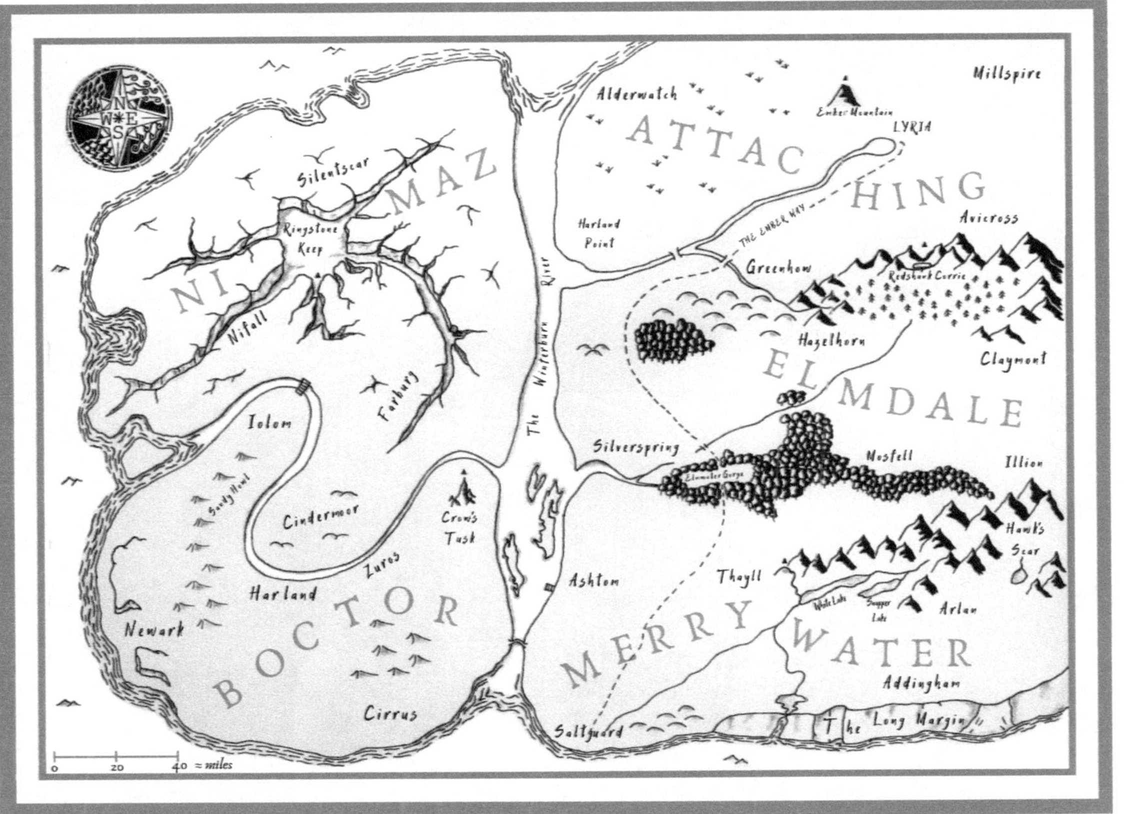

Millspire
Alderwatch
Ember Mountain
LYRIA
ATTAC
HING
Harland Point
THE EMBER WAY
Avicross
Greenhow
Redshank Currie
Hazelhorn
Claymont
ELMDALE
Silverspring
Elmwater Gorge
Mosfell
Illion
Hawk's Scar
Thayll
White Lake
Supper Lake
Arlan
Ashton
MERRY
WATER
Addingham
Saltguard
The Long Margin
The Winterburn River
NI
MAZ
Silentscar
Ringstone Keep
Nifall
Forburg
Iolam
Sandy Howl
Cindermoor
Crow's Tusk
Zuros
Harland
Newark
BOCTOR
Cirrus
N
W
E
S
0   20   40 ≈ miles

CONTENTS

For my Granma

Prologue
A Patrol

~Annah~

Ewan lifted the final piece of light armour bearing the King's insignia from his chair and strapped the shoulder piece on top of the rest. Annah shifted restlessly from where she sat on the bed, as he added his sword to the finished ensemble.

"I don't think you should go," she said, before she could stop herself.

"Annah," he said softly, "leading patrols is my job. I'm the Captain of the King's guard. I can't ask the rest of the men to leave without me."

"Even if others are not returning from their patrols?"

"Especially then," Ewan said, "we need to find out the reason why."

"I didn't expect to be able to talk you out of it." Annah sighed. "In that case, then I'm coming with you."

"You can't. I won't risk both of us. Not anymore."

"I won't wait here to see if you make it back or not." Annah's eyes flashed. "I'm not prepared to risk that either. You know as well as I do that with me there, you stand a much better chance. I can deal with anything we encounter out there."

"We have to think of our son now," Ewan said, "the worst-case scenario is worth thinking about, things do go wrong on these patrols. It's foolish to send a mother and a father out on an expedition together."

"It's foolish to let you needlessly put yourself in danger when I can protect you," Annah said, "that way we will both make it back here."

"I can protect myself."

"Not against everything. The soldiers that were sent out before you could protect themselves as well and yet they're still missing. You can defend yourselves against enemies armed with swords, but what about ones that fight with something else?"

Ewan fell silent and regarded her attentively.

"You think there is something more dangerous out there?"

Annah shifted on the bed. "I don't know. All I know is that if that is the case, I would never forgive myself if I wasn't there to assist you. You're the best fighter in the Citadel, and we can take on almost anything, but only as long as we're together."

"I won't ignore what you're saying. I have a bad feeling as well that there is more to this too, but I don't want to risk losing our family to solve the matter."

"It might not just be our family at risk, but everyone's if there is something out there rising up against the King. It's not just your job to protect the country from threats like this, remember it was mine once too."

"All right, you can accompany me," Ewan said, "but we have to leave soon."

"I'll be ready," Annah promised him.

A patrol of ten soldiers set out on horseback from under the city gates just a few hours later. As they passed beyond the wall, Annah looked back to see the King leaning upon the battlements, and beside him, a small boy with inky black hair stood on his tiptœs to catch a glimpse of his parents, as they rode out on to the plains beyond.

Suddenly doubting if she was making the right decision, Annah spurred her horse to catch up with Ewan and forced herself to focus on the task ahead instead. Soon, the sprawling city was left far behind them and nothing, but open ground fell underneath their horses' hooves for miles.

Ewan directed the patrol to the location of known encampments used by the King's soldiers, and they arrived at one of them that evening. The ground was littered with half-concealed remains of a recent campfire, and Ewan checked the surrounding area for signs of any hidden messages or caches left behind by a previous patrol. Finding nothing, they set up a watch for the night and pressed on early the next morning.

Eventually, they came to a river, but none of the party seemed willing to cross, not because the river was wide and fast flowing but because no report had come back from any patrol that had journeyed across to the other side. Ewan slithered down the bank to uncover a dwindling selection of rowing boats placed there for patrols to use, and with a new layer of unease, the soldiers left their horses to clamber into two of them and carefully make their way across to the far bank.

They crossed in the middle of the night, as the moon was high in the sky and the water of the river was dappled in silver around them. The wreck of another boat already awaited them on the other side, its oars long since washed away downstream. Annah climbed out beside Ewan, and they scrambled to the top of the embankment together, scouting out the way ahead, as the other soldiers tied off the boats.

Annah pressed herself flat against the uncomfortable stony bank and peered into the wilderness ahead. There was little to be seen in the darkness, but Annah was not searching using her eyes. She glanced sideways at Ewan, despite the circumstances, enjoying the fact that they were out on the open road together again.

"Do you think anything is out there?" Ewan mumbled to her.

"It looks clear," Annah answered, "but I still think we should be cautious."

Ewan softly whistled over his shoulder, and the patrol rose over the top of the bank together. They spread out across the rocky ground beside the river with Annah and Ewan directing the way, three soldiers watching the rear, two more on the left and right flanks and the final one in the centre of the formation.

Annah saw nothing beyond five feet in front of her in any direction, including in the sky above. Around her, the land was laid bare, as though someone had stripped it away in anger. Any tree or bush that tried to grow since had been cut down or withered over time.

Picking up the pace, Annah and Ewan strode on. While Ewan focused on tracking down any sign that a patrol had passed this way before them, Annah was concentrating on not being taken by surprise themselves. The moonlight provided him with enough light to track by, but it worried Annah that they were so visible themselves. Whether it was part of her imagination or not, she believed that somewhere ahead of her, there were noises in the night. Whenever she halted, they stopped, but as soon as she moved on again, they began once more. Finally, she felt like she had to say something.

"I think we should stop," Annah said, "I get the feeling that something is tracking us."

"From which direction?"

"In front of us."

"I don't see anything."

"Neither do I, but I still think there's something there."

"Annah, I can't halt the patrol for no reason."

"Wait." Annah grabbed hold of Ewan's arm. "They're behind us."

"How can they be behind us? You just said there was something ahead."

He drew his sword as they both felt a huge rush of wind at their backs, and turning, Annah saw that all three guards at the rear had disappeared.

"To me!" Ewan called out to the patrol.

Seeing what had happened to the others, the remaining soldiers drew their weapons and hurried back towards the group. Two of them did not make it, as Annah felt the gust of wind again and one was taken simultaneously into the darkness from the right and left of the patrol. She scanned around furiously for the source of the attacks and began to curse that it was so dark. The moonlight illuminated nothing, and their enemy clearly did not require it to see by.

Out of nowhere, something lanced across her shoulders, and she ducked just in time to feel the end of her hair become entangled in something sharp before she was wrenched free and thrown across the ground by the force of the attack. From the ground, she watched Ewan swing out with his sword against a dark shape, as another soldier behind him was simultaneously taken into the night.

Before Annah could attempt to get back on her feet, the moon above her disappeared from sight as two black silhouettes smothered her, enveloping her completely in darkness. In the same instant, she felt something blunt and heavy come into contact with her head, and that was the last thing she remembered.

CHAPTER 1
THE CARNIVAL

Sara woke early one morning to see a glimmer of sunlight filtering in through the open window of her room. A soft, cool breeze wafted gently through the air and it was just chilly enough to wake her up completely. As it blew into the room, it mingled with the scent of lavender originating from a cutting above her bed.

She got up and wrapped a warm blanket around her shoulders before wandering over to close the window on the opposite side of the room. Out of the corner of her eye, she spotted a blackbird perched on the window ledge and halted. The floorboard beneath her feet creaked and startled the bird which darted off into the sunrise, twittering away to a second bird that swooped up to join its companion. Together they danced off into the sky towards the forest.

Sara watched them disappear over the horizon where dark oak trees thronged high above the village borders. A determined-looking rabble of grim-faced, steely eyed woodcutters were marching up the grassy bank with axes resting over their shoulders. They hiked towards the outer boundary of the forest, following the river, and Sara saw the sunlight glint off their sharp blades. She traced the flow of the water back with her eye as it gently meandered down into the village below her house on the hill, gurgling under the bridge. The Spring River then ran off into the distance to join other tributaries of the vast main Winterburn River, miles off to the west, leaving her village of Silverspring far behind.

An overly large cockerel occupying the roof of a nearby farm abruptly interrupted the calm tranquillity of the dawn, proclaiming the start of the day for everybody to hear. The signal was repeated twice more by the bird, but the third time it was replaced by an ear-splitting horn, which resonated out and reverberated around the valley. Highly doubting that this had come from the rooster, Sara repressed a jump and scanned around quickly for the source of the noise.

A moment later she located its origin, emanating from a large party of bright figures descending on the valley from the north. They had begun to trail towards Silverspring and were heading for the village. Early dawn sunlight illuminated banners of red and gold from the borders of their group. But more interestingly, it also reflected off polished silver plates of armour worn by a select few members on the edges of the company. She could even faintly hear the jingle of bells and the accompaniment of drums.

Curiosity aroused, Sara briefly ran a comb through her brown-black hair and splashed her face in the small bowl by her bed. Glancing at her appearance in the faded mirror and the green eyes reflected at her, she was satisfied with it, and snatched a brown hooded cape from the end of the bed before sliding around the door, shutting it from behind with a hollow thud.

"Morning," a figure said over her shoulder. Her mother's voice rang out from the table as Sara flew by.

"We've got guests from the north," Sara informed her.

"Yes, I heard," Astrid replied, "wait a moment, and I'll join you."

Sara stood by the door impatiently, tapping her foot as her mother gathered her boots and cloak. Sara's mother was the local healer, but her swiftness at healing did not reflect her speed at getting ready. She was so infuriatingly slow that in the end, Sara had to drag her out the door, regardless of whether she had remembered her scarf or not.

"Sara. Just because you came of age last month does not mean you have the right to boss me around in any way you see fit."

"Come on!"

Her mother heaved a sigh of surrender and broke into a jog behind her as they made their way down the hill slope to the village. Sturdy houses loomed before them as they approached. Each was compact and designed to be resistant to the river water, constructed from stone, topped off with a neatly thatched roof and set far back from the floodplain. A churning water wheel rotated rhythmically on the house beside the bridge, and the water splashed back into the river noisily.

"Ah, Astrid!" an old man heralded her mother with a friendly grin on his face as they reached the bottom of the hill, "will my magical ointment be ready by tomorrow?"

"Yes, I'll come and deliver it in the morning!" she called back over her shoulder to the man, who tipped his hat in thanks.

Her mother had earned a reputation for being able to find a cure for almost any ailment. When Sara was younger, she had been fascinated by the skills her mother possessed. As she grew older, Astrid had taught her about different herbs and how to heal, but some of the things she did with healing Sara never thought she would be able to understand. Magic seemed like as good a description as any for it, if only such a thing existed, and naturally, Sara had grown up very healthy as a child.

Crossing the bridge over the stream in the centre of the village, they walked swiftly past the abandoned shops and houses to reach the far end of Silverspring. The town stood completely deserted since everybody else had had the same idea as Sara and Astrid. A small crowd of equally interested residents accumulated beside them as the village strolled forward to investigate the newcomers to their small community.

Open fields stretched out to the horizon, broken by green hills and a few beech coppices, but marching down from between the two hills nearest the village was a contrasting snake of gold and red. The group of travellers reached the fields just on the border of their settlement and halted there. Red banners fluttered gently in the morning breeze, and horses whinnied in the bright air.

Sara glanced at a board to her left and a brown poster that was crinkling at the edges. On the parchment was advertised the coming of the Carnival of Games to Elmdale. The notice depicted a painted troop of red and golden clad figures performing various athletics, with twisting flames curling at the edges and brightly coloured silken fabrics swirling all around. The Carnival came to Silverspring at the end of every summer to celebrate the changing of the seasons.

Sara and Astrid looked out again. The first travellers had begun to set up tents in the fields near to the village. Bright red tents were pitched, emblazoned with orange flags and golden shimmering designs that sparkled and blinded, even at a long distance. The Carnival had come down from Attaching, the region to the north, their banner decorated with a fiery wolf. The contrasting colours of these new arrivals transformed the once green fields, and as the sun rose, dotted around the tents and tacked up on posts, application forms for entering the competitions were slowly being laid out.

As the entire village appeared to have emerged onto the field, by midday the lists had almost filled up, with some people's names being signed twice, to be sure they would be able to compete. Astrid cast a glance over the entries for the healing competition and the prize of a leather-bound ingredients pouch and 100 golden pennies, before finally adding her name to the list.

Sara looked at the different competitions, but nothing caught her eye. She kept returning to the form for a riding competition entitled, 'The Quest to find the Golden Star', but all of a sudden a tall, surly man rather rudely whipped it out from under her gaze.

"Not for young girls, this one." He snarled and quickly scratched his name at the bottom of the long list before taking it away with him and handing it to a man dressed in burnished armour, half concealed by a red cloak. This man resembled one of the King's senior soldiers. Sara blinked in surprise. What were they doing at the Carnival? Her anger faded to curiosity as she took a second closer look and noticed a long, thin scar running from above his right eyebrow to the tip of his ear. Sara winced slightly, that scar looked as though it had been freshly cut.

"Sara, come over here!"

She hastily scurried away from the soldier as he smoothly whipped his cloak back down to conceal the steel plate beneath.

"Look," Astrid said, "horseback skills, men and women. You could enter."

"Hey," she began, unable to take her eyes away from the man, "have you seen...?"

"The soldiers?" Astrid raised an eyebrow. "Yes, it is strange. The Carnival has never needed protection before. I want to get another look, take your time over that form."

Sara took it from her and spent as long as it felt reasonable to read it through and add her name to the end. A horn blasted out nearby, and she jumped, ruining the last letter of her name in the process. Then a steady roll of drums boomed out with an almost warlike chant. The soldier departed swiftly towards the centre of the village, and the uneasy atmosphere faded with him.

"I wonder what that meant?" Sara said.

"Why don't we find out?"

Astrid set off at a distance, keeping her eyes fixed on the soldier. They crossed back over the small stone bridge that ran above the fast-flowing water and found the main stage of the Carnival. A circular games arena was undergoing hasty construction, and a large crowd had gathered around a raised podium where a tall man dressed in a deep red travelling cloak stood proudly.

Two more soldiers flanked him on either side. Each was wearing a red cloth to mask their face, leaving only their eyes visible. Both rested a hand on the hilt of their sword and scanned the crowd continuously, with the attentiveness of a hawk hunting for prey. Five more soldiers were patrolling at the back of the gathering. Sara met the gaze of a soldier on the left, and he glared back at her accusingly. She stared back at him for a moment until she felt her arm grabbed roughly, and she was steered deeper into the heart of the crowd.

"Keep your head down," Astrid hissed, "I do not like the expression in their eyes. Something dœsn't feel right here."

Alarmed, Sara stared at her mother. She could not remember ever seeing her so agitated before.

"Why?" Sara asked, "why are these soldiers so suspicious? Why are they even here? The Carnival is supposed to be a fun competition."

"Glad I'm not the only one to think something is wrong," a low voice said.

Astrid turned, one hand reaching out instinctively towards Sara but she stopped when she noticed who was standing there.

"Stephan!" Astrid almost managed to mask the relief in her voice.

The boy that Sara had known almost since she could walk stood across from them, with a wry look in his eyes.

"Did you think I was a soldier?"

Neither Sara nor Astrid answered him.

"They've stirred up things a bit, haven't they?" his expression turned solemn, "suspicion and soldiers, the village is full of it, and they've only been here a few hours."

"I wonder what's different this year?" Sara asked.

"They seem to be searching for something. Maybe the soldiers think there is something here we need protecting from."

"Like what?" Sara raised an eyebrow.

"These are the King's senior soldiers. They don't leave the city for anything less than serious."

"It's a long road from Attaching to here," Astrid said, "perhaps it is not us they are protecting, but the Carnival members."

"You think something might have happened to them on the way?" Stephan asked.

"One of the soldiers I saw looked like he had been in a fight recently," Sara said.

"If that's the case, I hope they haven't brought it here with them," Astrid said.

Sara stared at Astrid, suddenly feeling apprehensive, before switching her gaze to the distant horizon. Part of her half expected to see a giant black shape charging over the hill towards them, but the day was warm and bright. Nothing broke the line of blue, not even a cloud.

"Sorry I've got to go. I'll come by tomorrow," Stephan apologised, before saying goodbye and disappearing back into the crowd.

Sara watched him go with a growing sense of unease in her stomach. At the limit of her hearing, the Carnival member on the stand was explaining each of the contests and the rules of the Games, but to Sara, it only resembled a buzz of meaningless noise.

"...Twenty separate contests this year, ranging from healing to archery and fantastic prizes for the winners of each event. The regional champions will join others from across Meteorath for the chance to compete in Lyria before the King himself..."

"Come on, let's go. We don't need to hear this," Astrid said, leading Sara away from the crowd.

Sara was lost in thought as she walked away. She hardly noticed where she was going and barged into somebody going the other way, turning to apologise but the man had already gone. Her eyes flickered upward for a second, and she noticed that the soldier on the left of the podium had vanished. Sara dropped her gaze and hurried back through the streets, back home.

When they arrived back, her mother wasn't herself. Astrid was on edge and seemed to react to the smallest thing. She also was reluctant to confide in Sara, which was unusual. So finally, Sara gave up asking and wandered upstairs, leaving her mother alone.

The competitions began the next day. Astrid left early in the morning to compete in the healing, but Sara decided to stay away from the Carnival. Instead, she got dressed in her riding gear and padded coat to head out and find her horse, Arrow. Sara hesitated for a moment by the door and quickly grabbed a small hunting knife in a sheath from the rack by the door, sliding the blade down inside her boot. She heard the clatter of hooves behind her and saw Stephan ride up towards the house.

"Don't get off." Sara held up a hand to him. "I need to practise for the riding competition tomorrow."

"Then let's go."

They rode around the hills until the full extent of Carnival was spread out below them and Sara immediately noticed something else that was new this year. A broad, wooden lookout post had emerged behind the rows of flame-coloured tents, so it was practically invisible, except up here. The observation post faced back the way the Carnival had come from, and as they watched, two tiny soldiers far off down below took over the watch from their comrades beside them.

"That must be where the soldiers are staying," Sara said.

"All nine of them?" Stephan asked, "that thing could house more than thirty."

"What if there are more who we haven't seen?"

As Sara took in the length of the lookout, she realised just how easy it would be to conceal a large group of soldiers in there without a problem. The more Sara thought about it, the easier it seemed. The men could remain inside so that nobody would be alarmed to see so many of them in the village, but in the event of an emergency, there would be enough present to hold off an attack.

"I suppose you could be right," Stephan said, "the red masks they wear makes it impossible to distinguish one from another. They could easily swap places with without anybody paying much attention to who was who."

"Except for one. The man with the scar on his face, he is distinguishable from the rest."

"Do you think we guessed correctly then? They're watching for something coming from the road?"

"Perhaps. Could it be a wild animal of some sort?"

"There are plenty of wild animals living in the woods of Elmdale, but something like that shouldn't cause the soldiers from Attaching this much concern."

"Something human then," Sara said, thinking back to the soldier's scar. It had looked thin and sharp, so a sword or knife could have easily made it.

"But who would attack the Carnival?" Stephan asked.

Sara fell silent. Silverspring was a village in the region of Elmdale and Elmdale was bordered by Attaching to the north and Merrywater to the south. These three regions lived peacefully together, and the enormous Winterburn River bordered all three on the west. But beyond that was little more than a barren desert wasteland, home to people who were just as unfriendly to any who happened to set foot on their shores. Usually, the two western regions, Boctor and Nimaz, remained isolated from the remaining three. Occasionally attacks and raids were known to occur by people from Boctor and Nimaz, but so little was known about either of the regions, mainly because nobody wished to set foot there.

In significant contrast to the two regions that lay opposite them, grass, rivers, forests and colour blanketed the landscape in Elmdale, Merrywater and Attaching. Boctor used to be the same before it was won over by Nimaz and appeared to have suffered visually from its alliance with the darker region. All Sara knew of Nimaz was that deep ravines cut through it and barely anything but bedrock covered its surface.

Although all five regions together made up the one country of Meteorath, each was separated and cut off from the next by tributaries of the Winterburn River, which carved a natural boundary between each. Between

Attaching, Merrywater and Elmdale, the Winterburn was little more sizable than a stream in most places, but between the western three and the other eastern regions, its broadest width resembled more of a lake. It would take considerable effort for anything to cross into Elmdale from the other side.

"The Carnival travelled down from Attaching," Sara said, "perhaps the danger comes from up there."

"We could go down and ask the organisers of the events?" Stephan said.

For a moment, Sara considered going down to the Carnival and wondered why she felt so uncomfortable with the idea of just talking to the travellers from Attaching. She faltered when an image of the soldier with the searching eyes flashed into her mind, and she hesitated. Sara might be able to recognise that soldier, but she realised with some uncertainty that he might also remember her in return. No matter the colour of his armour, somehow he did not feel like a friend to her.

"Maybe tomorrow," Sara answered.

She turned Arrow and trotted back the way they had come, and Stephan left her to ride down to the centre of Silverspring. The moment she dipped again behind the crest of the hill, she sprang her horse into a canter and headed towards the house.

Sara busied herself for most of the afternoon, but as darkness began to engulf the horizon, she could no longer talk herself out of a new worry that had been growing for the last few hours. Astrid had not yet returned. On any other day, Sara would not have given her absence a second thought, but today Sara found herself beginning to overthink over what might have happened. Astrid had said that she would be back after the competition and that had finished this morning.

Sara made a snap decision and grabbed her cloak from behind the door. Pausing for a second, she hastily constructed a scribbled note and left it on the table in case her mother returned and headed out the door. She half ran down the hill to the outskirts of the village and ducked quickly behind the sidewall of a bakery as she spotted a soldier guarding the central passageway into town.

Nervous that it might be the soldier with the scar, Sara cautiously pulled her hood up to shield her face, before taking a long, winding route through the houses. All was quiet in the street outside Stephan's house, and she could see by the glow from his window that he was in his room. Sara took her favourite route into her friend's house and scrambled up the wall outside, before jumping to the oak tree and grabbing hold of branches that twisted their way towards his open window. Sara leapt silently from the tree into his room and suppressed a laugh as Stephan toppled backwards in surprise.

"Sara!" he exclaimed, before dropping his voice, "use the door, will you? What if one day I have a guest in here?"

Sara raised one eyebrow at him.

"What kind of guest?"

"You know, a girl, or something?"

Sara's raised an eyebrow.

"What? It could happen."

Sara's smile faded. "Stephan, I need your help."

"What's happened?"

"Astrid hasn't come home since she left for the competition. Have you heard anything? Normally I wouldn't worry, but..."

Stephan paused for a moment, thinking.

"Let's go to Hunter's Square. There are celebrations there every night of the Carnival."

"You're suggesting I forget about it and drink?"

"It is the best place in Silverspring to gather information. Most of the people in the village will be there, and someone might have seen her. Come on. I'll grab my coat."

As they left Stephan's house, it was almost entirely dark, except for the street heading towards the centre of the village which remained alive and busy. On the first day of the Carnival, there was an excitement that would only grow over the week. The brown stag carved into the central pole at the centre of Hunter's Square beckoned welcomingly, cast in the warm light of several fires outside. So Sara and Stephan slipped between the multitude of people, to find their way to the centre and the small bar that had been laid out alongside tables of travellers selling their handmade trinkets or local goods from Attaching. Stephan immediately struck up a conversation with the man behind the bar and asked if he had heard any news.

Sara took her drink and looked around the square on the slim chance that Astrid happened to be here as well. Out of nowhere, a stream of fire shot into the air and Sara's eye was drawn, along with many others, towards a duo from the Carnival now wielding a staff, which was alight at both ends, and his partner encircled by a hoop, adorned with six long candles placed at equal intervals around its edge. They began to twirl and dance around a small cleared area of the square, getting seemingly dangerously close to the crowd before retreating to the centre. Amongst the sea of faces in the group were many that Sara recognised, but none were her mother. She spotted Thalia, who had not long since become an apprentice of sorts to Astrid and approached her.

"Thalia!" she called, "did you enter the competition today?"

"Hey, Sara. I did."

"How did you do?"

"Well, I didn't win. Your mother took the first place but honestly, I am almost glad I didn't win."

"What do you mean?"

"All the winners of each competition were taken off to a tent, and they all came back saying that they had been questioned, almost as if the soldiers were trying to learn something from them. A lot have said it wasn't worth the prize to go through that interrogation."

"Do you know what they asked?"

"I have no idea."

"You haven't seen Astrid since, have you?"

"No, sorry. The last time was once she won. I saw being her led away towards the back of the Carnival camp. To be asked the same questions, I would imagine."

"All right, thank you."

Thalia turned back to the friends she was with, and Sara meandered slowly back to Stephan.

"Any luck?" she asked him.

"Not really."

Sara informed him of what she had learned.

"Do you think she's still in the soldiers' camp?" Stephan asked.

Sara thought about what Thalia had said. All the winners of the competitions had found themselves subject to questioning, but the others had returned.

"I don't know what to do. I mean, there is a chance she is at home and safe. Maybe I'm worrying over nothing."

A commotion at the back of the crowd interrupted their conversation as two soldiers bustled their way through into the square. Stephan took hold of Sara's arm and pushed her back into the third line of the crowd, so that they were more concealed from the illumination of the flames. The two fire dancers halted their performance, indignantly gesturing towards the soldiers who now stood in the centre of their arena.

"What is the meaning of this?" the barman asked.

"We are looking for one of your villagers," the soldier said, "the girl belonging to your village healer. Is she here?"

"Why do you want her?"

"We have some questions."

Sara took a step behind the man in the row in front of her, so that she had to peer over his shoulder to maintain a direct line of sight with the soldier. A small discomfort during the movement reminded her of the long hunting knife that she had concealed inside her boot earlier that day. Thalia hesitantly glanced over in her direction, and Sara panicked. Dropping lower to the ground, she dragged Stephan after her as she pushed through the crowd in the opposite direction and into the cover of darkness. The pair stole back to the outskirts of Silverspring, circling the houses to avoid lights and groups of people.

"Sara, why are the soldiers searching for you?" Stephan pulled her to a halt once they were clear of the village.

"I don't know."

"Is there something you're not telling me?"

"No! You know as much as I do."

Stephan's eyes glinted strangely in the moonlight.

"I promise you, I don't know anything," Sara insisted.

"I don't want to let those soldiers get their hands on you. I don't trust them."

"Me neither."

"You shouldn't go back into the village tonight."

"They must still have Astrid," Sara said, looking back, "I can't return to the house. What if there are soldiers there too?"

"Come back with me," Stephan said, "you can camp out at my house. You'll be safe, I promise."

Sara nodded uncertainly and followed Stephan back.

CHAPTER 2
INTO THE WOODS

Sara woke up before Stephan, feeling disorientated for a second before she remembered why she was not in her room. He was lying on the floor below her on a makeshift bed, and he was still dreaming. Sara rolled out of bed, tip-toeing over him. She had spent most of the night before she finally drifted off to sleep, developing a plan of how to find Astrid today.

Sara wandered over to the window to look out at the street below. It was still, with a pale morning mist hanging firmly off the edges of the houses and it was also deserted, which was good to see. She looked back at Stephan, and as if sensing her attention, his eyes opened. A loud trumpet noise erupted outside, and she instinctively turned to look out of the window again as an audible round of cheering began, signalling the start of competition far off in the distance.

"I half expected you to be gone already," she heard Stephan say behind her.

"If you had slept longer, I might have."

"Do you have a plan?"

"Not a good one."

"I'm coming with you."

Sara hesitated for a moment and then nodded.

"I want to check the house first. Just in case I have been worrying about nothing."

They left the house as silently as they could, with hoods pulled up to attempt to remain anonymous. The route to Astrid's house was easy, as the village could be avoided entirely if the right path was known. The pair of them emerged on top of the hill at the back of Astrid's house and sprinted across the grass to the back doorway. Both horses stood in the stable and the house was just as quiet as when Sara had left it the previous day. She ran inside and did a quick search of the rooms for a note, or something that might indicate Astrid had been there, but the house was devoid of clues. With a sigh, Sara turned to Stephan.

"Then she must be with the Carnival," Stephan said.

"Thalia said the soldiers took the winners behind the main tents. We'll start there."

They left the house and took a route around Silverspring towards the field of Carnival tents. As they drew closer, Sara noticed that many of the shelters here had been hastily patched up and repaired. They ducked behind a stack of food crates to avoid a pair of passing soldiers, and Stephan pointed out a sizeable cart nearby decorated by long, deep scrapes down one side. The marks were enormous, more striking than any Sara had seen made by a wolf or bird of prey, and so she darted forward to have a closer look.

"Can I help you?" a voice asked from over her shoulder.

A Carnival woman was standing next to the cart, holding a large wicker basket. Inside the container, Sara could hear the scurrying sound of something unquestionably alive.

"Oh, um," she said, thinking rapidly, "I just was wondering how you got those marks on your cart. They look pretty deep, and I just wondered what had made them. My father fixes all sorts you see. If anything is broken, he can mend it."

Her heart thrummed as she waited for the reply while praying that she didn't sound too nosy. The woman looked at Sara suspiciously, but her eyes kept darting around, and she seemed to be nervous herself.

"Got stuck in a ditch," she said, "must have scraped it on the way out."

"Oh, of course," Sara replied, "unlucky that. Well, sorry to trouble you. I'll be on my way."

She felt the woman's eyes fall darkly on her back as she walked off as quickly as possible to re-join Stephan in the crowd towards the centre of the field.

"Whatever it was that happened, it has scared the people from Attaching," she said.

"I don't understand why they would want to keep hold of Astrid," Stephan said.

"Well, she won the healing contest. Maybe they need a healer for something? Perhaps somebody was injured, somebody important?"

"But then why did they want to find you?"

"I don't know."

Before Stephan could speak again, Sara drew up her hood and walked purposely through the crowd of Carnival applicants, towards the tents of the soldiers at the back of the field. She knew Stephan would still be following her, so she turned her mind instead to how best get her mother back. They reached the far line of tents when suddenly Sara felt Stephan drag her back out of sight.

"What?" she whispered.

"Look." Stephan indicated back the way they had come.

Two soldiers appeared into view on either side of a villager from Silverspring. The man they were escorting looked a little bewildered as to what was going on and to why he was here.

"I don't understand," he said, "I don't see why I have to be taken back here to receive my prize."

Sara ducked lower out of sight beside Stephan until the soldiers had passed them. Silently, she indicated to Stephan that they should follow the trio. Keeping a safe distance, they stalked behind as the soldiers directed the villager further and further away from Silverspring. It was becoming harder to remain undetected themselves, Sara observed, as the Carnival workers thinned out and just the accompanying soldiers remained. Only they would have reason to visit this part of the field. Sara was considering abandoning their trail when the soldiers turned the villager towards a red tent and disappeared inside.

Sara and Stephan crouched behind a nearby tent, in sight of where their target had withdrawn inside. The outpost that they had seen the previous day loomed closer and Sara saw that she had got the scale wrong. The structure was much larger than their original guess, and it made her nervous. There was no other entrance to the outpost except for the guarded front door, and even if she ever made it past that, she had no skills to free her mother, if Astrid was trapped inside. She crouched silently, trying to decide what to do and her hand strayed to the knife concealed in her boot.

Sara's train of thoughts shattered as the soldiers re-emerged from the tent. This time the man from the village was not between them. It was Astrid. Sara felt a rush of relief to see that her mother was here and unharmed until she noticed that Astrid's hands were bound in front of her.

"Sara..." Stephan tried to caution her from doing anything rash.

"What are they doing?" Sara whispered.

"Wait. Maybe we'll find out."

"She's a prisoner," Sara hissed. Not knowing what she was doing, Sara leapt to her feet and ran forwards over the grass.

"Hey!" she cried out.

Sara heard Stephan cry out in dismay behind her. She caught the attention of the soldiers instantly.

"What are you doing here? Leave this area at once."

"Sara?" This time, her mother spoke, surprised to see her daughter there.

"Why are you holding her captive?" Sara heard her voice waver.

"Take her," one soldier said.

Both soldiers moved around so that they were in between mother and daughter. Astrid stepped forward as the first soldier drew his sword. Sara felt her heart race, feeling way out of her depth. The man moved forward, but just as he was about to touch her, the ground began to rumble under Sara's feet. Unsteadily, she stumbled out of arm's reach of the soldier as she saw his own eyes widen in fear. The second soldier rushed out of nowhere, with his sword swung up high. The air seemed to still, and there was a faint flash of green from somewhere. At the same time, Sara felt her stomach lurch as though she had just leapt off something high. There was a loud boom, and both of the soldiers surrounding her were flung off in separate directions before they could harm her. Sara was knocked back as well, but not quite the same distance. She sat up shakily, not knowing what had just happened. Astrid stood unharmed in the centre of all the chaos.

"Sara. Free me now."

Still trying to make sense of the events here, Sara was slow to respond.

Her mother looked up at the guard post in concern.

"Sara, hurry."

Sara scrambled forwards and brought her knife out of her boot, cutting the rope binding her mother.

"Do you know what just happened?" she asked.

"There's no time to explain. I will give you answers I promise, but not now. We have to leave."

Sara watched Astrid anxiously as they ran back to the Carnival, her mind racing. She had not done anything, at least not consciously. Did that mean that Astrid had? But what? As they reached the village, her mother finally turned to look at her and Sara saw Astrid's mouth twist guiltily, presumably at the expression on Sara's face.

"Everything will be fine," Astrid said, almost to herself.

"Maybe we should get out of the village," Stephan said, glancing at Astrid.

They strode straight through the centre of Silverspring and back in the direction of the house. Once at the top, Astrid stopped and turned to face Stephan and Sara, and there was sadness mixed with the urgency in her eyes.

"Stephen, we need to leave Silverspring," she said.

"All right." He took a deep breath. "Let's go."

"No," Astrid objected, "not you. You can't come with us. I cannot take you where I intend to go."

"And where is that?" he asked.

She smiled grimly. "I can't tell you that either."

"You're just going to leave?"

"You saw what happened back there," Astrid said, "Silverspring is no longer safe for me, or Sara."

"You can't stop me from following you," Stephan said.

Astrid paused. "Sara, go inside and pack two bags for travelling. I will saddle the horses and meet you there."

Obediently, Sara followed her orders. She rushed to her room and stuffed extra clothes and food into two leather satchels. Pausing at the door, she turned back and then hastily grabbed a small amulet from under the pillow. She thrust it over her neck and hid it from view underneath her shirt. It was her good luck charm, a gift from her father.

"Sara! Get out here, now."

She threw the bags over her shoulders and ran out to where her mother held the reins of her horse out for her. She scrambled back onto Arrow, surprised to notice that Stephan was gone.

"Where's Stephan?" she asked, "and where are we going?"

"Just follow me."

Astrid rode off, and Sara had no choice but to hurtle after her. They galloped away over the fields high above the village, in the opposite direction to the Carnival. It was not long before they reached the cover of the trees and had to slow slightly to navigate the narrow, winding track.

"Are we being followed?" Sara asked as she ducked her head under a tree branch.

"I assume the soldiers will come after us."

Surprised that she had received an answer to her question, Sara dared another.

"When will you tell me what's happening?"

"When we are safe. Hurry!"

They rode on for an hour, with no sign that anybody was actively pursuing them and Sara relaxed a little. Astrid, however, did not, and kept up the same pace since they had left the house. They travelled all afternoon through the forest until the paths that Sara knew gave way to unknown territory. Under cover of the trees, she had no idea which direction they were travelling in anymore and could not even guess at their final destination. All was quiet around them until the sound of faint thundering hooves in the forest alerted Sara a few minutes later.

"Do you hear that?"

"This way," Astrid ordered, moving ahead.

She steered her horse right off the track and into the forest undergrowth. Astrid halted once they were far back off the road and dismounted.

"Wait here. I'll be back in a second."

Sara opened her mouth to object, but Astrid was gone. Left with the two horses, she strained her ears for any sound but heard nothing. A noise in the undergrowth a moment later signalled Astrid's return, and to Sara's surprise, she saw that Stephan accompanied her. It seemed he had indeed followed them. He stood before her with his arms folded.

"You never said goodbye to me," he said.

"Is that why you came after us?"

"You two have one minute," Astrid said to him with a sigh.

She left to guard the road and Stephan ran forwards. Much to her surprise, he immediately took her into a hug.

"Where are you going?" he asked.

"I don't know," she answered.

"This is madness."

"You're right," she agreed, "I have no idea what is going on. Astrid is keeping things secret."

Stephan leaned in closer and lowered his voice.

"I'm worried about you," he said, "are you sure Astrid is all right? What happened back there at the Carnival?"

Sara looked at Stephan in surprise. "I don't know, but I have to trust her. Once we're safe, she promised to tell me what's going on. But you should turn back. I don't want to involve you in whatever this as well."

Stephan did not look convinced.

"Were you followed?" she asked.

"No." Stephan's expression was smug. "The soldiers were pursuing you, but they have ridden off in completely the wrong direction."

"Make sure they don't run into you."

"Don't worry. I can look after myself."

"We won't be away long," Sara tried to reassure him, "just until the Carnival leaves Silverspring. Then I'm sure we'll be back."

"Make sure that you are."

"I...I'll miss you, Stephan."

"I'll miss you too, but I will see you again. I promise."

"Time to go." Astrid returned from the path.

Stephan's took a step back as Astrid mounted her horse and stood next to Sara.

"Stephan," she said, "thank you for helping Sara over the last few days, and I am truly sorry that you can't come with us."

"I will go back to Silverspring, for now."

Astrid nodded and nudged her horse into a walk. Sara followed reluctantly, not taking her eyes off Stephan until they rounded a corner and removed him from sight.

For the rest of the day, Sara rode after Astrid in silence, after trying to talk to her mother twice more but getting no response. She still did not know where they were going, but at the moment, she did not care. Her thoughts churned around Stephan, and however hard she tried, she could not rid the last image of his face from her mind.

The wind had picked up, and as the temperatures dropped, Sara shivered and huddled down inside her cloak. Peering ahead, up at the silent figure of her mother, she found herself realising that the person riding up ahead of her now was not the Astrid she recognised. It was approaching late afternoon now, and the sun was steadily sinking in the sky. Sara suddenly felt weak and remembered that she had not eaten all day. Just as the evening snatched its last rays from the forest around them and her stomach let out an audible grumble, Astrid finally spoke.

"Here," she whispered, "we're stopping."

Blearily, Sara sighed.

Fumbling around in the near darkness, they brought out some cold food, and as they ate, Sara risked a question.

"Where are we going?"

In the darkness, Sara felt a steady gaze on her.

"I'll explain properly tomorrow," was the hesitant reply. "For now, let's say that we're going to my brother in Merrywater. Bear with me just a little while longer, Sara, and I promise I will explain everything to you. Now, get some sleep."

Sara's eyes widened in the darkness. Merrywater. She had heard Astrid talk about that region before and the way she had described it had always made Sara bubble with excitement. Fuelled by a new intrigue, her worries about Astrid subsided slightly. Hopefully, she would be able to get her mother to open up more tomorrow. Astrid's answer to this question, however, had only succeeded in opening up a whole new range of queries, giving Sara a new list of things to think about, instead of sleeping.

CHAPTER 3
TRAVELLING

~SHUMUTI~

Shumuti's father had been in the room for two hours now. He had bolted the door shut and reminded her several times not to disturb him until he came out. Shumuti was sitting outside under the old yew tree in the garden, waxing her bow, now and then glancing up at the window to the room where her father was. She leant back against the rough bark of the tree and sighed. Despite everything about who he was, she could not help worrying about him and wondering what it was that he was doing. All he had said to her was that he had had a feeling something was going on far away and that he needed to find out what it was. He had asked for her help in the beginning, but he had been in that room for two hours now. It was too long.

There had been rumours though that something had been happening in both Merrywater and Elmdale, on the western banks. Scouting groups had spotted several attacks on villages and also on their patrols. The assailants remained unknown because so far there had been no surviving witnesses, but they did know that the raids were happening increasingly closer to Shumuti's village. After every report, Shumuti could see her father becoming tense and uneasy and consequently, it made her so, too. Whether this connected to what he was trying to learn today, Shumuti did not know, but she couldn't bear to wait much longer.

All thoughts were cast aside, as her father came rushing out of the house and over to her tree, his silver hair flying behind him. She scrambled up quickly and slung her quiver of arrows over her back, ready for whatever he was about to ask her to do.

"Shumuti." She was alarmed at how anxious her father sounded.

"What is it? What's happened?" she asked, her mind conjuring up a whole host of terrifying scenarios.

"My sister is coming over."

"I...What?"

"My sister, Astrid. She is running from something. I have seen her just now, but she's not safe, and she is going to need some help."

He looked pointedly at her.

"And you want me to go find her?"

"Yes."

"Now?"

"Yes."

"Right," Shumuti said, still slightly caught off balance, "I'll get ready then."

"Thank you," he replied.

She strode inside, with her quiver bouncing on her back, and grabbed some food from the cupboards. Then she searched out her dark coloured travelling cloak and put both the food and the coat into the saddlebags of Fynne, her horse. Shumuti had already got a riding skirt on, as she had been out that morning, and a long leather jerkin over her shirt, so she collected her wrist guards and strapped her bow to her back. Her fingers hesitated for a second by her sword, but she decided against it. A bow ought to do for this rescue mission, and a lighter weapon meant she could travel faster. Satisfied that she was ready, Shumuti walked out of the house to meet her father.

"Where exactly am I going?" she asked.

"Here, I'll show you." He came over to her and placed his first and last fingers onto her forehead. She closed her eyes and felt an image entering her mind. Shivering slightly from the touch, Shumuti concentrated on seeing what he was showing her and gradually the resemblance of a clearing in the forest emerged, wreathed by a border of flames. Shumuti smiled and opened her eyes. She knew that place very well.

"That's where you'll find them," he said.

"Them?"

"I saw another girl with her, somebody I have never met. She was young. Perhaps your age."

"Does Astrid have a daughter?"

"Maybe so, I haven't seen Astrid for years," he said, "something pursues them, but I am not sure what it is. Good luck."

Shumuti rode off down the track, hearing horse hooves clattering on the stone. She could tell Fynne was glad to be out. He was eager to go fast so, giving her father a final wave goodbye she let Fynne go. His dark figure, topped with silver, vanished into nothing as she descended the hill from the house. They galloped over the rolling hillocks and streams, enjoying the thrill of the speed and the rush of the wind. It whipped through Shumuti's hair and danced in Fynne's mane, and he whinnied with joy. Shumuti grinned, and they picked up more speed.

The gradual sinking of the sun began in the afternoon, and Fynne slowed to a trot. They navigated a tricky network of small streams in the centre of the little valley and Fynne leapt the last one with ease. After a while, clouds began to close in, and it looked like it might rain. Shumuti groaned. It didn't look like they would make it to the trees in time to avoid getting soaked.

"Faster, Fynne!" Shumuti called, but he seemed to have run out of speed. She grumbled as they slowed to a walk and dug out her cloak from the saddlebags. The rain hit them a few minutes later and as Shumuti pulled her hood up in disgust. Fynne began to increase his pace again. Thankfully, they reached the borders of the forest soon after, cold and dripping wet.

Shumuti dismounted Fynne once they had reached the cover of the trees and led him on the winding path up the bank to the proper start of the forest, which cut into the crest of a hill. She breathed a sigh of relief as the canopy of the forest alleviated the constant downpour of rain, even if it meant that the individual drops under here were more considerable in size. Shumuti estimated that they would reach the clearing that she had seen the next evening. It wouldn't have taken so long if it were not for the enormous gorge that lay in between her and the clearing that she had to bypass around the top. That would take half a day at least. She was used to hunting and tracking animals here, but she had never searched for any humans in these woods before.

Shumuti could not see the sunset that evening, but she felt the world grow colder, so she and Fynne settled down for the night under a rocky outcrop a few metres from the track. Fynne stood disgruntled and soaked to the skin, staring out into the forest back towards home where there would have been a nice dry stable for him and a comfy bed of hay. He shook his head feebly and gave Shumuti a sour look. She got up to brush the tangles out of his mane and attempted to dry the rest of his body with a small rag. He made a slight, disgruntled noise when she had finished and folded his legs up under him to lie down on the comfiest patch of grass. She gave him a comical look before wiping the saddle with the rag and finally twisting the water out of it.

Placing the saddlebags next to her, she settled down to go to sleep, with her cloak wrapped around and her head on Fynne's saddle. She dreamed enviously of her father at home in the warm house. Rain fell once again during the night, and Shumuti woke up with her cloak and face sodden once more. She saw with a glad heart that enough time had passed for the morning sunlight to be filtering through the leaves and branches to dry the ground on the forest floor. Fynne was up, and he snorted once or twice when Shumuti replaced the saddle and saddlebags.

As the sun rose higher, the light illuminated every dewdrop on the spiders' webs dotted about here and there, and there was a fresh smell drifting on the breeze. She led Fynne for the first part of the morning, munching an apple as she went. The trees slowly began to spread out, and so she fed the core to Fynne and clambered up onto his back, placing her feet in the stirrups and gathering up the reins. They walked quite steadily because the path was thin here, and also because a slower pace meant easing the sore, aching pains in her legs from the fast riding yesterday. The sun was slowly drying her clothes, and Shumuti laid her cloak over the end of Fynne to dry, turning him into a walking washing line.

As Shumuti travelled, she thought back on what her father had said. He had mentioned his sister was in danger and was running from something or someone. She considered then that the threat lay in front of her and became more cautious, keeping her eyes and ears open. If she had been following them and not coming to meet them, this would have been much easier, Shumuti thought. She had always been good at following a trail, but this time the only clue she had to go on was the image Seaglen had given her.

Late morning found Shumuti breaching the slope that led to the beginning of the route around the gorge. She stopped for a moment to figure out the best course to take that would keep her under some cover and provide her with a swift and easy crossing. The deciduous trees interspersed amongst the conifers of the forest had become tinted with shades of orange and deep red. The wood was at its most beautiful as autumn set in entirely and just before leaves began to fall idly to the floor.

Dropping down slightly over the hill, she nudged Fynne along the track that was cut into the side of the gorge and hid her in the shadows away from the hot sunlight. This decision was a relief to Fynne as it decreased the number of flies that swarmed and tormented his eyes and ears. They drifted up to Shumuti as well, considering if she was a likely snack, but it seemed they preferred the taste of horse, so Shumuti covered him as best she could, and they carried on.

Halfway along the pathway, Shumuti pulled out her bow and strung it, just in case. A few dark dots were circling high above in the sky as though they were tracking prey. It seemed to her that before the day was out, she would be meeting Astrid and therefore, the danger from which she was fleeing. Curious about the other person travelling with Astrid, Shumuti began to wonder if she did have a daughter. If that was the case, then Shumuti realised that would make her a cousin. She smiled happily at the prospect. She had never had a cousin before.

Lost in thought, it took her longer than it would usually have to reconsider the birds. For some reason, Shumuti was no longer sure that was what they were. So far she had seen two of them; they circled overhead for a minute before shooting off back into the distance, only to re-materialise a few minutes later. They resembled vultures, but even at range, they looked huge, too large for conventionally sized birds.

Once or twice they had flown almost over her head, and she had felt the need to steer Fynne off the path and into the cover of nearby bushes. For reasons she could not explain, Shumuti did not want to be seen by them, they gave her a prickly feeling of deep unease and was glad when they eventually disappeared for good. It also seemed that she was not the only one disturbed by their presence, not a single bird sang that whole afternoon, and the very air felt cautious and stifling. All in all, Shumuti was glad when darkness fell, and she reached the empty clearing as owls began to hoot and swooped out to catch their prey.

She jumped down from Fynne and looked around. The glade resembled the image Seaglen had shown her accurately. The dell was composed of two sections and was connected in the centre by a narrow path, overhung with winding branches. From the air, the overall outline formed a figure of eight or an hourglass. Trees grew tallest on either side of the linking pathway, and their entwining branches had slowly grown to criss-cross over the top of the path.

To the majority of people who visited the meadow, Shumuti presumed it would feel entirely ordinary but a select few, like her, would be able to detect the Magic held within it. Magic was like energy, and it flowed through everything natural, allowing rivers to run and grass to grow. That energy was everywhere, Shumuti could even feel it saturated into the bark of the trees around her, the concentration of it giving them an unnaturally fast growth. She had felt the presence of Magic in her surroundings her whole life, and it was an ability she had gained from her father. He had told her there were only a handful of people in the whole of Meteorath who had ever had that power and they kept their talent a secret from everybody else.

Magic was a curious thing, each person who used it had a speciality in one of four different elements; fire, water, air and earth, which they could use to manipulate Magic to suit their own needs. As her element was air, she could easily borrow a little from the environment around her to say, increase the power of the breeze that was blowing through the clearing or even still the air completely. But there were consequences. Take too much out from the tree beside her, and it would wither. Take all the Magic from the clearing and everything growing would die, taking ten times the amount of time to regenerate than the single tree would have.

As a result, the use of Magic had to be limited. That was the most important lesson she had ever learnt. This fact was also the reason nobody could ever know of its existence apart from those who wielded it because Magic needed to be protected to prevent misuse in the wrong hands. The difficulty of using Magic was in knowing where the invisible line lay that would prevent damage from being created. It had taken Shumuti many years to learn how to find the correct balance.

She wondered whether Astrid, or the girl who travelled with her, would have the same abilities. In the haste to leave, Shumuti cursed herself for forgetting to ask her father. Astrid was her father's sister after all, and from what Shumuti knew, the ability tended to run in families, but he had very rarely mentioned her in the past.

A slight movement in the trees brought Shumuti back to the present. She reached for an arrow, but it was only a small rabbit that jumped up from the grass. Shumuti shifted her feet, and it pricked up its ears, noticing her for the first time. With a leap and a hop, it shot off back into the heart of the forest where there would be no travellers to disturb its evening meal. Shumuti kept her arrow out, alerted now to any sound and prepared to wait in the sheltered archway. Despite her horse's gentle protests, she kept his saddle and saddlebags on, in case they needed to get away quickly. She brought out some food for them both instead, but Fynne declined it and chose instead to munch calmly on some grass, so Shumuti silently leant against the trunk of a tree with her bow in one hand and her nocked arrow in the other.

There was a gentle calmness in the glade that evening. Everything was still, except for the occasional hoot of an owl or flutter of bat wings. If anything was going to enter their little camp, Shumuti reasoned that Fynne would be aware of it long before she was. She relaxed a tiny bit.

Instead, she stared up at the night sky. The stars up there glittered like silver jewels on a luxurious fabric that blanketed the world. Despite the peace of the night, a worry had been nagging at Shumuti recently. It felt to her as though the world was changing somehow and almost that somewhere, something new was coming.

Something was coming, Shumuti realised with a jolt, heading towards her through the forest. Fynne's ears had sharpened, and he was staring dead ahead into the trees at the end of the meadow. Shumuti sprang up and lifted her bow, feeling the beat of her heart increase slightly and the hairs on the back of her neck rise. Everything was silent for a minute, but then there was a rustling in the trees and a faint panicked whinny.

Slowly, Shumuti drew back the arrow and peered around the side of the tree, using the trunk as a shield. The noise increased, getting nearer, and she heard the beat of hooves rumbling in the direction of the glade. She sighted down the shaft towards the direction of the sound as Fynne shifted beside her and snorted gently. For a moment, Shumuti thought he was going to bolt, but he stayed where he was. Then there was another higher cry, but it was human this time. Finally, she heard a high-pitched shriek, similar to a large bird.

Two riders burst from the cover of the trees on her left, and she tracked them with her bow before a large, black shape shot out after them. The taller rider dragged the girl's horse aside as the form streamed past them, elongated talons almost rendering the side of the animal. Wings shot out to steady itself, and the shadow twisted round to attack again. The taller rider had her back to the oversized bird.

"NO!" cried the girl.

Shumuti fired her arrow.

The creature halted in mid-air and spiralled to one side before slamming into the ground. It shrieked in pain and plucked the shaft out of its shoulder with a clawed foot the size of a small boulder. Shumuti whipped out another arrow, suddenly wishing she had brought her sword and leapt out of the cover of the trees. The bird crawled to its unnaturally large hooked feet, and Shumuti took in what she was facing. As it stood, she saw in horror that it was a mutilated combination of the shape and size of a human but the beak and wings of a jet-black vulture. Shumuti took in mottled hands and a body that alternated between scaly and smooth grey skin, alongside a vulture's beak that twisted into a patchy face, composed of both human and animal. Darkness covered portions of the creature's body in pure shadow. She had never seen anything like it.

It let loose a long, low hiss.

The vulture spread its enormous wings and launched itself towards Shumuti at lightning speed, taking advantage of her momentary paralysis. She was swept off her feet by an unseen force just as the bird reached her and in a panic, she let loose an arrow into the foot of the animal. The bird's claws just caught the fabric on her chest as she fell, ripping it, but just glancing her skin. It flew up into the sky as Shumuti's back slammed into the grassy earth, disappearing over the trees with a final scream.

Shakily, Shumuti got to her feet, gasping for the breath that had been knocked out of her by the fall and turned to face the two riders. One of them she thought she could place with the descriptions given to her by her father, but the other one she did not know. Although, as she glanced between the two of them, it was clear there were definite similarities.

None of them moved or spoke. Shumuti checked the rip in her clothes to make sure she was unhurt. Suddenly aware that her weapon was still out, Shumuti quickly stowed the bow away on her back. The woman whispered something to the girl and then handed her reins over and walked towards Shumuti, plucking her first arrow from the grass as she came. Her other hand was on the hilt of a long knife that rested beside her hip.

"Shumuti?" she asked, offering her back the arrow.

"Yes."

She sighed, and her hand slipped from the knife.

"You know me?"

"I knew that that was to be the name of Seaglen's daughter. You are his daughter, aren't you? You have his look..."

Shumuti smiled. "Yes, and you are Astrid?"

"Yes."

"Seaglen sent me. He thought that you might need help."

Shumuti paused uncertainly. She had been sure the thing she had felt throw her over just before the creature attacked had been Magic. As she took in her newly discovered aunt now, she felt the same energy radiating from her that she did from all around the glade.

"Thank you for saving me," she added.

A flicker of hesitation and surprise crossed her face before Astrid nodded. "You're welcome."

The girl appeared beside her mother.

"This is Sara," Astrid said.

"How did you know to find us?" the girl asked.

"My father knew you would be here," she said.

"What do you mean?" Sara asked, in confusion.

Shumuti hesitated. Did Sara not know about Magic?

"Thank you for coming to meet with us," Astrid said, "I'm not sure if we would have made the journey otherwise."

"I'd been watching those bird-like creatures all afternoon," Shumuti said, "I have never seen anything like them."

Sara frowned briefly at the change of topic but remained silent.

"Neither have I," Astrid said, "Seaglen was always the one I asked to help me identify creatures."

"I doubt even he would be able to recognise what just attacked us. It didn't look like any animal I've ever seen," Shumuti said.

"We should keep an eye out in case it returns."

"I can take you the rest of the way to our house. I know my father is excited to see you."

"Are you sure he dœsn't mind us coming?"

"He would be glad of some new company. But we may as well stay here tonight and carry on tomorrow. We should be safe in the trees. I can keep a lookout while you two get some rest."

Secretly, Shumuti wanted to stay here because it would be an excellent defensive location. If the creature did return, there was more than enough surplus Magic here to drive it away and Shumuti would be able to do much more damage than she had with her bow. Astrid nodded, and they began setting up a small camp underneath the overhanging branches of the entwining archway. Astrid set up a fire and Sara got out some food for them. Shumuti took off Fynne's saddle now, and he tossed his head happily. The three of them sat around the fire and by unspoken consent, too tired to talk, they both fell asleep beside their weapons, while Shumuti stood guard, with her on one side of the fire and them on the other.

CHAPTER 4
THAYLL

The next morning, Shumuti and Astrid were the first two awake. Astrid beckoned Shumuti over to a small rise that looked out above the trees, across the gorge towards Merrywater. Curiously, Shumuti wandered over, leaving Sara sleeping by the smoking embers of the fire.

"How is Seaglen these days?" Astrid asked, "it's been so long since I last saw him."

"He's good," Shumuti answered, "I doubt you'll think he has changed very much."

"I can see he passed on his talents to you."

Shumuti turned to look at her.

"I need to talk to you about Magic," Astrid continued, "I did wonder whether the ability would pass on through a family."

"So it hasn't in your case? I mean, I think I already knew Sara didn't have the same abilities. Usually, I can tell just by looking at someone."

"Shumuti. I haven't even told her of its existence. I thought I had left that part of my life behind. I have hardly touched Magic for years until recently."

"She dœsn't know?"

"Please, keep it quiet for now. I was going to try to explain it all once we were safe in Merrywater. But I wasn't expecting you would come and meet us on the road, and I need some time to figure out how to explain it all."

Shumuti looked back uncertainly to Sara's sleeping form, as she shifted slightly in her sleep.

"All right."

Astrid nodded gratefully.

"So, what did happen to you in Elmdale?" Shumuti asked.

"I don't fully understand it myself yet," Astrid said.

Shumuti opened her mouth again, but at that moment, Sara sat up.

"We'll tell you the non-magical side of the story on the road," Astrid said.

She gave Shumuti a final glance and went to greet her daughter.

With Shumuti only knowing of eight people ever in the history of Meteorath to have been able to use Magic it was hardly surprising to her Sara could not, Shumuti thought, but in the two cases she knew, it did seem to be passed down from parent to child. Shumuti thought about back home and realised that Sara would be living with three people who could use Magic and winced, wondering what her reaction would be to it all. There was no way they could keep their secret hidden for long.

The three of them ate and packed up the camp, erasing all signs that they had been there, before starting back on the track around the gorge that Shumuti had traversed the day before. As they rode, Astrid explained what had happened to them over the past few days as they travelled, culminating in the escape into the forest.

"It wasn't until yesterday that we first saw the birds," she said, "once we had entered the forest, we noticed them more frequently, but they couldn't get near because of the closeness of the trees. Only when we got close to the glade did the canopy open up enough for them to dive through."

"What happened to the second bird?" Shumuti asked, "I saw two yesterday."

"It left yesterday afternoon," Astrid said.

"Sounds like the other may have been a messenger," Shumuti said.

"Do you have any idea what they were?" Sara asked.

"I have no idea," Shumuti replied, "vultures the size of humans, but they were something more than that. Perhaps my father will have an idea. But why they were following you?"

"We don't know," Astrid said, "they appeared after we fled the Carnival."

"When will you tell me what happened when the soldiers questioned you after the tournament?" Sara asked her mother.

Shumuti was curious to hear those details herself.

"You said they kept you overnight?" Shumuti said.

"They did," Astrid said, "if it hadn't been for my escape, I think they would have still had me held captive. Only, I would not have been a prisoner in Silverspring, but on my way to the city of Lyria."

"The Carnival would have taken you back to the King, in Attaching?" Shumuti said.

"I believe that was their intention. They did not reveal to me why they took the other competition winners and me aside. All they said was that they were searching for 'unusually talented individuals'. They asked a lot of questions about my background and when I came to Silverspring, where I had learnt my healing skills and that sort of thing. But it is my fault too. I should not have won the competition so flamboyantly."

"They were looking for skilled people?"

"I was reluctant to answer them when I didn't know what they planned to do with me. I told them as little as I could, and they became less friendly once I made it clear I was not going to cooperate. It was soon after that that they bound me and led me off to a tent alone. I considered trying to break free then, but I didn't know what had become of you, Sara. They told me that they had you."

"Could the soldiers have sent that creature after us?" Sara asked.

"I don't know if there is a connection between the Carnival and the creature," Astrid said.

"But if the vultures weren't with the Carnival, why would they come after us?" Sara asked.

Shumuti exchanged a glance with Astrid and slipped into silence. She did not want to mention it, but the vulture had emanated Magic when she had fought it. Not that they could use Magic but they were somehow connected to it. Was it just a coincidence that the vultures were hunting a Magic user? Or was this to do with something entirely unrelated? Then there was the matter of the Carnival and their connection to it all. What was the King searching for in Elmdale? She wanted desperately to discuss everything with Astrid, but at the same time, she wanted Seaglen there as well, to learn what he thought about it all.

The travellers rode in silence for a while. They had nearly bypassed the gorge into Merrywater and would soon be back into the cover of the trees. Shumuti would be glad of them because they were far too easily spotted out in the open. Shumuti and Astrid had decided to remain an extra night under the protection of the forest, rather than ride on over the plains in the dark. When they stopped that night, they decided to take watches once again. Astrid went first, so Sara and Shumuti fell asleep under their blankets. Shumuti could not sleep, so after a while, she gave up and walked over to Astrid.

"Shumuti, you should sleep," she said, without turning around, "you need some rest."

"I can't sleep," Shumuti said, "and besides, I want to talk to you."

Astrid shifted and glanced at her daughter before turning back to face Merrywater.

"Why dœsn't Sara know about Magic?"

"She can't use it. I never thought I would use it again either until I escaped from the Attaching soldiers."

"But she is your daughter."

"And part of a life that is completely unrelated to Magic."

"Not completely. Sara said you won a competition for healing. I know the talents of someone gifted in earth Magic. Your skill at healing comes as no surprise to me."

"I have hinted to her that it exists."

"But dœs she believe you?"

Astrid paused.

"I don't think she dœs."

"Do you think she'll ever be able to use it?"

"I used to think she would, one day. But I have never seen Sara display any sign that she would be like me. Every day my belief gets less and less. I don't think it will ever come to her."

"Hardly anybody can use Magic."

"But you can. Why would I not pass it down to Sara the same as Seaglen did to you?"

"I grew up my whole life around Seaglen practising Magic. Maybe that's why I picked it up. Perhaps if we show it to Sara, the three of us, she'll start to learn. My friend, Aurielle, is like us, and Seaglen taught her at the same time as he taught me. Aurielle's father can't use Magic, but I think her mother could."

"There was no need for me to keep using my abilities. We used them to fight in Nimaz long ago. After that was over, having Magic was only ever a hindrance to trying to live a normal life again. To me, it belonged with the past."

"I've heard a little about what happened, from my father. But he was always reluctant to go into the details."

Astrid nodded, and they stood in silence for what felt like an age. When Shumuti knew Astrid would also say no more, she turned away.

"Whether Sara can use Magic or not, she will have to learn about it soon," Shumuti said.

"I know." Astrid kept her attention focused on the moonlit view of Merrywater through the gaps in the trees. "Just please, give me time."

"All right. I will."

She got up and walked back to Sara, leaving Astrid on watch.

Shumuti talked mainly to Sara the next day, getting to know her and finding out about her life. Astrid rode a little way ahead, so they were left on their own. Sara told her about being in Elmdale and her village. It seemed like she had enjoyed growing up there, but often she mentioned the boy named Stephan and the guilt she felt at leaving him behind.

They reached the edge of the woods at midday and broke out onto the open plains. Shumuti was relieved to notice no dark shapes in the sky, which meant they were no longer being followed. The horses were glad to be free of the closeness of the forest and so the three of them set off at a canter, with the warm sun beating down on their backs. They streaked out over the plains and Shumuti heard the thunder of hooves either side of her as Shumuti, Sara and Astrid rode level with each other over the hills together, turning the grass beneath their feet into a blur of green.

They reached Shumuti's village, Thayll, at dusk. Behind the town, Shumuti could see the start of the mountain ranges that lay beyond and the silhouettes of mountain peaks that glowed white. The settlement sat much higher up than the forest and was therefore much colder. The horses slowed to a walk, and apart from a few curious glances at Astrid and Sara, they passed through unhindered. A variety of familiar and different smells, of wood smoke, leather and curing meats passed them by on the road.

"It's so different from Silverspring," Sara said, "why are the roofs of your houses so large?"

"They overhang to catch the snow in winter," Shumuti answered, "otherwise we would all get snowed inside each year."

Sara's eyes brightened. "It snows a lot here?"

"Every winter."

Sara was staring up in wonder at the wooden houses. Boxes of bright red and pink flowers adorned most of the windowsills and brightly painted shutters were thrown open on either side of the windows. But the group soon left them behind as they ascended the foot of a winding track that wound up the slope to Shumuti's home.

"It's like our house," Sara said, "on a hill high away from everybody else."

"Seaglen and I always had the same ideas," Astrid replied.

Shumuti dismounted when they reached the single house at the top and led the way around to their small stables. When the horses were safely inside and fed, Shumuti brought Astrid and Sara back to the front of the house. She opened the door inside to find her father sitting at the table, sharpening a sword with a whetstone. For a brief moment, he gripped the sword hilt until he realised who was there. Shumuti felt slightly troubled at the sight of his sword, he had not brought it out in a long while.

Seaglen laughed with what Shumuti could not help thinking was relief at seeing his daughter, before putting the weapon on the table and standing up. Then he noticed Astrid and laughed again, giving Shumuti a grateful hug.

"Well done," he said to Shumuti, before turning to Astrid. He regarded her for a moment before cracking his face into an even fuller smile and throwing himself into another embrace.

"It has been far too long," Astrid said.

Her father held Astrid's gaze for a second longer, before turning to the third person in the room.

"And who is this?"

"This is Sara," Astrid replied, "she's my daughter."

Sara looked up at him nervously and Seaglen contemplated her for a moment, as if he was searching for something.

"Aye," he said, "I did wonder."

Sara shifted uncomfortably under his scrutinising gaze and glanced away.

"What happened to you?" Seaglen asked, noting the tear on Shumuti's shirt.

"It's nothing."

He walked over and inspected the rip with concern. Shumuti noticed disconcertingly that the frayed edges of the fabric had blackened and disintegrated slightly, and was doubly thankful that the claws had not made contact with her skin.

"Something large did this." Seaglen looked up at her for an answer.

"A creature in the forest," Astrid said, "Shumuti saved us from it."

"It was something I've never seen before," Shumuti said, "an unnatural creature made up of a man and a vulture. I shot it with an arrow, and it flew away."

Seaglen's face darkened.

"It pursued us from Elmdale," Astrid said, "but what it is, I have no idea."

"I have not heard a description of anything like this before," Seaglen said.

"It nearly managed to get me in the forest," Sara said, "what if it comes to Merrywater?"

"Have you been taught how to defend yourself?" Seaglen asked.

"Not from something like that," Sara said.

"Then perhaps it would be a good idea for you to learn while you are here," Seaglen said.

Sara's eyes drifted to the sizeable two-handed blade resting on the table.

"I could teach you a thing or two while you are here," Seaglen said.

Astrid opened her mouth. "Seaglen..."

"Not now, of course," Seaglen said, "you look like you need rest, all of you. But where to put you, I wonder?"

"I'll show Sara," Shumuti said, "she can sleep in my room."

"Good," Seaglen said.

As Shumuti led Sara away, she heard Astrid say, "I need to talk to you-" but the door slammed shut before Shumuti caught anything else and, knowing her questions would have to wait another day, she instead guided Sara along the corridor.

Shumuti opened the door to her room and walked in. She took off her wrist guards and placed them with the rest of her small collection of armour before lighting two candles so that they could see clearer. She rested one gingerly on a bare patch of her desk in its holder and the other on the window ledge so that the whole room became illuminated with a flickering light. Next, Shumuti went over to her bed and pulled out a concealed mattress beneath it, padded with feathers. She dragged it out on the floor next to the bed so that they both had somewhere to sleep.

"This is yours," Shumuti said, "here, you can use these as a cover, it's not much, but it is better than the forest floor."

Shumuti handed her some blankets.

"It's a bed," Sara said, "that's more than I've had for a few days."

Shumuti stood up and felt the room sway slightly. She had forgotten how little sleep she had got since she had left the house.

"I'll show you around tomorrow, I promise."

"Shumuti?"

"Yes?"

"Was your father serious about training me?"

"Probably. If you want to learn, there are lots of things he could teach you, like fighting skills, riding. Just useful things you might need while you're here. It's just the way he is. He loves passing on knowledge. There are lots of other things as well, and my father is a good teacher. He taught me almost everything I know."

"I have so many questions." Sara looked up as Shumuti yawned. "But they can wait for tonight."

Shumuti got under her blankets and glanced over at Sara from across the room, wondering how much the girl had guessed. She was not the only one who wanted some answers, Shumuti thought. They each blew out a candle and darkness descended around them, but it was a long while before Shumuti heard the footsteps of Seaglen and Astrid going to bed.

CHAPTER 5
TRAINING

Sara awoke the next morning to see bright sunlight streaming in through the window as it bounced off the motes of dust lazily drifting through the air in the room. Shumuti's bed was empty, and there was a pile of freshly brought out clothes on the end of her mattress. Sara glanced around the rest of the room, her eyes taking in all the maps on the walls, surrounded by drawings and notes. There was a small collection of weaponry in the corner, including a sword, bow and arrows.

She got up slowly and reached out for the clothes at the foot of her bed, presuming that they were meant for her as they looked as though they had not seen use for a long time, but were also relatively unbeaten and unworn. Sturdy-looking leather formed the outer layer of the outfit which looked like it might be able to sustain some amount of damage with sacrificing any manoeuvrability. She lifted a cotton shirt, and a small note fell out, spiralling gently onto the bed.

Your training gear, it read.

At that moment, Shumuti came into the room.

"Hey, you're awake."

"This is for me?" Sara held up the shirt.

"Seaglen found them for you. I've no idea where from though. He said if you're ready, he can take you out for a few hours today, but I'll show you around first."

"I'm ready." The attack in the forest was still fresh on Sara's mind.

Sara looked down at the clothes once more before scrambling to her feet and gathering them up. She had a quick wash and then pulled on her new outfit; the shirt, a hard-wearing brown pair of trousers and a plain leather surcoat that was split down the front. She followed Shumuti's example and tucked the left side of the surcoat under and buttoned the right side over, securing the ensemble in place with a black belt around her waist. There were also a pair of leather boots and a set of wrist guards to match. Shumuti looked up from a drawing of a map when Sara walked back in and eyed Sara's gear with an approving look.

"You suit them."

"Thanks," Sara replied, evening out her collar slightly.

Shumuti led the way downstairs. Still unsure of the layout of the house, she directed Sara away from a corridor that seemed to do nothing apart from halt abruptly and instead led her through the small parlour they had been in last night and out through the front door. They walked past the stables and out to an overlook beside the track that ran down to the village. A fresh, alpine breeze ruffled Sara's hair as she stepped out.

"You can almost see back to Elmdale from here." Shumuti pointed towards the way they had ridden yesterday.

Sara looked out, feeling strangely homesick, so instead, she turned to face the other way, in the direction of the towering mountains brooding in the distance to the north.

"I'd heard Merrywater was nothing but mountains and lakes," she said.

Shumuti laughed. "Just like Elmdale is nothing but trees."

Sara smiled.

"Thayll lies at the fringes of the mountains," Shumuti said, "to the south, it's nothing but open grassland until you reach the sea."

"I like it here." Sara nodded in approval.

"Come on," Shumuti said, "Seaglen and Astrid are around the back of the house."

Shumuti led her to a gate at the side of the house that led into a small garden, with a large yew tree at the centre. The sun had bathed the garden in bright morning light, and Shumuti led the way towards the tree, where Seaglen was sat cross-legged with a sketchbook on his lap and a stick of charcoal in the other. Astrid sat from a gnarled, handmade swing that hung down from one of the thick tree branches above. Sara could see a half-drawn image on the paper, and she recognised her mother immediately from the half-sketched picture.

"Ah, you're dressed for action," Seaglen said.

"Yes," Sara said, "that's an amazing drawing."

"It is merely a hobby of mine," Seaglen said.

"He has to update the family records every now and then," Astrid joked, "you shall have to draw Sara as well at some point."

Sara raised an eyebrow as she and Shumuti sat down on the grass. She had never had anyone draw her before and was not too sure about the idea at all.

"Naturally," Seaglen said, "but I think we shall be rather busy as it is. I take it from your attire that you would be interested in me teaching you how to fight?"

"I am," Sara said. She had seen the way that Shumuti had dealt with the creature they had met on the road and wished she had been able to defend herself as well.

"Well, you'll have yourself a good teacher," Astrid said.

"The best," Shumuti added.

Sara looked around at this new family she had discovered; a new cousin and an uncle. She was excited to get to know them better and had the feeling that she didn't know them at all. Sara looked at Astrid and found that she had lately been wondering the same thing about her mother. Astrid had agreed once they were safe that she would explain everything to her, but here they were now distracting her attention with talk of learning how to fight.

"Wait." Sara held up her hands. "Before I start anything, I have some questions. You promised me."

Sara directed her words at her mother, who looked back at her, saying nothing. Seaglen continued to draw with his charcoal, slowly and expertly sketching the tree into the background of the image.

"Astrid and I have been trying to piece it together," Seaglen said, "the Carnival of Games seems to have been nothing more than a cover-up for some other purpose. Whatever the creatures you met on the road have to do with that, if anything, we still don't know."

"At the moment, we know very little," Astrid said, "Seaglen leads some patrols from the village down below and is going to spend the next week or so expanding them further afield to see if we can learn anything more."

Seaglen finished a final stroke of shadow and set the drawing aside. "But for now, it seems like it would not be a terrible idea to make sure that all of us present have the skills to take care of themselves, in case something like these vultures were to appear again."

Sara's heart skipped a beat. "Right now?"

Her body was aching from riding the last few days and the general tiredness that came from continually running for days. She realised she had not felt entirely safe since the Carnival had arrived in Silverspring and that had taken its toll. Seaglen slid the completed drawing back into his sketchpad and stood up. His hazel eyes stared down at Sara expectantly. She rose to her feet slowly, to face him.

"Don't worry," Astrid whispered, as Sara passed her, "he knows you're still tired."

Sara tried to give her a reassuring nod, before she followed Seaglen out of the garden. Seaglen walked over to the stables and brought out a tall white horse, with speckled grey flanks. Sara went to get Arrow, and they were both daunted by the size of Seaglen and his horse. The sight did not improve her self-confidence.

"Shumuti!" Seaglen called back into the garden. "Remember the task I set you for today! Bring Aurielle with you."

"I won't forget!"

He turned to Sara. "Off we go then."

As they left the house, Sara remembered she still had more questions to ask. Suddenly, it felt too intimidating to raise these to just Seaglen alone. Even though he probably held the answers to almost every query she could think of, she was too daunted by him to ask. So she did nothing but follow after him silently across the fields.

Seaglen led the way up the grassy slope and into a small, shaded coppice of conifer trees, where pinecones crunched under Arrow's hooves as he walked. They rode upwards on a short, twisting path for a few minutes, before emerging out into the sunlight once more. The brightness of it burnt Sara's eyes and forced her to blink. It was a few moments before she managed to see again, but when she did, a silent gasp escaped her mouth.

They were on top of a high crag, and the visibility ran for miles. Gazing out into the distance, she caught a glimpse of a band of sparkling blue water on the faraway horizon, and recognised the Winterburn River. Looking the other way, the north-western region of Merrywater stretched out below her, as if on a map. From here, they stood on the highest point around Thayll. Rolling green fields and mountains covered the earth, and two long, bright lakes stood out in the centre of her vision, with streams that ran out like a ribbon from either end.

A pair of large birds circled in the sky above them, searching for prey in the mountains, and she instinctively crouched a little in the saddle.

"It's all right." Seaglen was watching the birds with a trained eye. "That is only a pair of eagles. You are lucky to have seen them."

Unbidden, a vision of the vulture creatures flashed through Sara's mind. Even now they could be swooping over the land to deliver their news to whœver might have sent them.

Seaglen gruffly interrupted her grim contemplation. "We will walk from here."

Sara dismounted without a word and obediently followed Seaglen to the overhang of the rock face, wondering where he was planning on going now. Oddly enough, she could swear that she could hear running water, a crashing noise that sounded like a waterfall. But there was no water anywhere nearby.

"Follow me closely," Seaglen said.

Apprehensively, she watched him walk towards the end of the cliff...and took one final step promptly over the edge. Sara gave a half yell and leapt forwards when he stepped off, but to her amazement, he did not fall. Instead, he just hovered there next to the top of the crag, and all Sara could see of him was his top half. Amazed, she shuffled forward to the edge and peered over the top. Cut into the side of the crag was a narrow stairway that wound down the rock face like a jagged, broken snake. The width of the stairs was little more than the spread of

Seaglen's feet. Sara gulped, with an ominous feeling in the pit of her stomach.

"Are we going down there?" Sara asked, dreading the answer.

"Of course," Seaglen said.

"Couldn't we train here?"

"My equipment is down below."

"Oh, right."

Sara cast around for some reason to prolong going down, and her gaze fell on Arrow.

"What about the horses?"

"They'll be safe here."

Safer than I am going to be, Sara thought miserably.

"Do not worry," Seaglen said, with a glint in his eye, "you will be perfectly fine."

Sara bit back a reply to that as fell the colour drain from her face. Seaglen began to descend the so-called stairway, and Sara crept forward to the brink of the crag and knelt on the grass above the precipice, examining the route. Dubiously, she swung her legs from beneath her and lowered one leg over the edge while gripping on the cliff top for dear life. On the path, Sara realised it was a little wider than it had looked previously, and there were good handholds in the rock. She shifted her weight until she was standing firmly on the stairs. One step to the right or one false footing, and Sara imagined for a second plunging through the air and landing on the rocks below, cracking her head and breaking bones. She screwed up her face, cast the thoughts from her mind and began the descent at a snail-like pace.

As Sara inched her way down, hugging the rock, she heard it again. Water. It sounded like a waterfall. As she pressed her ear against the stone, the noise almost seemed to be coming from inside. Sara shook her head and decided to focus on it later. At the moment, there were more important things to consider.

It didn't take as long as she first thought it would to traverse down the rock. They were about halfway down the cliff face when the stairs opened up into a small, rocky platform. Sara was busy concentrating on the last section when Seaglen spoke up.

"Sara, hurry up!" he shouted, almost sending her flying off the stairs. Sara's head shot up, and she suddenly felt afraid when she noticed a small trace of anxiety in Seaglen's eyes. He was staring at the sky above her. When she was near enough, Seaglen grabbed hold of her arm and dragged her through a crack covered by tangled curtain of ivy. It swung still once more after Sara had brushed through it and all light was cut off, plunging her into pitch blackness.

"This place is secret." Seaglen's voice spoke into her ear. "We do not want to be seen entering."

Around her, Sara could see nothing, but there was a thunder of water pounding in her ears and covering them with hands did little to block out the noise. She did not dare move, partly because of Seaglen's unease and also because she was not entirely convinced what would happen if she took one step in any one direction.

Sara tensed as a flame flickered up. Seaglen was holding a torch in one hand that he had taken from a bracket on the wall. She looked around in the orange light that cast wavering shadows on the rock walls and saw, at last, the waterfall. It was an enormous crashing wall of water, and the sound echœd and reverberated off the walls, resonating and amplifying the level of noise. Sara looked up at it in awe, its edges illuminated in a golden, fiery light.

"This way!" Seaglen called once more, over the noise.

They walked on a path around the edge of the waterfall until they arrived opposite the point they entered. Spray threw itself from the waterfall at random intervals, coating Sara's new clothes in a misty film. Seaglen stopped at the other side, and Sara cautiously peered around him to see why. The path had ended abruptly, but Seaglen did not seem too bothered by that as he turned to the rock face. Putting one hand on the stone, it briefly flickered red underneath his hand. Sara blinked, unsure if it had just been the torchlight she had seen, but then a sharp grating noise vibrated from the rock, and her eyes widened with surprise as part of the stone grated outwards slowly to reveal a hidden room. Sara walked through the rock-door after Seaglen, wondering what would be coming next.

Seaglen closed the door behind her, and the noise of the waterfall cut off instantly. The echo of it rang inside Sara's ears for a minute and then gradually faded to silence. The floor of the room they were in was small, but it was incredibly high, and Sara could barely see the ceiling. Cracks of light illuminated down from the roof to create fragmented shapes on the floor and walls, which meant that the top of the room reached the top of the cliff.

Scattered around the wall of the room were metal brackets that each occupied some kind of weapon, useful for both long-range and close combat, except for the few that contained torches. Seaglen used his flame to ignite the brackets on the wall and cast a warm glow over the room. Two cupboards rested up against opposing ends of the room, but elsewhere the space was bare.

"This is my training room," Seaglen said, "I will mainly teach you here, but there are occasions where it will be more useful to go outside."

In the semi-darkness, the firelight glinted through Seaglen's hair and face and shadowed his figure. Sara peered across at him in wonder, speculating about how he had come across this hidden cave in the first place. Of course, she did not dare to ask him.

"Now then, first off, I am going to give you a small test."

"What sort of test?" Sara asked.

"Just to see what you can do."

Seaglen detached a bow from the wall and then pulled back a grey curtain that blended in as part of the wall, revealing a circular target board.

"Have you ever used a bow before?"

"Occasionally," Sara said, "I think I'm better at it than I am with a sword."

"Let me see how you do then." Seaglen handed over a quiver of arrows.

Sara stood opposite the target board and fixed an arrow to the bow. Drawing the string back to her cheek, she fired at the target, sighing with relief as she heard a low thud. It had hit the second ring in on the target board. Her next two arrows landed in the outer ring, though the fourth hit the ring around the centre and Sara heard Seaglen shift behind her. Fuelled with confidence, Sara fired the fifth arrow, and it missed the board entirely, rebounding off the wall to fall limply onto the floor. Slightly embarrassed, Sara turned to Seaglen, who looked at her wryly.

"I've seen worse."

Sara walked over to the target board and plucked out her arrows.

"Here," he instructed, "stand like this so that you are facing perpendicular to the wall."

She turned her feet at right angles to the target and twisted back to look at the board. She placed them shoulder-width apart and then Seaglen showed her how to hold the bow up and keep her bow arm straight. He told her that one of the three shafts of the arrow was different and that it marked which way the arrow should enter the bow.

A mixture of brown and white-flecked feathers decorated the flights of Seaglen's arrows.

"Now try again. Try to aim with your distance from the target in mind. Sight down the arrow and take your time."

So Sara did. She drew the bow back to her ear, keeping her elbow high and closed one eye to focus better. She fired six more rounds into the board and with Seaglen's advice, noticed her aim steadily improve. No more arrows fell outside the third ring after her second round.

"Good work," Seaglen said.

"Thank you." Sara smiled, feeling slightly more confident.

He considered her for a moment.

"Keep practising."

Seaglen walked away from Sara dismissively and over to a cupboard. Feeling deflated, she yanked out her arrows more force than they needed.

Time passed, and Sara lost track of it. They switched to swords and even briefly to hand to hand combat, before returning to the bow. Early afternoon approached when she noticed the sunlight through the holes from the roof became brighter and more intense. Her aim had withered away into nothing as she lost concentration and it was a moment before Sara realised Seaglen was tapping her on the shoulder.

"That is enough. Let's go back outside. There is one more thing I want to show you before we end today."

He turned and opened the door again. The rush of the waterfall echoed through into the room, filling her ears and deafening her. Seaglen gestured for Sara to bring the bow and to follow him. Thankful to get out into the fresh air once more, she gathered up the bow and quiver of arrows, before rushing out of the door.

Going up the narrow stairway outside was only slightly less demanding than it had been going down. Sara shouldered the quiver of arrows after sliding the bow inside with them so that her hands were free to grab the rock and steady herself. Only when they reached the top of the climb did she notice that her fingers were aching for gripping to the rock so tightly.

Arrow stood grazing in the same spot that Sara had left him. Seaglen mounted his own silvery, grey horse and Sara followed suit after him. Seaglen led the way down through the woods back towards the direction of the house. As they approached the house, Seaglen swerved around to the right and entered a long field, and Sara turned Arrow sharply to follow him.

Scattered around the field were wooden poles. They were sticking out of the grass and cut at various lengths and thicknesses. Curiously, Sara leaned over in her saddle as she passed by to get a closer look. The leather saddle creaked beneath her and she jolted upright, in case she might fall. Small puncture holes riddled the poles and crawled over every inch of the wood, giving it a twisted and wounded appearance.

"The poles are getting old," Seaglen said, "like me."

Sara looked up. It was odd, but ever since she had first seen Seaglen she had not once thought of him as old, but there was no denying the silver of his hair and beard showed that he was no young man.

They practised for a few minutes shooting the bow from horseback. It took a moment for Sara to get used to the difference from standing on the ground, but she eventually managed to start hitting some of the larger targets scattered about the field.

"Right then." Seaglen came over to her, taking the bow and one arrow. "This is what I want you to do. I'm not expecting you to get this first time around, but it's something to aim for."

Sara stepped Arrow backwards out of the way, as Seaglen turned around to face down the field. He set off cantering down the centre of the paddock, but as he approached a shorter pole, Seaglen nocked an arrow to his bow. He rode past the pole and then turned in the saddle, firing the bow at the same time. His shaft sank deep into the wood and Sara stared on in disbelief.

Seaglen trotted back.

"Now it is your turn."

"I can't do that!"

"Just give it a go."

Reluctantly, Sara brought out an arrow and got it ready to fire because she knew there would be no way that she would be able to accomplish that while she was moving. Then she steadied herself on Arrow and set off, juggling the bow and reins in both hands. Arrow picked up speed, and Sara selected the tallest and widest pole in her path. As she got there, she swung around as Seaglen had done but only got halfway round when she lost her balance. Both the bow and arrow flew out of her hands. The arrow embedded itself deep into the ground, and the bow skidded along the grass.

Sara's right foot came out of the stirrup, and she clung desperately to Arrow's saddle as they thundered down the field. Frantically, she scrambled back upright and twisted around, struggling to get Arrow back under control. She had no chance. Arrow skidded to a halt as he reached the end of the field, neighing in panic and Sara gracefully slid off the end of him to land in a heap on the ground.

For a while, she just sat there feeling slightly stunned until she heard Seaglen's horse's hooves vibrating through the ground towards her. Further off, she caught the sound of cheering and some clapping. Sara grimaced and pushed herself up out of the grass. Standing by the fence were Shumuti and Astrid. Another girl accompanied them who Sara had never seen before.

"For your first go, that was not bad," Seaglen said from his horse.

Sara stood up. "Honestly?"

He smirked. "You ought to have seen Shumuti's first time, she does not dare talk about it."

Sara grinned, despite a winded pain in her stomach, where she had hit the ground. "I'll bet she doesn't if it was any worse than that."

"Are you all right?"

"Fine," Sara answered.

"Then that will be it for today," Seaglen said, "I will be teaching you the tricks of doing this, along with much more. You will pick it all up soon."

Sara nodded. "Thank you, for deciding to train me," she added, not sure why she had said it.

"We shall see what else I can teach you soon enough," he said, stroking his horse's neck.

Sara waited for elaboration to his comment, but nothing was forthcoming. Seaglen inclined his head and rode away. Seaglen had grown less scary in the last few hours, and she was almost beginning to look forward to having him as a teacher. She gave Arrow a pat on the neck, taking the time to ponder on the unexpected turn her life had taken.

CHAPTER 6
THE LAKES

Shumuti cheered in Sara's direction from the far side of the training field, while Astrid whistled loudly beside her.

"So, she is your cousin?" a voice asked, to Shumuti's left.

Shumuti nodded to her oldest friend, Aurielle, who stood beside her.

"That must be a good surprise to find you have a new family." Aurielle smiled.

"It is."

As Shumuti watched Sara training with Seaglen, it struck her how well Sara was doing for her first day. She had a lot of talent, and Shumuti knew that her father would find the best way to utilise it. She knew that Seaglen had wanted to spend some time with Sara to test whether he could discover anything magical about her, and a part of Shumuti wanted to run and ask him what he thought. He had never once trained anybody who was not talented in Magic.

"Hey, Shumuti," Astrid said, on her other side, "I was wondering what the two of you thought about maybe showing Sara and myself around Merrywater this afternoon?"

"Oh, that's a great idea!" Aurielle said.

"Of course," Shumuti said.

"We could go out to the lakes?" Aurielle said.

"Ah, they were my favourite place," Astrid said.

"Sara!" Shumuti called her over, seeing Seaglen ride off.

Jerking her head to the direction of the noise, Sara mounted Arrow and rode over to the small party by the fence.

"Are you done for the day?" Shumuti asked.

"I am." Sara breathed a prolonged sigh of relief.

"Do you fancy doing some exploring?" Shumuti asked, "we were going to take Astrid up to the lakes and see what she can remember. Oh, and this is Aurielle, by the way, my friend."

Shumuti pointed out Aurielle and Sara gave her a small wave. Aurielle grinned cheerily back.

"I'll come," Sara said, "but I need to sort Arrow out first."

"You can drop her off at the house on the way there," Shumuti said, leading the group away from the field.

"All right," Sara said, "I'll ride ahead and meet you once I'm ready."

Sara rode off towards the stables. Curious to ask about the first day of teaching, Shumuti quickly detached from Aurielle and Astrid, who seemed to be getting on well together already and darted back to the house to find Seaglen.

"How did she do?" Shumuti asked, bursting in through the door, "I thought she looked good."

Seaglen wearily ran a hand through his wild hair and looked up from the chair he had just sat down at. "She has done extremely well, considering it has been her first day. Almost...as good as you were."

"Then, you've found something?"

Seaglen gazed across out of the window. "Nothing to do with Magic." He tapped the wood grain on the table. "But she is talented. I am curious about her and will not give up my search just yet."

The door opened behind Shumuti, and she exchanged a final glance with her father as Astrid and Aurielle joined them.

"What do you think of her?" Astrid asked. She sounded almost as eager as Shumuti.

Shumuti caught Aurielle's eye and jerked her head towards her bedroom. Aurielle smirked and took the hint, realising they would be having a long conversation.

Aurielle and Shumuti had been friends as far back as Shumuti could remember, though Aurielle was just over a year older than her. Seaglen had trained them both at the same time, and their skills were almost equal. Aurielle had grown slightly taller than Shumuti had, much to her annoyance and she had bright golden hair that contrasted with Shumuti's deep chestnut colour.

"What do you think?" Shumuti asked, sitting down on her bed.

Aurielle sank into a seat on the window ledge and stretched out.

"About what?"

"About how Sara can't use Magic," Shumuti said, "I guess I had always assumed it ran in families."

"Family dœsn't mean anything," Aurielle said, "just because we can both use it dœs not mean it's always guaranteed. Besides, if she were magical, she would have shown it by now."

Shumuti nodded slowly.

"I just hope Astrid decides to tell her about it soon," Shumuti said.

"We've kept Magic a secret for the whole of our lives."

"I know, but this time it feels wrong."

"At least Seaglen will teach Sara how to defend herself," Aurielle said, "then she can come and join us out on scouting patrols."

"I don't even know if they will stay here in Thayll," Shumuti said, "once the threat of that creature's attack has died down and the Carnival has returned to Attaching, there's no reason for them not to return to Silverspring."

"Well, we saw no sign of anything on patrol this morning," Aurielle said.

"I know Seaglen wants to get to the bottom of where the creature came from and why it attacked," Shumuti said.

"So do I," Aurielle said, "I'm intrigued about what you said that it might link to Magic in some way."

Alerted by a creak at the bottom of the stairs, the pair instinctively fell silent. Aurielle folded her arms in thought and turned her attention to gaze out of the window. A minute later, Sara reached the top of the stairs and strode into the room. She greeted them, before almost immediately collapsing onto her bed.

"Hi," Aurielle said, "you looked good out there. Seaglen says you're doing brilliantly."

"Thanks," Sara said, "I'd quite like to sleep for a week now, but Astrid said she was ready to head out, if you both were?"

"One minute," Aurielle said, gathering up her coat.

Shumuti and Sara waited for Aurielle a moment. Out of the corner of her eye, she saw that Sara fiddled unconsciously the string of a small necklace around her neck that Shumuti had not noticed before. The four of them left the house and walked up to the winding track, leaving the village far behind them. Sara began talking to her mother up ahead, and a moment later, Aurielle materialised out of thin air beside Shumuti.

"So, do you think Seaglen is right to be worried?"

Shumuti said nothing for a second.

"I do." She sighed heavily. "I know well enough that when my father is on edge about something that I certainly ought to be."

Shumuti cut her conversation short to concentrate instead on not walking straight into Sara and Astrid, who had stopped abruptly on the path ahead. She glanced out, realising that they had reached the hill overlooking the Merrywater lakes. The lakes cradled the foot of the mountains, surrounded by steep precipices on every side, and coniferous forest that clung impossibly to the edges of the rock. On the crag above, exposed patches of white stone gleamed and trails of the broken off scree zigzagged down to the waterside below. The rocks at the waters' edge infused the colour of the lake closest to them, turning the edges white. The two vast bodies of water shimmered a bright blue in the sunlight today, reflecting the mountain peaks and the occasional fluffy cloud that passed overhead as sharply as glass.

The lakes were named Snapper Lake and White Lake, and this spot was a popular draw in the height of summer for both travellers and locals alike, for their size and beauty, not to mention for the abundance of fish contained within the waters of Snapper Lake. The lakes were a calm place, and occasionally Seaglen would bring Shumuti down, but they only came either in the early morning or at night when nobody else was around. Luckily, today they seemed to have the lakes all to themselves.

"Ah!" Astrid said, "now these I do remember."

They meandered casually down to the shores of White Lake. Pebbles interspersed the light sandy beach, some of which had the occasional strand of lichen draped over them. The gentle waves of White Lake rippled gently in a half-hearted sort of way, and underneath the water, Shumuti could see the point where sand and rocks were swallowed up by the murky darkness of the deepest part of the lake.

Aurielle was talking enthusiastically to Astrid, who was recounting her memories of Merrywater, so Shumuti looked for Sara and found her sitting on a large rock turning a pebble over and over in her hands and sat down beside her. Sara glanced towards Aurielle and Astrid with a sad look in her eyes.

"What's the matter?" Shumuti asked.

Sara stared at the pebble and opened her mouth before closing and re-opening it, trying to find the right words.

"Can I ask you something?"

"Of course," Shumuti replied, hiding her worry.

"And you'll promise to give me a straight answer?"

"Tell me the question."

"All right." Sara thought for a moment. "Well, what do you know about Magic?"

"What do *you* know about Magic?" Shumuti asked her, thoroughly caught off guard.

"Whatever it is, I know it's something that links to my mother." Sara took a deep breath. "But now I'm betting that you, your father and possibly even Aurielle have a connection to it as well."

"How did you find that out?" Shumuti asked.

"I heard you and Astrid talking, the morning that we met you in the forest."

"Oh." Shumuti slumped back against the rocks. "Then you guessed the rest?"

"I'm fairly confident your father did something with it to open the door to the training room."

"He took you down the path in the cliff?"

"I'd call 'path' a bit of a strong word."

Shumuti was astounded. Not only had Seaglen risked Sara's life by taking her down those stairs, but he had also shown her Magic even though she could not use it herself. Had he revealed it to her on purpose? Shumuti made a mental note to confront him the moment they got back, but in the meantime, she could think of nothing to say.

"Am I right?" Sara asked, "is that what my mother used on the soldiers at the Carnival?"

"Yes."

"And you can all use it?"

"Yes."

"You all have this...ability," Sara said, at last reaching the heart of the thing that she wanted to talk about, "but I don't."

"No."

"What is it?"

Sara was twisting the string of her necklace again, utterly unaware while she stared at Shumuti sadly. She realised how down and confused Sara must have been feeling when essentially her whole world had been flipped over in a matter of days. Shumuti shook herself and tried to form a better answer for Sara.

"It's true, we have access to this power that we call Magic. It's a connection we have to the world around us and that connection lets us control it, to some extent. You may well have the same skill, Sara. Seaglen is looking for it in his training with you. In Aurielle's case, and mine, we learnt it when we were very young, but there is no set time when the ability might come to you. I'm sorry that we kept it from you though, about what we are. You see, we've always kept that side of ourselves hidden and I know Astrid wanted to wait so she could explain it to you properly. But we were wrong. We should have told you earlier."

Shumuti thought her words might have made a small difference, as Sara relaxed a little. They sat in silence for a bit, listening to Astrid and Aurielle happily chatting when Sara spoke up again.

"I can't believe she never told me what she could do." Sara stared across at Astrid.

"I think your mother was happy in her life in Elmdale with you," Shumuti said, "where there was no need for it."

Sara gave a small nod in reply.

"I still don't really understand," she said, "what is it? Can you see it?"

"No," Shumuti said, "you see only the effects of it. But I can feel it everywhere around me, in the cliffs above and down to the bottom of the lake. Look."

She raised one hand and pointed to a cluster of rocks by the water. Shumuti reached out with her mind for the energy that was coated over the pebbles beside the lake and extracted the tiniest amount from it. Directing the Magic at the pile of stones, out of nowhere she created two spirals of air that lifted the rocks and suspended them in a miniature tornado. Sara watched on at the spectacle in awe. A second later, Shumuti released the Magic, and the pebbles clinked back down onto the beach.

"That's incredible," Sara said.

"Shumuti!" She heard her name called out indignantly.

Astrid and Aurielle had realised what she had done and broke off their conversation to march over.

"What do you think you're doing?" Astrid said.

"She already knows," Shumuti answered, "she's known since the encounter in the forest, perhaps even before that something wasn't right."

Astrid looked across at her daughter with a mixture of guilt and anger on her face. Shumuti knew she had wanted to tell Sara herself, but she had just taken too long to do it.

"Sara," Astrid said, "I'm sorry. I'm the one who should have told you."

Sara remained silent.

"You must have a lot of questions," Astrid said.

"I do."

"Maybe we should answer them at the house," Aurielle suggested, "otherwise it will be dark before we get back."

Shumuti looked down at her shadow on the beach and noticed how long it had become. The lake was now a rainbow of sunset hues, more beautiful than ever. Sara and Shumuti scrambled to their feet after one last look and set off after the other two.

They climbed steadily back up the slope and reached the village of Thayll just as darkness fell. A few thin, snaking tendrils of smoke wound their way up from Seaglen's roof, high on the hillside, the smoke drawing them in towards the house. Seaglen was visibly nowhere inside until Shumuti heard his footsteps upstairs.

"I'll go and get him," she said, eager for an opportunity to talk to her father alone.

Shumuti headed up the stairs and barged into Seaglen's room upstairs, finding him studying a pile of dusty old books.

"Did you show Magic to Sara?" she asked outright.

"Yes," he replied, just as bluntly.

Shumuti stared and then burst out in anger. "She figured out all about it and that everybody can use it, except for her. Why did you show her? She looked so miserable when we were down by the lakes."

"I knew she was working it out," Seaglen answered, "I just gave her a small push in the right direction."

"I told her she might one day have the same abilities. Do you think that's true?"

Seaglen looked at her evenly. "What I believe will make no difference as to what will happen."

"That's not an answer."

"No. All we can do is wait to see."

Shumuti refrained herself from arguing any further.

"Sara and Astrid are waiting downstairs."

They left the room and rejoined the others. All five of them sat around the table, wondering who should begin.

"So, Sara," Seaglen said, "now it is time for us to speak openly."

"I have so many questions that I don't know where to start," Sara said.

"I can understand," Seaglen said, "perhaps the best way to explain Magic to you would be to show you."

"Shumuti already did," Sara said.

"Why don't Shumuti and I organise a Magic lesson of sorts for you?" Aurielle said, "give us a little while to put something together, and we can try to teach you about what we can do."

"All right," Sara agreed.

"It sounds like a good idea to me," Seaglen said, "is there anything you want us to answer now though, Sara?"

"I don't know. I'm still trying to take it all in. Shumuti answered a few earlier."

"We promise to answer any questions you have whenever they come to you."

"We need to figure out how to explain it to you as well," Shumuti said.

Aurielle ate with them that night, but left soon after, so the four remaining family members sat by the fire, with Sara and Shumuti on the rug and Seaglen and Astrid on the two chairs. Everybody felt relaxed and sleepy and not in the mood to do very much. Sara and Shumuti stared into the warm, glowing flames listening to Seaglen and Astrid catching up, until Sara turned to Shumuti with a question.

"Can Aurielle's parents use Magic?"

"Her mother could," Shumuti answered, relishing the fact that there was no longer a need for secrecy, "she was called Lyria, but she disappeared a long while ago. Nobody truly knows the details of what happened, but Aurielle believes that her mother walked out on her. Her father can't, but he knows what Aurielle can do and keeps it to himself. It affected him badly when he found out, though."

"I understand. Who else is there who can use it?"

"Nobody."

"Nobody?" Sara was shocked.

"Nobody else here. Years ago, before we were born, there were six in total. They were friends of Seaglen and Astrid, but they live far to the north if they're still alive. I think at least one of them is dead, but Seaglen has lost contact with them."

"Oh."

They drifted back into silence and Sara returned her gaze to the fire. The sparks and small flames next to the hearth flickered about in a wild, frenzied dance with each other, crackling and hissing occasionally. Shumuti reached out and added another log to the flames, wondering if Sara would continue to deal with this new situation as calmly in the days to come.

Chapter 7
Magic

~Sara~

It was a while before Sara received her lesson. The others answered her questions on Magic and what it was, but she knew she had barely scratched the surface. Shumuti kept repeating was how strange it felt to talk about something she had never spoken about freely before, so she knew the others were getting used to the idea of sharing their secret as well.

For Sara, the next month or so of her new life gradually settled into a routine. Every morning she would head off up to the underground waterfall with Seaglen, where he would teach her new skills, and she would train. Most of the time, she would practise alone, but occasionally Shumuti came along to challenge whatever new techniques she had learnt.

She knew though that there was something else behind the training she was undergoing. Secretly, Seaglen was hoping to unearth some hidden magical ability in Sara, but so far he had been unsuccessful. Gradually, Sara was beginning to understand more and more about the talent that the others had. The more she learned, the more she was sure the same was not a part of her. Aurielle and

Shumuti had tried to tell her about the theory behind what they could do, but she still had no idea how it worked practically.

Nevertheless, only when Aurielle was with them that Sara completely felt like the outsider. It did not matter how friendly everybody was to her; she did not share the same connection that they had. Half of her tried to learn about what they could do, but the other half almost wanted to cut herself off entirely from something Sara knew she would never have. Whenever she was instructed by Seaglen to research a subject for a few hours in his study, she knew it meant that the four of them would be heading up to the waterfall to practise Magic. On one such morning, Shumuti approached her while she was getting ready for the day.

"Listen," Shumuti began, "Seaglen can't teach you today because he's been called out on a scouting patrol near the northern border of Merrywater. He'll be gone all day."

"So I won't be training?" Sara asked.

"Well, how about you come out with Aurielle and me?"

"Really? I mean that would be good." Sara had never seen Aurielle fight before, and she was curious about how Shumuti's friend compared.

The pair of them met Aurielle above the house and rode up to the track to the training room. Leaving the horses to graze on the grass, they descended the slender stairway and on to the platform below. Sara had become almost adept on the stairs by now, but when Seaglen had smiled and suggested adding in the extra challenge of seeing how fast Sara could go down them blindfolded, she had blankly refused.

Once inside the cavern, Shumuti led the way through the darkness to the stone door. When she pressed her hand against the rock, there was a flash of silver from underneath her fingertips instead of the red Sara was used to whenever Seaglen opened the door. The stone door creaked shut behind them as soon as all three were inside, and she felt the familiar eerie silence every time the noise of the crashing water was cut off.

"Right," Shumuti began, glancing at Aurielle furtively, "so we had an idea of what to do today, but whether we do is up to you."

"What?" Sara stared between them, wondering what was going on.

"Basically," Aurielle said, "we thought it might be a good idea to show you how we use Magic. What do you think?"

"Are you serious?" Sara asked, "you know I'm not like you."

"Let us explain why," Aurielle continued, "you may not be able to use it, but being surrounded by the four of us, there's little chance you can escape from it. Besides, there is a still lot to learn, if you're willing."

"But I thought Astrid and I would be leaving soon," Sara said, "heading back to Silverspring now that the danger from the creature has gone."

"Well, that's just the thing," Shumuti said, "that's the reason my father has gone on patrol today. There's been another sighting. Further north, but close to the border with Elmdale."

"It's back?" Sara asked.

"It's not safe for you and Astrid to leave here yet," Shumuti said, "it's too dangerous on the open road."

"Do you think it's still looking for us?" Sara asked.

"Yes." Shumuti hesitated. "We think the creature links to Magic and it chased after you because Astrid has the same ability. You need to understand why we want you to stay here, Sara. We don't want to keep any more secrets from you."

"All right." Sara agreed with that part wholeheartedly.

"I was worried it would be the last thing you would want to learn about." Shumuti admitted.

Sara didn't want to acknowledge that it was not far from the truth but she also knew if these creatures were going to keep hunting Astrid and her, she knew she needed to gather more information. So instead, she took a breath and dove in.

"You say you think these vultures are connected to Magic, does that mean that they were created by it? They didn't seem natural."

"We think it's a possibility," Aurielle said.

"There is also some link between the creatures and Attaching," Shumuti informed her, "it is a dark thought to think that the King would have anything to do with this, but you said his men were acting very strangely at the Carnival. The thought that the King might be aware of Magic is an unsettling one."

"If there used to be others like you, could the creatures be linked to one of them?" Sara asked.

"We don't know," Shumuti answered, "Seaglen lost contact with them over the years, but two of them did eventually settle down up north."

"If the ability is passed down, there could well be more of you now, if the others are still alive and had children," Sara said.

"Maybe, but you are proof that might not be the case."

"So, were Seaglen and Astrid born with the ability?"

"No, they were about our age, or a little older when they first could use it. It's odd, Seaglen has little memory of how it happened. All he can remember is that he was in the city of Lyria, in Attaching when it happened, and met a peculiar stranger there who he never saw again, who gave him the ability to wield Magic. From the moment he realised what he could do, he was told that there was a job to go with it."

"What do you mean?"

"There was a threat from Nimaz that couldn't be dealt with by the regular army. Seaglen and the other five went to deal with it instead."

"A magical threat?"

Shumuti nodded. "Since their success then, they've still been able to use Magic."

"But I don't remember hearing anything about this. If they defended Meteorath, surely it was a big event?"

"Nobody knows about it," Aurielle said.

"People have no clue," Shumuti said, "the whole operation was carried out in secret in the heart of Nimaz. Everything to do with Magic has always remained a secret."

"Why?" Sara asked.

"Because it's a dangerous thing to use," Aurielle said, "if it fell into the wrong hands."

Sara cast a confused expression between the two of them.

"We told you Magic is inside nature and everything living," Shumuti said, "like a source of energy. It's what keeps rivers flowing and trees growing. Our skill is that we can take some of that power and reshape it, alter its form. If we take a little of that energy, it can replenish itself easily, but take too much and you begin to destroy what's around you, not to mention hurting yourself. If you don't know what you're doing or don't care about the consequences, then you can create a lot of uncontrollable damage or unintended effects. That's the reason Seaglen always impresses on us the importance of keeping it secret because it is safer the fewer people know of its existence. Over time, depleted Magic will naturally begin to accumulate again, but the more you use, the greater the damage dealt and the longer the land takes to regenerate."

"We think the vultures are an example of the misuse of Magic," Aurielle said, "something like that should not exist naturally."

"Do you see, Sara?" Shumuti said, "what we can do comes with a lot of responsibility. We can't just use Magic recklessly, whenever we want to."

"I get it." Sara nodded slowly. "But it is hard to understand something when its existence is based just on your word. Is there no way that I can see it around me?"

"Not the way we can, I don't think," Shumuti said, "you can see the effects of when we use it, like with the door here or when I lifted the rocks on the beach. For us, I guess it's like having an extra sense, along with being able to see, hear or smell. You're always aware that it's around you. Like here, I sense it in the walls and floor, in the air. If I focus harder, I can begin to manipulate it and transform it into whichever element I can wield."

"You told me there were four elements," Sara said.

"We either specialise in the earth, air, water or fire," Aurielle said, "I use water for my Magic, and Shumuti uses the air, Seaglen can use fire and Astrid uses earth. We don't get to choose, and we can only ever control one out of the four."

"That is why the door to the training room glows silver for me, but red for Seaglen," Shumuti said, "silver is sometimes associated with air Magic and red with fire."

"But why does the training room door glow at all?" Sara asked, "is there something special about it?"

"There is, actually," Shumuti said, "there are very few locations in the world where Magic is abundant. Where there is almost an endless supply of it and the use of Magic costs almost nothing, this room is one of those places. It's no coincidence that this is where Seaglen decided to settle down and set up his training room."

"Then you can do anything you want to in here?" Sara asked, looking up and trying in vain to detect something other than what she could visibly see around her.

"Limited only by our imagination and our ability," Shumuti said, "it's also taken us years to become any- where near skilled in using Magic. Even now, there is still so much that I don't know."

"It doesn't help that Seaglen and Astrid are trained in controlling fire and earth, whereas we use water and air," Aurielle added, "there is only so much that they can teach us."

"That is something else unique about this room," Shu- muti said, "all four elements are present here. There is earth in the walls, and above us on the cliff, the waterfall supplies water, and the torch brackets can be a source of a fire. Air is also all around."

"So, do you need your element to be present around you to use Magic?" Sara asked, "like Seaglen would need a lit torch to be able to use fire?"

"No." Shumuti shook her head. "when you are starting, it is easier if there is something nearby, like a river for Aurielle, something to draw on, rather than creating your source of water from nothing. But after a while, you no longer need that assistance."

"I moved from needing the waterfall to a stream, to a water drop, to creating water from nothing," Aurielle said, "once I fully got to understand my element."

"This is a good training room then," Sara said.

Shumuti nodded.

"But outside of here, what you can do is limited?" Sara asked.

"It is all about knowing the point not to cross," Shumuti said, "Magic enriches some areas and remains sparse in others, so it depends on your location and what you intend to do. It takes a while to learn when you're close to the point where you should stop. If you go too far, it's not long before you start to see the effects visually around you. For instance, plants die, the ground cracks, and the air becomes dry."

Sara voiced a question she had about her mother. "Did Astrid use her Magic to heal people?"

"Yes," Aurielle answered, "healing is one of the skills attributed to the earth element."

"She used Magic to heal people without them knowing?"

"Yes."

It struck Sara then that Astrid could have used Magic on her too anytime she ever fell ill. Her whole life and she had never once been aware. Despite herself, Sara felt a sudden sense of misgiving. There was no way of knowing when either of them was using Magic, or what they could do, and she had no concept of what the limits of Magic even were. They could do anything, and Sara would be completely unable to stop them. She bet they could also kill with Magic. Struck by the thought, Sara asked them.

"Yes, we could use Magic to kill." Shumuti appeared reluctant to reply. "The same as you can use a sword or a bow, but we never have."

Sara was beginning to realise why they had decided to keep the existence of Magic a secret. She doubted that the majority of strangers would understand what they were and take kindly to them, knowing what they could do.

"Can the vultures use Magic?" Sara asked.

"It's unlikely," Shumuti said, "otherwise I'm sure they wouldn't have fled the clearing so quickly."

"Can you even defend from a magical attack?" Sara asked.

"Only with Magic," Aurielle answered.

"We could protect you by creating a ward to defend from most attacks, which forms a magical barrier," Shumuti said.

"Could you show me?" Sara asked, curiosity getting the better of her.

"Are you sure?" Shumuti asked, with concern.

"Maybe just protect yourself. I'll stand back out of the way."

"All right. In that case, I'll create it. We need an attacker, so Aurielle, you attack me with Magic, and I will try to defend myself."

Feeling suddenly apprehensive, Sara backed away to the wall and watched Aurielle step away from them and face Shumuti across the room. Everything fell silent until Sara heard a slight creaking sound. She whipped her head round to where she heard the noise from and then watched, enthralled by what was happening. A single drop of water fell onto her face from the darkness. From high above Shumuti, a creaking sound became a rush of water, similar to the noise the waterfall usually made. Sara glanced at Aurielle to see her face set in concentration. In front of her, Shumuti tensed, as though preparing for something. Out of the pitch black of the top of the cave, a new waterfall appeared out of thin air, aimed directly at Shumuti.

Sara thought she saw a flash of silver as the water connected with something invisible in the air. Shumuti stood calmly staring out at Aurielle as dry as she had been a few minutes ago. A few feet above her head was an invisible barrier that deflected the water like a shield and sent it crashing harmlessly to either side. Veins of silver occasionally glinted through the shield that Shumuti had created, so Sara could see it extended to the floor on all sides, encompassing her in a dome of safety.

"You see?" Shumuti turned her head back, calling over the sound of water. "It's a good defence."

"Is it hard for you to do that?" Sara asked.

"It used to be," Shumuti replied, "but not anymore. If the attack is more powerful than my casting though, it will break through. Fortunately, Aurielle is being kind."

The flow of the unnatural waterfall ebbed away into nothing, leaving nothing but pools of water scattered across the training room. Sara noticed after staring at them for a moment that they were evaporating much quicker than water would typically take to disappear.

"I got wetter than you from that," Aurielle commented, as she rejoined them and the silver cage faded into nothing.

"So you both are still learning?" Sara asked.

"Always will be," Aurielle said, "the more adept you become, the more new skills there are to learn. Even Seaglen can still learn a thing or two if he chooses. You have to remember that Shumuti and I are only the second generation of Magic users to have ever existed. Seaglen once said that anything we can imagine, we could try to figure out how to do with our Magic. The only limit is our imagination."

"What happened to the others then?" Sara asked, "Aurielle, Shumuti told me your mother was one of the original six that there were."

"Her name was Lyria." Sara watched Aurielle stiffen slightly. "That is almost all I know. My father refuses to talk about her, and I can see it brings up bad memories. Seaglen has told me a little more. The last time he saw her, she was heading to Boctor when I was very young, and that is the last I heard."

Sara fell silent, suddenly wishing she had not asked the question.

"I know that one died during the battle they fought in Nimaz," Shumuti said, "the other two stayed in the north after, while Seaglen, Astrid and Lyria all moved south."

Reluctant to ask any more questions, Sara began to digest all the information she had just learnt. Subconsciously looking around the room, she noticed that the floor had now entirely dried out once more.

Sara could tell the other two did not want to overload her with information any further and so they spent the rest of the day practising with swords and bows. She discovered that she should not have been surprised by the fact that Aurielle was as equally talented as Shumuti using a sword, if not with a different, slightly more aggressive style.

As evening began to fall, they traversed the cliff to join the path that would lead home. They gathered the horses on the cliff top and galloped down through the trees and back to the house, to see whether or not Seaglen had returned yet. As they approached the house, a lone rider came up from the track from the village to meet them. Shumuti moved ahead to see who it was, but Sara recognised the horse immediately. Picking up speed, she rode past Shumuti to greet Astrid.

"Has Seaglen been to see you?" Astrid asked Sara as soon as they met.

"No," she answered.

Astrid looked worried.

"Why?" Sara asked.

"Is everything all right?" Shumuti asked as she caught up.

"Seaglen's patrol has still has not come back," Astrid replied, "they were meant to return this afternoon."

"That is unusual," Shumuti muttered.

"I've come from the village. No one there has heard any news," Astrid said.

"Let's get back to the house," Shumuti suggested.

The house was dark and silent when they returned. Seaglen's horse was not there when they stabled the rest. The four of them sat silently down at the table, each wondering whether they should be concerned or what was the best thing to do. Stood by the window, Sara cast a glance out down the darkened road, but it was empty. An image of the vultures flickered again into her mind, but she kept her thought to herself.

"Sometimes the patrols do stay away overnight," Shumuti said, "but only when they are meant to. Usually, I would not worry, but what with what has happened recently, I wonder if I should go out and try to find him."

"He can handle himself," Aurielle said, "plus we have no idea where to look for him and little chance of finding him in the dark. He may return before morning."

Sara watched as Shumuti nodded and absent-mindedly picked a small sliver of wood away from the table.

"Couldn't you use Magic to find out where he was?" Sara asked.

"If it was the other way around, maybe." Shumuti grimaced. "Seaglen can detect the distant location of other Magic users, but neither Aurielle nor I have managed to pick up the skill. We can tell from a short distance away, but Seaglen is well out of my range."

"We might be worrying over nothing," Aurielle said, "the patrol may just have found something out there that they needed to stay overnight to look at."

"Either way, if there is any news, we will learn of it first in the village, not here," Astrid said, "I am going to head back down there. If the need arises, I will head out and try to find him."

"We should come with you," Sara said.

"No, there's no sense in all of us trailing around, maybe over nothing," Astrid said.

"I do normally worry about him when there is no need," Shumuti admitted.

"In that case, the three of you ought to get some rest," Astrid said.

Once Astrid had left, they ate some leftover stew that had been bubbling near the fire and tried to settle in for the night. Shumuti took up a seat on the windowsill, watching the road silently. However much she might say she was not concerned, it was clear how she felt.

"I would rather stay up for a while just in case," Shumuti said eventually, "there is little chance I would get to sleep."

"We may as well stay here until Astrid returns," Aurielle said, "if we go to a proper bed we'll have to lock the door, and that would mean locking your mother outside. I don't think she'd appreciate it."

"Oh, I don't know." Sara yawned. "A night in the stables wouldn't do her any harm."

"I'm happy sleeping here," Shumuti said, "if somebody comes, the chances are that one of us will wake up."

The hours passed by slowly as their conversation finally faded to nothing, failing to mask the disquiet that each of them felt. Nobody wanted to admit how much they were on edge waiting for Seaglen to re-appear. Eventually, tiredness took hold, and the three of them fell asleep where they were sat, settling out either on the windowsill or with top halves on one chair and legs draped across another.

CHAPTER 8
THE GUARDIANS OF MAGIC

~SHUMUTI~

Shumuti woke up blearily, running one hand over her face, to feel the imprint of the window grain engraved there. Curled up by the fire, just visible under a heap of fur and blankets were Sara and Aurielle, both of whom were still asleep.

A figure Shumuti had not noticed before crept into the room around the doorframe. The sunlight was shining directly through the open door, and she raised a hand to shield her eyes. The figure moved, so that they were blocking out the light. Shumuti's heart skipped a beat, and she sprang up. Leaping up and over towards them, she cried with joy and wrapped her arms around her father with more enthusiasm than she realised.

"What's this in aid of then?" he chuckled.

"Where were you?" Shumuti demanded, pulling back.

"Let's wait until everybody's up," he suggested.

Shumuti turned back to the room and then realised that somebody was missing.

"Where's Astrid?" she asked.

"I slept in my bed," came her voice from behind them, "like a normal person."

Astrid stepped into view. At the same moment, Sara sat up from beside the fire, waking up Aurielle. Both of them squinted upwards at the scene occurring above them, trying to work out what was happening.

"What happened to you?" Aurielle asked Seaglen, scrambling to her feet.

"Tea, anybody?" Seaglen asked, picking up the kettle. His eyes were ringed with tiredness and it seemed like he had not slept at all.

They each had a mug of tea made with some of Astrid's herbs to wake them all up, before sitting back down at the table and looking expectantly at Seaglen. Nobody touched their drink. He scrutinised all of their faces and deliberately took his time to put his mug down. They waited impatiently to hear him talk.

"All right," he began, "I'll tell you what happened. Five patrols in total went out yesterday morning, and each had five men in them. I was to lead my patrol over towards Elmdale near to the Winterburn River. We rode to the boundary of the forest and then to the river. Everything was normal there, so we patrolled back over to the hills, but all the while I felt that something was not entirely as it should be.

"Further on, we heard shouting and a scream, so we abandoned our original route to investigate. I halted my men on the crest of a hollow. Another patrol was in the shallow of the hill, and they had crouched over something in the middle of a circle."

Seaglen spat out his next words in a mixture of disgust and regret. "We weren't quite quick enough. We reached the other patrol members to see what they had been protecting. Slowly they all stood back to show us the bodies of two dead villagers from a town close to the river, slaughtered."

"What killed them?" Shumuti asked.

"We don't know," Seaglen answered, "the other patrol had reacted the same way we had, and neither of us had got there in time."

Seaglen's breath misted in the early morning air as he sighed. "I spent the rest of the day overseeing a search of the area for traces of the attackers or other victims. But there were no tracks to follow. I fear the attack never came from the ground."

Silence greeted his last words as they listened intently. Shumuti felt Sara shift beside her.

"Was it the same creature who followed us from Elmdale?" Astrid asked.

She turned at Seaglen, awaiting confirmation.

"It is what I suspect."

"It is because of us being here that they are causing damage in Merrywater," Astrid said.

"I think it may be time to start actively dealing with them," Seaglen nodded.

"Did you find anything else?" Aurielle asked.

"No. We brought the two bodies back to their village and held a ceremony for them in the evening. I talked to many people in the early hours of this morning, and they all told me they now fear lands close to the river. It is not the first time something like this has happened, but this is the first time people have died."

They were interrupted all of a sudden by a knock at the door. Seaglen got up in surprise and left the room to answer it. Shumuti, Sara, Aurielle and Astrid listened in silence as the front door creaked open.

"Morning Seaglen." They overheard a grim voice. "We're handing these around after yesterday. The rangers told me to pass on that it would be valuable to have you with them."

"Give them my word I'll be there," Seaglen replied, after a moment of silence.

"I need to be getting back."

After a scuffle of footsteps, the door swung shut with a firm thud and Seaglen returned to the room with a brown parchment in hand, sitting down to read it silently.

"There is a meeting to be held in the village," he relayed finally, "they need more patrols, that is the gist of it. More trained men to deploy to the more vulnerable settlements near the borders. After the meeting, the rangers will send a detailed account of the attack and our current situation to the King himself. The last few lines read: *A threat to our longstanding peace in Merrywater has begun to surface. You would be advised to sharpen your swords.*"

"But they are trying to fight an enemy that is too strong for them," Astrid said with concern.

"I will begin to lay my plans as well," Seaglen said.

"We thought the creatures might have come from Attaching," Aurielle said, glancing between Shumuti and Seaglen.

"I do not think the King would be ordering attacks on his people." Seaglen furrowed his brow. "Merrywater and Elmdale still fall under his rule, even if they are outside the borders of Attaching."

"Can we all go to the meeting?" Sara asked, "I mean, this is what the training has been for, right? So I can fight as well as the rest of you?"

"You're not ready for that just yet, Sara," Astrid said.

Seaglen's face was hidden behind the parchment as he read the words over. It seemed to Shumuti as though he was contemplating something.

"No," he muttered, "she's right. You are ready."

Sara stared at him in surprise and Astrid began to open her mouth in objection.

"Ready for what?" Shumuti asked, feeling there was more to this.

"Seaglen..." Astrid sounded wary.

"They're ready," he repeated, glancing between Shumuti, Aurielle and Sara, "all three of them."

"Three?" Shumuti questioned.

Seaglen stood up. "Come on, all of you, follow me."

Shumuti turned to Astrid, but her face was unreadable. They followed Seaglen in single file as he walked down the corridor at the far end of the house. It faced towards the hill up to the waterfall, but the passage had only ever led to a dead end. Shumuti remembered Sara trying to go down here on the first morning she arrived, but she had only ever known it to lead to nowhere. Dubiously, she continued after Seaglen down to the wall at the far end.

Darkness shrouded the passageway because there were no windows. Shumuti had always thought of this corridor as being out of place with the rest of the house and had always avoided it when she was younger. Torch brackets, similar to those in the training cave decorated the walls. Seaglen took one of these and lit it so that a warm, red glow settled around everybody and allowed them to see properly. He then detached another and lit it off the first, before handing it to Shumuti with a meaningful look in his eye. The flame flickered and diminished before rising again as a red blaze.

Without a word, he then turned to face the blank, stone wall at the end of the dimly lit passage and ran one hand over the rock until he appeared to find what wanted to find. He pressed inwards with that hand, and there was a small grinding noise, before a circular section of the wall rotated and swung inwards.

"This way," Seaglen said, before heading into the dark tunnel that had emerged beyond the corridor.

He and Astrid disappeared into the tunnel, and the three of them followed silently behind. It was like walking into a cave. There was a chill wind blowing in Shumuti's face. The composition of the stone wall became slowly interspersed with bedrock as they walked forwards until eventually, it became an underground tunnel that was carved directly out of the earth.

The remnants of Seaglen's torch were just visible ahead, and Shumuti led the other two in the direction of the light at a brisk pace. The tunnel lowered and gradually started sloping steadily upwards. Soon, even Shumuti and Sara had to bend their heads to continue along. Shumuti could not help wondering if the tunnel got so low that they could not go on, but Seaglen ploughed ahead, and she chose to place her trust with him. It took Shumuti a second to realise that he had halted and peered over Astrid's shoulder to see what was coming next.

This time, entry into the next section was through an ordinary door. One-by-one, the group walked through, and Aurielle shut the door behind them with a snap. The room they were now in was of a very similar design to that of the training room, except that the construction of the floor appeared to be out of concentric circles. Each one cut a further level into the floor, in a ring towards the centre, like an amphitheatre. Cobwebs hung from the rafters, and a considerable amount of dust had gathered amongst the stones. Spaced at regular intervals around the walls were collections of leather armour with faded fabric under layers, just visible against the rock. Five sets were present in total and complimenting each one were half broken or decaying weapons, the steel dulled from lack of use.

"Now this," Seaglen said, "is a room that hasn't seen any use for a very long time."

"Nothing's changed," Astrid muttered.

"You've been here before?" Shumuti asked her in surprise.

"Oh, yes. I could never forget this place."

"I haven't put much effort into maintaining this room," Seaglen confessed almost apologetically to Astrid.

"So what is this room for?" Aurielle asked.

Seaglen walked down to the centre of the room and looked up at them.

"This," he announced, looking back up at them, "is the home of the Guardians of Magic."

Shumuti saw Sara look at her with a bemused expression on her face, but Shumuti was none the wiser herself. Guardians of Magic?

"How come you've never shown it to me before?" She frowned down at Seaglen.

"There was no need," he replied, "this is a room of war. There was no use for it during times of peace. Only now, perhaps things are beginning to change. This room was our war council chamber and armoury."

"What are the Guardians of Magic?" Aurielle asked.

"That was our name," Astrid said, "the first six users of Magic. We were meant to protect Meteorath and the Magic that runs through it, so guardians felt like an apt name."

"I wanted us never to forget what our responsibilities to Magic were," Seaglen explained, "we had been allowed the use of Magic and it was our responsibility to make sure we protected it and prevented its misuse."

Astrid turned to the six sets of dusty armour that adorned the walls. "That set was mine. The one beside it was Seaglen's. Then the next one was Lyria's. Then Annah's, Jemina's and finally Dagaz's."

"Dagaz died during our final battle," Seaglen said, "the last I heard of Lyria, she had travelled into Boctor. Annah and Jemina settled down to live in Attaching, but I heard news that Jemina has also died. Annah, I am not sure, but I have not heard from her for years now, either."

"That was our emblem," Astrid said.

She pointed to the floor, and Shumuti saw that there was a dim symbol of a spiral that formed itself almost into a number six. Five other smaller spirals formed a circular border around the main one, but the pattern had faded over the years, and the swirling lines had become faint and almost indistinguishable.

"But now the room will be used once more," Seaglen said, "for the next set of Guardians."

"There's two of us," Aurielle said.

Seaglen ignored her and unhooked a set of leather-clad armour from the wall and almost reverently handed it over to Shumuti. The amour looked as though it would provide her lighter protection but with the bonus of not adding too much weight. Besides, Shumuti thought, her Magic could protect her far better than armour ever could. Overlapping plates of leather ran diagonally down the chest piece and the armour also offered additional protection over her shoulders.

"We had to have two sets of livery made," Seaglen said, "we were a lot older when we went out to battle, and this was our first gear. I hope it fits you, but the pieces are adjustable. This one once belonged to me."

"There is a blacksmith in town who can make alterations as well," Astrid added.

Shumuti took the outfit and looked at Seaglen gratefully, noting small nicks and marks on the shoulders and chest piece. He then turned back and unhooked a second set for Aurielle.

"Was this my mother's?" Aurielle asked.

"It was."

Aurielle took the set and turned it over as Shumuti had done.

"I remember when I fitted into that," Astrid said, staring at the armour Aurielle currently wore.

Astrid then took down what Shumuti assumed to have once been her armour and walked over to Sara.

"But I'm no Guardian," Sara said.

"I want you to have it," Astrid said, "to protect you."

Sara silently accepted the offering, handling it like something precious. Shumuti eyed the three remaining sets of armour on the walls.

"There is some new information I have not revealed to you yet," Seaglen said.

Shumuti turned his way, with all of her attention focused on him.

"You know that I have some ability to detect other Magic users," he began, "well, while I was travelling north on patrol, trying to track the vultures, I discovered something entirely unexpected."

"What?" Shumuti asked.

"I noticed the presence of a source of Magic."

"Where?"

"In Attaching."

"That is far away," Shumuti remarked, "I didn't know you could detect Magic over such a distance."

"I only noticed it for a moment," Seaglen said, "whœver it was used a great deal of Magic very quickly. It was almost like an explosion."

"It must have been a lot for you to catch it, two regions away," Aurielle added.

"Worryingly large," Seaglen agreed, "if it is in Attaching, there is also a chance it may link to Annah in some way."

"You think it is worth investigating," Shumuti said.

"It sounds like somebody is using too much Magic up there," Aurielle said, "and it's our responsibility to find out what is going on."

"If somebody is using Magic up there who is a threat to us, you and Aurielle need to deal with them," Seaglen said, "if Annah is in trouble, I want you to find her and bring her back to Thayll."

"Aurielle and I will head out to Attaching and find out what the source of all this is."

"Sara, you should also accompany them," Seaglen added.

"Me?" Sara said, "but I'll be no use if I can't do Magic."

"No use?" Shumuti said, "you haven't been training for nothing, have you, Sara?"

"Everybody's paths may be laid out for them, but you choose which turnings to take," Seaglen said, "remember that, Sara."

"I will try my best to help." She nodded.

"Astrid and I will remain here," Seaglen said, "to protect Thayll and the other villages from the threat of these vultures. We will try to track it down if we can."

"We will have to tread carefully in Attaching until we know what is going on," Shumuti said.

"My advice would be to steer clear of the King and his guards," Seaglen said, "at least until we know what his intentions are and whether he is involved with these creatures or not. If the situation up there is more serious than we have envisioned, you must send word back to us. It will be safer if the King has no idea you are in his region."

"But I was planning on starting our search in the city of Lyria." Shumuti sighed. "It's the only large settlement around. If we can't learn anything there, I don't know where we can."

"The city, I would advise visiting," Seaglen agreed, "the Lyrian Citadel, you should keep your distance from, for now."

"So we should leave for Attaching?" Aurielle asked.

"In the next few days," Seaglen said, "but there are some things that I must teach you first. Things I never hoped I would."

Shumuti looked at Seaglen and saw how downhearted he looked. He gave her a small smile, but she understood he never wanted this to happen. He had trained her, her whole life to defend herself, but she could tell he thought he would never have had to revisit this room. Shumuti only hoped that she was ready herself.

CHAPTER 9
FINAL PREPARATIONS

Sara lost Seaglen as her teacher a week after they had visited the Guardians of Magic room, as a result of Shumuti and Aurielle's need to learn new skills that might be necessary for the journey. Strangely enough, this did not bother Sara. She still felt excluded whenever they did Magic or talked about it, but she had come to a decision that she should stop brooding about her situation and at least put on a front of not caring before the others. Perhaps then, in time, it would not bother her as much. Instead, she threw herself into completing her training, which to Sara's delight was taught to her by her mother.

As well as the fighting training she had received from Seaglen, Astrid taught her more about herbs and healing. The magical side of Astrid's abilities was forgotten entirely as Sara instead improved her knowledge about what plant was most useful for which purpose and where she was most likely to find each of them. After a few long, intense sessions and detailed note taking, she felt as though she could pose as a partially qualified medic for the group.

However, despite her joy at the new skills she was gaining, Sara remained curious about what Shumuti and Aurielle were learning. One evening while Astrid was preparing a meal, Sara found herself at the start of the corridor to the blank wall. She knew Seaglen, Shumuti and Aurielle must be inside because their training was regular as clockwork. Astrid was occupied and would be for the next half an hour at least. Sara's heart began to thump loudly in her chest as she slowly crept forward along the dark passageway, inexplicably drawn towards the wall at the end.

When Sara reached the dead end, she paused and slowly lifted a hand to the wall. She had memorised the exact spot Seaglen had pressed inward. Sara hesitated; having decided to distance herself from Magic, what was she doing here? Her fingers hung there, an inch from the wall. She closed her eyes. Then touched the wall.

It was solid. Disbelieving, Sara ran her hands over to search for some crack. Somewhere where she could get through to the other side. Nothing. Of course, Seaglen still had some barrier to prevent any outsiders from gaining access. Angry with herself for even being here, Sara turned away, trying to forget what she had tried to do, and walked back up the corridor feeling dejected.

On the final day before they were due to set out, Sara was alone in the training cave with Astrid. She had never taken her mother for much of a sword fighter, but after a few sparring sessions, she realised how much she had underestimated her mother.

"Your technique has improved," Astrid observed, slightly out of breath when they eventually stopped.

"It has?" Sara was pleasantly surprised. "I hardly noticed."

"You've worn me out." Astrid smiled, with a hint of tiredness.

"Why don't you go back for the rest of the afternoon? I can practise alone with a bow."

"I suppose. I'll leave the door ajar so that you can get out. Remember to close it when you leave."

Astrid left the room with the door open just enough so that the noise of the waterfall was audible. Once alone, Sara put away the sword and pulled out a set of bow and arrows. Pulling down the target board, she stopped all of a sudden as she heard a noise. Cautiously, Sara turned and looked around the room. Everything was as it should be. Then she heard it again. A shout, accompanied by clanging metal.

The noise was not coming from outside the room or above. It was coming from the opposite end, somehow within the wall. The only thing present on that side of the room was the tall cupboard. Curious, and slightly bewildered, Sara nocked an arrow to the bow and stalked towards the wooden doors. As she approached, the noises became louder. Outside the front, she stopped tentatively and listened. There was a shout. A name was called out, and it sounded oddly familiar. Sara kicked the doors wide open, still holding the bow in her hands.

With the entrance open, she stood back, puzzled. Sets of training armour and boots hung up in rows inside. Propping the bow up against the wall, Sara swept the rows of clothes aside and stepped inside to the back wall where she noticed a small, discoloured square, where the wood was slightly out of place.

She pushed the square in to try to remove it, and it clicked outwards. Taking hold of the sides, Sara drew the whole thing out and rested the square on the floor. A pane of glass lay in its place now. Sara put her face to the window, and through it, she observed the Guardians of Magic room where Shumuti and Aurielle trained.

Sara quickly looked away with an intake of breath. Staring at the darkness of the cupboard wall, she heard Shumuti shout something and could not help but return her eyes to the window. Seaglen, Shumuti and Aurielle were all there, and Seaglen was facing the two girls across the central circle of the room. Shumuti and Aurielle were holding hands and around them glowed a faint aura of silvery blue.

"Now," Seaglen was saying, "this was designed to involve double the amount of people, so naturally I do not expect the three of us to succeed here. I want you to get an idea of the concept. Linking Magic like this makes it more powerful and is useful when one person or one single element is not sufficient. One thing to keep in mind though, this form of Magic requires everybody present to have a full level of control. If not all your Guardians are properly trained, the results can be devastating. But I think it will be safe for us to give it a go."

He placed a rock on the floor and went to join Shumuti and Aurielle. Once he took Shumuti's hand, the glow around the three of them intensified, and this time there was a tinge of red mingled with the silver and blue.

What happened next occurred so quickly that Sara almost missed it. The glow from Shumuti and Aurielle disappeared, and instead, Seaglen became encircled twice as brightly. Then a twisted stream of fire accelerated out from him at a savage velocity and as soon as it reached the stone, the rock shattered into hundreds of pieces. The force of it reverberated around the room and caused the windowpane to vibrate. A crack appeared in the glass and, not wishing them to notice her, Sara hastily replaced the wooden covering and stepped back out of the cupboard.

Behind the wall, she heard Aurielle exclaim something and the sound of Shumuti laughing.

That evening Seaglen confirmed what everyone around the table had been thinking.

"You are ready," Seaglen announced, "Shumuti and Aurielle have received the extra training, and you have completed your own, Sara. There is no sense to delay any further. We must get to the bottom of this vulture business before anybody else gets hurt."

"You said you were going to think of the best way for us to travel," Shumuti said.

"I did," Seaglen agreed, "the most direct route for you to take is to go along the Winterburn River."

"Won't we be too exposed out on the river?" Aurielle asked.

"There is the chance that you will not make it to Attaching without some encounter, but the majority of incidents have happened inland, close to the villages. Besides, Astrid and I intend on holding the vultures' attention."

"We can handle anything we meet," Shumuti said.

Seaglen folded his arms. "Then we will go with you for the boats tomorrow."

On that night, the five of them separated. Aurielle returned to her home for the evening, and Seaglen took Shumuti aside into his study to talk further about the journey ahead of them. Sara realised then that she needed to make the most of these last few hours with her mother, so Astrid and Sara decided to take their horses out at sunset and rode them up to the track to the clifftop above the training room. Wrapped in their cloaks, Astrid and Sara made a small fire and sat on the grass, watching the stars and darkening landscape of Merrywater below them.

"I am sorry, you know, Sara." Astrid broke their peaceful silence. "For never telling you what I am, for never sharing any of this with you."

Sara stared across at her mother in surprise, under the glowing light of the fire.

"It's all right," she replied, "I miss Silverspring and my old life, and especially Stephan. I wouldn't have changed the way things were growing up, at all."

"I am glad of that at least." Astrid smiled slightly as she stared out into the night.

"Can I ask a question about Shumuti? Do you know what happened to her mother? Has it always just been her and Seaglen?"

"Ah," Astrid replied, "you see, Shumuti's mother died giving birth to her. Seaglen barely ever speaks of her, I think it still hurts him too much. I came to Thayll when I heard what had happened, having just had a miscarriage myself. We helped each other recover I think, and then when he no longer needed my assistance in raising Shumuti, I set off for a new start in Elmdale."

Sara said nothing, hit by two new revelations at the same time. She turned back to the fire instead, not feeling like she could ask Astrid for any further information.

"Do you wish we never came here?" Astrid interrupted her musing a minute later.

"I used to," she admitted, "now I worry that I'll be a burden to Shumuti and Aurielle. Surely they would be better off without me?"

"They both want you with them, Sara. You three have become good friends, correct? There are more important qualities needed in travelling companions than an ability to use Magic, and I would say you're more than qualified in those areas. Do not let your worries and fears cloud your judgement of what matters."

"I won't. Thank you."

"I will miss you, though."

"I'll miss you too."

Early the next morning, Seaglen's house was a hive of activity. Sara and Shumuti dashed about, collecting various items that they might need on their voyage. Aurielle arrived while it was still dark. As the sun cautiously peeked out from behind the tip of the hill, they were ready.

The group padded softly through the village. The first few farmers were up, but no one else. As they left Thayll and ascended the hill leading towards the river, Sara leant forward on Arrow to avoid tumbling backwards. Seaglen set a brisk pace at the head of their party to ensure they reached the river basin in good time. On the second day, as the midday sun emerged from between the clouds, the Winterburn River spread out ahead, and Sara could not help but gaze in awe of how wide it was. Assembled down by the water's edge was a single, solitary hut, the only sign of human presence for miles.

They dismounted the horses and strolled them down to the large, rickety wooden clad cabin. Attached to the log chalet, overhanging the water, was an additional shed. As they entered, Sara saw row upon row of boats with varying sizes and shapes inside, and all lashed together by strong, thick ropes. It was almost dark within, and the only light found its way from outside through holes in the panels of wood, causing the dark blue water to cast undulating reflections on the walls. A voice could be heard muttering from around the corner inside.

"Now this shipment is for Barbara," a man was saying, "it's the pig iron that she didn't paint..."

"Aye, sir," came another voice.

A young man hurried out past them, clutching a heavy-looking parcel in both arms. He looked momentarily surprised to see such a large amount of people inside the cabin, before nodding and speeding past. Seaglen pressed on further inside.

An older man came emerged into view, kneeling next to one of the larger boats and meticulously applying a coat of varnish to the wood. He was a curious-looking fellow, quite short but with spindly legs and muscular arms. A large tuft of black hair ran down his forehead, almost concealing his eyes as if it was trying to escape from the top of his head. His face was weather-beaten, and he had the look of a man who had journeyed out to sea for a long while, on multiple occasions. He twisted round to face the newcomers, and his face immediately broke into a craggy smile, revealing a set of crooked and stained teeth.

"Ah, Seaglen! It has been too long!"

"It has. I came to ask for your help. I am after a boat."

"Aye, naturally. Nobody comes here for much else." He winked. "Did you have any in mind?"

"It will need to be quite big, able to carry three and potentially one more if needed. Also, it needs to be able to undertake a journey to Attaching and back."

"Attaching, eh? What business brings you up there?" he inquired.

"Dœs it matter?"

The mariner looked Seaglen keenly in the eye. "It matters if this journey incurs a risk of danger to one of my vessels. I've been less willing to lend out boats bound for that direction of late. Fewer and fewer are returning."

He gestured to several empty bays behind him, and Sara also noticed one or two fishing boats that were in need of repair.

"You know that I would not risk any danger to any of your boats. That I would take care."

He huffed.

"You'd best stay true to your word. Otherwise, I'll be on your tail. Mark my words! One scratch on her an' you're a dead man! Now! Come and choose your craft."

He led Seaglen off to the store of the larger boats and Astrid went with him.

"That's Ed," Shumuti muttered to Sara, "I daresay that he probably loves boats more than he loves people, but that does make him the best man for his job."

They watched Seaglen and Astrid being shown around by Ed, when a thought occurred to Sara.

"Do either of you two know how to work one of these?"

"Yes," Shumuti replied, "Seaglen used to go sailing quite a bit, and he taught me when I was younger. I've tried to teach Aurielle..."

Shumuti's gaze withered on her friend.

"With limited success," Aurielle finished, laughing at a memory.

Seaglen settled on a boat and handed over a small pouch of gold as payment.

"You'll get it back in one piece," Seaglen re-affirmed.

"Very assuring," Ed grunted, but he untied the boat.

Seaglen beckoned to them, before climbing up a ladder into the boat. They clambered after him, some more gracefully than others. The sides rocked just as Sara was stepping over the top and she clung onto the wood, knuckles white.

"You ought to watch out for that one." Ed eyed her warily from the decking, "it doesn't look as though she's got her sea legs."

He pushed them off with his pole and the boat rotated gently round to face the entrance of the shed and the open river. A pair of carthorses stood ready to help them out of the shed and on to the open water. Seaglen took up the tiller at the back of the boat and steered them safely out of the boat shed and out into the broader river. Astrid handed Shumuti a long pole, and the two of them helped push the boat away from the path of obstacles on the shore.

"Now we're out into wider water, we can put the sail up," Seaglen instructed them, "we'll travel south for a small test trip before Astrid, and I leave you."

Sara took a good look at the boat, now that it was out in the light. It was large and high above the water, requiring ten paces to cover the length of it. The boat was fashioned with a raised section in the middle of the deck, while a gangway constructed from layered and varnished wood ran around the sides. Within the central, raised decking was a door that presumably led to a small cabin inside. Around the entire outer perimeter of the deck was a railing of wood to prevent anybody from falling over the edge, of which Sara was glad.

Together, Astrid and Aurielle had brought out a russet red mainsail, and under Astrid's instruction, they were busy attaching it to the mast they had just hoisted up. Sara pushed herself to her feet to offer to help and misjudged the movement of the boat again. She gave up and sat down, feeling decidedly unsteady.

"Ed was right," Shumuti said, putting down the long pole and sitting down next to Sara, "we will have to watch out for you. Here, this will help."

She handed Sara a waterskin, and she drank from it gratefully.

"I've never experienced this before." Sara frowned in annoyance "I can barely even stand up. How will I get anything done?"

"You'll get used to it soon." Shumuti laughed. "Then it'll get to the point where you're so used to living on the water that you'll step onto dry land once again and that starts to feel like it's moving."

Sara leant over one side to look down at the water below. Now that the sail was up, the boat cut smoothly through the water. There was a board fastened onto the boat's side, just below the level of the deck. Sara leant over to read it before realising how far she was over the water. Hastening backwards, she sat down on the raised cabin. The plaque showed what she guessed to be the name of the boat, 'Stannair'. She liked it already.

Suddenly, the boat lurched violently, and the water nearly slipped out of her hands.

"Sorry!" a voice cried from the back.

"Oh." Shumuti sighed. "Aurielle's steering."

They got up and made their way to the back of the boat. Aurielle was indeed steering, her face set with concentration, and her body was rigid.

"Relax a little," Seaglen advised.

"I almost capsized us last time," she answered, gritting her teeth.

"Perhaps try someone else?" Astrid suggested.

Shumuti looked at Sara.

"Have a go."

Uncertain, Sara gingerly took the tiller from Aurielle.

"Right," Seaglen began, "do you see the triangular flags of fabric on the mast? They will show you the wind direction and therefore, the direction in which you need to point the boat. You must turn at right angles to the wind for the fastest course. If you want to turn left move the tiller to the right and if you want to go right push it to the left."

Sara looked ahead. The flags were fluttering towards Elmdale so she pushed the tiller left as the boat sped up. They started to drift slightly towards the eastern bank, and Sara continued to push gently. Nothing happened, so she added some more weight, and finally, the boat swung round to travel back on course. Filled with confidence, Sara steered towards the centre before again turning it back towards the right. She glanced at the smooth tiller under her palm, noting that it was made up of layers of wood skilfully crafted together and shaped into a curve.

"Now we're going to try a tack," Seaglen coached, "when I say, move the tiller all the way over to the right, as far as you can go. Shumuti, come back from the boom, it's going to swing."

At Seaglen's command, Sara pushed the tiller as far as she could, and the boat lurched around. Sure enough, the boom swung across the whole deck and the sail billowed out in the opposite direction, buffeted by the altered wind. After a moment of panic, Sara corrected their course, and soon, the boat was speeding forward in the direction of the opposite bank. It was easy. There was no other word for it. It came naturally to her, and she hardly noticed the sway of the boat when she was concentrating on steering it.

"Well, you two," Seaglen observed quietly, "I think you've found Sara's new job."

"No complaints there," Aurielle agreed.

"I think we will stop for a bit and I'll explain everything to you. There's a good spot coming up. Take us into the bank gently Sara."

Spotting the location that Seaglen was talking about, she altered the course of Stannair. Seaglen went away to give orders to the other two, but Astrid stayed by her side.

"Uncoil the ropes and fetch out those...Shumuti, there. By your left hand. Get two. You'll need one each."

Sara gripped the tiller and slowly turned the boat, so it swung into the bank.

"When I give the word..." Seaglen was saying.

The boat's back end swung around, and the gap between them and the riverbank closed in fast.

"Now!"

From opposite ends of the boat, Shumuti and Aurielle leapt over the wooden barrier, with ropes streaming out behind them. Each landed firmly on the grassy bank and looped the rope around two large, metal pegs they had been carrying. Driving these into the ground, they pulled on the lines and Stannair was dragged sideways towards the shore. Fenders on the side of the boat nudged gently against the bank as they slowed to a halt.

"Make sure the ropes are secure," Seaglen said, "and then get back on board. There's a lot to teach you."

The party re-joined one another after descending a ladder into the cabin below. It was cosy below deck, and largely one room, made up of a small kitchen and two benches running along either side, upholstered in a deep blue fabric. Two doors ran off from this main cabin, one towards the front of the boat and the second under the ladder they had descended in by.

"There are two beds in the front cabin and one at the back," Seaglen said, "Ed said the seats here in the middle will also double as beds if need be."

"What's this?" Aurielle asked, her hand on a thick cord tied to the wall.

"Release it," Seaglen said.

Aurielle unhooked the rope and slowly loosened. Down from the ceiling, a table descended between the two bench seats.

"To save space," Seaglen said.

The bench seats lifted up to reveal storage space for food and gear. Sara was beginning to like this boat more and more. The worries she'd previously had about going on this journey fizzled away, and instead, she found herself starting to get excited.

Seaglen opened a long hatch on the deck and told them that this was where to keep the sail. They would have to use it all the time because it was the only means they had to travel up the river. As autumn was approaching, the winds would be more frequent and stronger, which was good and meant that they ought to reach Attaching in good time. When there was no wind, they would have to stay in one place, although it was possible for Shumuti and Aurielle to work the wind and the water to provide them with some movement if it was an emergency.

Once Seaglen had finished, they turned Stannair around and sailed back towards the boat shed to drop off Seaglen and Astrid. As they approached, Shumuti and Aurielle secured Stannair again on the bank while Sara steered. This time Ed was outside when they arrived.

"Good heavens!" he cried as they approached, "what have you gone and done, Seaglen! Putting her at the helm! Take it easy lass, one scratch on my paintwork, and I'll have your head."

With the utmost care, Sara manœuvred Stannair to a safe halt. Lost in concentration, she looked up to see Ed staring back with his mouth wide open. He shut it with a snap and then grinned.

"Well I owe you an apology lass, I underestimated your skills. If you're after a job..."

"She's not," Astrid said firmly.

"Well, it's open to you." He looked at her and Sara was surprised to realise he was serious.

"Well, have a safe journey." He waved and vanished back inside the shed, giving Sara a nod before turning away.

"We'll be careful," Shumuti called back to him.

"Yes, you will." Seaglen arrived next to Shumuti. "You can't afford to damage Stannair."

"Stannair?" Shumuti looked puzzled.

"It's the name of the boat," Sara informed her.

"You noticed?" Seaglen observed with approval, "good."

Sara faltered slightly, realising the time had come to say goodbye, and turned to Astrid.

"Take care," Astrid said, "all of you. We need you returned in one piece."

"Remember everything I have taught you," Seaglen added, "it may just save your life. Be careful."

"You too," Shumuti said quietly. She had a worried expression in her eyes.

Seaglen nodded.

"Remember. Stay clear of the Lyrian Citadel in Attaching and avoid the King at all costs if you can. I'm not sure what he would do if he discovered you in his city, but if the events at the Carnival are anything to go by, you would be wise to be cautious."

"I know," Shumuti assured her father.

Seaglen and Astrid exchanged final goodbyes before gathering up all the horses. With the last wave, they turned and galloped back down the track towards Thayll, leaving Sara, Shumuti and Aurielle entirely alone.

Chapter 10
A Voyage Upstream

It wasn't until Seaglen and Astrid had disappeared from view over the fields that the three of them even considered continuing their journey. Aurielle watched them ride off, surprised at how sad she was to see them go. Seaglen had become like a second father to her over the years, and she had grown fond of Astrid too, over the short time Aurielle had known her. They just naturally made each other laugh, and the words flowed smoothly between them, arguably better than with her own family. Aurielle's eyebrows furrowed as she thought back to her farewell with her father, the night before.

"So, you're finally doing something with all this training you've been receiving," he had muttered gruffly when she had relayed the news.

"Yes." Was all Aurielle had said.

"Well, don't do anything foolish." Her father, James, then softened his tone. "You are all I have left, and I have already partially given you to Seaglen. I will not try to stop you leaving, but make sure that you return won't you, Aurielle?"

"I will," she had answered determinedly, before they had shared a rare hug.

Aurielle had left the house the next morning and shouldered her pack over her cloak before he had even woken up. Her father had never been good at expressing much of his feelings, but he was her family all the same.

"Shall we set sail?" Shumuti's voice brought her back to the present.

"Let's go." Aurielle nodded finally.

Shumuti stood at the tiller today and following her advice, the three of them soon had the boat out on to the open water and underway, with a good wind to transport them upstream. The breeze buffeted them along at a relaxing pace that required little work to keep their vessel propelled onward. Once everything was under control, Aurielle turned to Shumuti with a question.

"What is your plan when we get to Attaching?"

"We should head straight for Lyria," Shumuti answered, "from what I have heard of the city, news and rumours travel fast there. I am hoping that there was some visible sign of whatever caused the Magic that Seaglen felt. With some luck, something out of the ordinary will have occurred, and it should be the clue we need to progress further."

"Let us hope our trail doesn't lead us in the direction of the Lyrian Citadel then," Aurielle said, "do you think the King can be trusted?"

"Honestly, I don't know." Shumuti sighed. "Weren't we always taught not to trust anyone when it came to dealing with Magic? To choose the safer option."

"We seemed to have ignored that rule when it comes to Sara."

"True, maybe Seaglen is wrong about how people would react to Magic after all."

"I'd say it depends entirely on the person," Aurielle said, "in the case of the King, I don't think he would let something that powerful continue to exist unchecked by him. He would want to control it."

"That is what Seaglen fears," Shumuti said.

The first day drifted into the second and past the third, as the trio sailed on. Slowly becoming accustomed to life on the water, Shumuti and Sara took turns at steering while Aurielle undertook any extra job that was required. Before them, the Winterburn River stretched out to the distant horizon, and their destination lay directly north. The water stretched out almost as far as could be seen on either side as well. In places, the Winterburn became more of a lake in this reach of the river, with northern Boctor on one side and Merrywater on the other, it was at its widest. Throughout this segment, small, deserted islands emerged within the central channel of the river.

When the workload had dissipated entirely later that afternoon, Aurielle went and collected her cloak and headed to the prow of the boat. They had drifted slightly to the west over the past few hours, and on the now visible western bank, she could see a bleak plain emerging out on the horizon, decorated with a few scrubs and crumbling rocks. Further out were darker, hazy outlines of eroded remains that once formed giant mountains. As she continued to stare, Shumuti appeared at Aurielle's shoulder.

"So, that's Boctor," Shumuti remarked with curiosity.

"It's exactly as bleak as I'd imagined," Aurielle commented.

The contrast of landscape between the western and eastern bank of the river was stark. The land in Boctor appeared as though it had fallen to desertification and disease. The King had no control over that region since the previous King had fought to try to prevent Nimaz from invading Boctor. During the fighting, it had become clear how divided a region Boctor was when half of the people there had turned to fight on the side of Nimaz and half against it. Realising the futility of defending a territory that did not want to prevent Nimaz from overtaking it, the old King had retreated in defeat back to Attaching, taking as many that wanted to be saved back across the Winterburn River as he could. Over time since then, Boctor had descended into an unknown and uncontrollable wilderness.

Merrywater, on the other hand, bloomed in beauty. Grasslands covered the landscape and birds flocked to the banks on the eastern shores. As Aurielle glanced between the two different worlds, both just about visible together, she noticed strangely that the presence of Magic in the landscape on the right bank was higher than that on the left. She had thought that it had been the wars and desertion of the land by people that had stopped prevented anything from growing in Boctor, but now that she looked, it felt as though something had drained the Magic from the landscape as well. Whether it was subconsciously or not, Aurielle could not help noticing that Sara had turned to steer Stannair edging back towards the Merrywater bank.

Stannair sailed northward, and soon the banks of Boctor were lost from view once more. Sara took the boat out towards the centre of the river where the winds were highest. The sun suddenly broke out from behind the clouds and illuminated the water beneath them. Aurielle watched a small school of jet-black fish dart beneath the starboard bow of the boat. She peered down over the side of Stannair to catch them as they shot beneath the bow and lost sight of them as sun flashed black all of a sudden, as if a dark cloud had suddenly covered the sky. Shielding her eyes, Aurielle stared upwards trying to see what had caused the temporary disturbance, but there was nothing but blue skies overhead. Behind her, there was a long ripping noise.

"Aurielle!"

She turned at the sound of her name. Simultaneously, she was engulfed in darkness and knocked to the ground, enveloped by the confusion and weight of red material and rigging as everything went dark.

"The sail!" she heard Shumuti exclaim.

Confused by the sudden outbreak of activity and fighting to break free of the cloth that was smothering her, Aurielle tried to remember to breathe with what little air remained available and not to panic. The sound of Shumuti and Sara shouting mixed with the rushing of water and the noise of what Aurielle thought to be wing beats, creating turbulence in the previously calm water. The boat swayed, and river water crashed over her. Then a slash of light broke into her vision.

She threw herself towards it and through one of several long tears in the fabric that had ripped itself free from the mast. Shielding her eyes from the brightness, she beheld the chaotic scene of Shumuti and Sara trying to reach her from the other end of the mess that was once the clean deck of the boat. Stannair was dangerously close to keeling over, and the wooden floor had turned into a steep obstacle course between where she stood and Shumuti and Sara. Busy grappling with the tattered sail, neither of them noticed a second shadow pass over the deck.

"Behind you!" Aurielle yelled out.

Shumuti swivelled, but their attacker had been aiming for Sara. A frighteningly quick black blur collided with her directly, slamming her into the floor before shooting up into the sky, beyond sight and trailing a large length of red material in the sky behind it.

"Quick!" Aurielle shouted, "we have to get under cover! Inside!"

Stannair righted itself and threw Aurielle forward as she fumbled to her feet and broke even more of the wrecked sail. She scrambled her way hastily over to the other two, keeping one eye on the sky. Grabbing an arm each, they dragged Sara down the steps into the cabin below, sealing and locking the hatch door above them. Shumuti collected her sword and drew out the blade with a ring, moving over to the entrance of the cabin.

"Sara, are you all right?" Aurielle asked, propping her up against the wall.

"Ow," she mumbled, with a trickle of blood running down her forehead.

"There are some dressings in the box next to the food," Shumuti said, from the door.

Aurielle went to search for them. As she hastily rummaged through the carefully packed drawer, Shumuti stood unwaveringly on guard, watching up through the window in the hatch.

"Can you see anything?"

"Nothing," Shumuti replied, straining to see out of the porthole.

The boat rocked around them, drifting in circles with no sail to guide them. Several minutes later there was a sudden, sickening crunch as the side of Stannair came into contact with something substantial and finally fell still, rocking gently but firmly held in place. Shumuti swung back around the pole she had grabbed to avoid being thrown off her feet entirely and returned to her watch position, straining to see what had happened. Aurielle rubbed her shoulder from where she had knocked into the first aid drawer and gingerly limped back over to Sara.

CHAPTER 11
REPAIRS

~SHUMUTI~

"Is it safe to go out?" Aurielle asked, standing up from beside where Sara was recovering.

"You two stay here," Shumuti replied, after a minute of deliberation, "I'll go and check."

"Not a chance," Aurielle replied, "you might need somebody to watch your back out there."

"I'll be fine," Sara reassured them, "both of you go."

Shumuti took a second to agree, before the two of them climbed slowly out of the hatch door, swords in hand. They edged across the decking, eyes fixed on the sky. Above them was clear and bright once more, and the sun fell on their faces, as though nothing had caused an interruption. Shumuti carefully wound her way to the front of the boat, stepping with care over what remained of their sail.

Once at the bow, she leant over the side to inspect the damage. It was better than expected. There were no holes in the boat and brambles had only scraped the sides and damaged the boat's paintwork. A tangle of spines and withered branches growing out from the riverbank had trapped the boat securely. So securely in fact that they had become embedded into the embankment and without the sail, their hopes of immediately continuing by water had been extinguished.

Satisfied that they were not about to sink or capsize, Shumuti glumly traversed her way back to the others. Sara had emerged on deck as well now, wearing a look of despair on her face. She shook her head and sat down, her face pale, as Shumuti took a seat next to her.

"We didn't even manage a week downstream without wrecking the boat. What are we going to do?"

"I don't know," Shumuti answered.

As the pair of them stared, demoralised, at the sail, Aurielle joined them at the tiller, satisfied that they were no longer about to be attacked.

"What was it?" she asked, "did either of you two see?"

Both of them nodded, but it was Sara who answered.

"It moved too fast to see any clear shape. But when it attacked me, I tried to fight back and tore out this."

She held out two long, black, oily feathers.

"They've found us already," Shumuti said, her face dropping.

"It came and went so quick," Aurielle said, "I don't understand why it only tore the sail. It took us by surprise and easily had the opportunity to hurt us. Why didn't it?"

"Maybe it was afraid of you?" Sara suggested, "or perhaps it was following specific orders."

"But, surely we can fix the sail?"

Shumuti laughed and ran one finger down the length of the torn fabric. It was split almost from the top of the mast to the bottom and a large section of it was missing.

"Not right here, I think is the plain answer," she replied.

"Where exactly are we?" Sara asked, "are we near a village?"

Shumuti scanned around to look at their surroundings, and her heart sank another notch. A desert landscape dominated the view, scattered with rocks and bare vegetation.

"We're on the wrong side of the Winterburn," she said quickly, "this is Boctor."

"What?" Sara cried, standing up in horror.

The three of them stared silently out at the alien expanse before them.

"There is no way we can swim safely to the other side of the river here," Shumuti said, "it's at its widest, and the current is strong."

"We can't go into Boctor either," Aurielle said, "couldn't we work the wind and the water to move the boat?"

"For a short time," Shumuti answered, "but to keep it up would begin to cause damage. We might be able to get across to the other side of the river, just about, but there's nothing over there that can help us. We're level with the wrong bit of Merrywater on the far bank. There are no settlements or villages for days in either direction, just grassland."

"We need a new sail," Aurielle said.

"And how are we going to get that?" Shumuti asked.

Aurielle looked around thoughtfully. "I saw smoke from a settlement when I was looking out earlier across to Boctor. I think it might be under a day's walk from here."

"No," Shumuti said.

"But we can't exactly do anything else."

"Going into Boctor would be crazy. It's a dangerous region we know barely nothing about."

"But we need to get to Attaching," Sara said.

"Isn't there a spare sail anywhere?" Shumuti asked.

"I think there was at one point," Aurielle answered, "I had a look at the supplies before we left. Ed is a tight man. I guess he needed it for one of his other boats and never got around to replacing the spare."

Shumuti gave a deep sigh. "Aurielle, are you sure what you saw?"

"Certain," she answered.

"All right. We go to this village and try to get a new sail or at least new material for one."

"Right," Aurielle said, "I'll start packing some supplies."

"Fine," Shumuti uttered, in a resigned tone, "it will be dark soon. We'll set off tomorrow morning."

Shumuti crawled down the ladder into the cabin to lie down and think for a while. Worry was beginning to grow in her mind that the vultures had meant to leave them stranded on the wrong side of the river. What if there was something else planned for them once they set foot on land? Trying to remove the worrying thoughts from her mind, she decided to block them out and shut her eyes for a minute.

Aurielle woke her what felt like a second later. The porthole windows of the cabin were pitch black.

"Was I asleep?" Shumuti asked.

"Yes," she replied, "we decided to set a watch tonight. It's your turn now, and you'll need to wake Sara in three hours."

Shumuti nodded and mechanically stood up.

"Did you see anything?" she asked.

Aurielle shook her head.

Shumuti clambered up out on to the deck and felt the bite of the frosty, autumn wind. Pulling her cloak around her and the hood up, she huddled against the raised wall of the cabin, staring out at the dark wilderness of Boctor. Perhaps in the next few hours, she could concoct an alternative plan to save them from trespassing into this unknown land. Her best thoughts and ideas had always come at night. However, the next three hours passed by uneventfully and Shumuti was no nearer to an alternative master plan, so she handed the watch over to Sara and fell back into a troubled sleep.

The next morning, Aurielle and Shumuti decided to expend a small amount of Magic to protect Stannair from anyone or anything that might happen across the boat while they were gone. They set up a system of wards running in the air and beneath the water surrounding the craft. The Magic was an invisible net once cast, except for a flicker of silver and blue glimmer, and would remain hidden until something came along and triggered it, causing the protection to rebound on the intruder. This kind of Magic was useful as would only cost anything if the trap were sprung. The wards could exclusively be removed by whœver made them or broken entirely, but that would take strong Magic beyond anything they hoped they would encounter on the shores of Boctor.

When they had finished, Shumuti checked over their protection of Stannair. They had done a thorough job that Seaglen would have been proud of. Shumuti had conducted one last hopeless search for another sail, or a mending kit but there was nothing designed for the repair of a sail. Reluctantly, the trio set off just past dawn and left Stannair floating, wounded, in the tangle of bushes. Shumuti scanned up at the sky frequently, but it was a bright blue once again, with no clouds to hide any potential airborne assassins from view.

They trudged across the barren earth, and soon their boots became coated with a layer of sand and dirt. The straps of Shumuti's pack cut into her shoulders, and she had never thought to check what Sara and Aurielle had put into it. They walked in an uneasy silence. Shumuti had her ears pricked for any sign or shadow of life watching or following them. Her new armour felt almost like a second skin to her, for which she was glad. The leather could almost be mistaken for a sleeveless coat and she was glad it did not too obviously stand out.

The afternoon sun beat down softly on her back, and Shumuti clasped her hands behind her back to rest the weight of her pack on. They dipped behind the crest of a hill and the Winterburn River disappeared from view.

It was silent here. Not a single bird chirped overhead or any animal at all emerged out of the wilderness, as the trio walked. The landscape was wholly foreign to Shumuti. It was extraordinary what difference lay on each bank of the same river, wide as it was. She was used to lakes and lush grasslands, but here there was barely a drop of moisture around. The land was arid, and the air was as well. But the difference she felt most strongly here was the lack of Magic. That fact scared her a little as well. Just by coming to Boctor, they were weakened, in terms of being able to fight back.

A few hours later, the skies overhead began to darken. As they continued to walk, an unwelcome rain began to drip down on them steadily. Shumuti pulled her hood up and pressed on, feeling the water drip onto her shoulders and run down her cloak. On the positive side, she was thankful that the rain made it harder for anyone to track them and she hoped that the vultures would have an aversion to flying in it too. She could not believe their bad luck that the creature had found them so soon and realised that Seaglen and Astrid's efforts to track the vulture down in Merrywater would be futile now, but least the attacks in Merrywater would come to an end.

Shumuti's gaze was fixed at the ground before her feet as she noticed the comparatively more fertile soil closer to the river change to gravelly rock and only the odd tuft of spiky grass forced its way through the earth. Shumuti knew the danger was going to increase as they travelled further into Boctor. Aurielle was walking in front of

Shumuti, and she noticed friend had become more alert. Shumuti concentrated on every sound and sight around her, determined not to be caught off guard again.

"Is it far from here?" Sara asked.

"I don't think so," Aurielle answered, "if we can get onto that hilltop, we can get a view of the area."

Looming mountains were also appearing now, a lot closer than they had seemed from the river. Shumuti scrambled up the narrow pathway after Aurielle, and they breached the hilltop together and looked around. Aurielle had been right. There was the village nestled down in the valley.

"Well done." Shumuti congratulated her with marked relief.

The evening was now falling around them, and the light was growing dim. "We should be able to reach the village before it gets fully dark," Aurielle said.

"Do you think they will help us?" Sara asked.

"We should be prepared to retreat out of there at the first sign of anything we mistrust," Shumuti said.

She stared down at the soft glow of the village lights below them. From this visibility, they almost could be surveying Thayll down there. There was no way to tell what might await them.

"Can you hear a noise?" Sara's voice had abruptly softened to a whisper.

"No..."

"Shh! There! Didn't you hear it?"

Unsettled, Shumuti strained her ears to listen. A flapping sound broke through the night on her left.

"Aurielle..."

Unconsciously, Shumuti found herself attempting to gather Magic. Something swooped overhead, and Shumuti cried out. Her blade sprang from its sheath in a flash of silver. She wheeled around in the murky dusk but saw nothing.

"Stay together!" Shumuti ordered. Aurielle and Sara grouped near her to form a triangle. Shumuti searched the skies, but she was none the wiser. Even if it was possible to raise an attack, it was impossible to pinpoint where to aim - fluttering again! She spun to face the noise and leapt backwards, flashing her sword before her. It was no use. It was like fighting air.

"Can you see what it is?" Shumuti called out.

"No!" Aurielle replied, "Shumuti, what are we going to do?"

"Help!" Sara yelled.

Her grip on Shumuti's arm vanished. Her eyes widened in shock.

"SARA! Aurielle, where has she gone?"

"I'm here!" That was Sara's voice. "Get them off me!"

Shumuti took a second look at where Sara had been standing. The air seemed to be moving. She had not disappeared. She was still there, underneath a cloud.

"We're coming!"

Shumuti sprinted towards the black cloud and felt instantly battered by a thousand wings. Wings! Battling through, Shumuti found Sara's arm and pulled her down. They threw themselves on the grass, face down, while the dark cloud wheeled overhead. Shumuti heard a shout from Aurielle, and a minute later she was down beside her. Shumuti almost couldn't breathe as the mass above them was so thick and close.

Then an exclamation rent the air. A high voice cut through the flapping, and there was an odd, echoing sound. Then, silence. Shumuti counted to ten, before slowly lifting her face, gripping her sword in one hand. The cloud had departed, but there was something else that had taken its place.

CHAPTER 12
THE WITCH OF DUSK

Ouch, Sara thought miserably. Her face and arms had been torn, it seemed, by what felt like thousands of tiny, sharp wires. Her skin burned from the cuts and laying face down in the prickly grass was only aggravating the dozens of small wounds.

It had been Shumuti that had saved her. She was sure of that. She had pulled her down to the ground. In the chaos, Sara was not even sure what had happened to Aurielle. Beside her, Sara felt Shumuti roll over and stiffen. Grateful to get the gravel out of her cuts, Sara lifted her head to see that Shumuti was transfixed at something behind her. Sara poked her head around the side and opened her mouth in astonishment.

Standing a few feet away from her was, what Sara presumed to be a woman. In the darkness, her outline was hardly distinguishable from the rest of the night. She was garbed from head to toe in black, and even her hair was, as far as Sara could tell, the colour of black jet. However, the feature that caused Sara's eyes to remain transfixed was the lure of the woman's eyes. Bright lilac, they shone out through the night, unnatural but beautiful at the same time, and entirely unnerving.

On Shumuti's right, Aurielle stood up, and she held her sword ready in one hand. Slowly, Shumuti rose as well, and so did Sara. She shivered as something brushed past her cheek. Then Sara realised that they were still encircled by their previous attackers. The woman took one step forward and the sound of fluttering intensified.

"You will come with me." Her tone was deadly serious. "Now."

No other option seemed available, as the circle of enemies tightened all around them, forcing the three of them to walk forward to avoid being cut again. Aurielle glanced over in objection at Shumuti, who shook her head slightly and took a step after they mysterious woman. Maybe they could sense something she could not, Sara wondered, as she shuddered and followed the other two, escorted by the fluttering cloud.

From the slope they were travelling on, she guessed that they were gradually moving uphill, which meant they were travelling away from the village. Sara strained to identify the shapes by her side, but there were so many, and they moved too fast. The night air was cold and sharp, making Sara shiver inside her cloak, from both cold and fear. Keeping one hand on the hilt of her sword comforted her, though she had no idea what use it would be against something she could barely see. At least Shumuti and Aurielle were able to use Magic, but the woman's control over these creatures seemed to be an equally inexplicable talent.

They climbed upwards for what felt like hours until, eventually, the woman brought them to a halt. Sara went to stand by the other two, and once again they faced the dark figure uncertainly.

"Inside," she ordered. Her voice was slightly raspy, but it had a certain flow or musical quality to it.

The three of them walked obediently forward together to enter a large cavern constructed into a dome, with a high ceiling. The cavern was lit at the bottom by faint torches, but above there was only darkness. More black shapes flittered into Sara's view and lit by the flames of the torches, she finally realised what they were.

"Bats!"

A flicker of something that almost felt like amusement passed across the woman's eyes as she looked back over her shoulder at Sara. They passed through the large cavern and entered a smaller, better-lit one. The woman followed them in and shut the door behind.

In the brighter torchlight, they could now see her appearance clearly. She was indeed dressed in a long black garment, which was made out of a curious and unnameable material, like nothing Sara had seen before. Woven into her clothes were carved beads and ivy leaves that draped from the folds of her sleeves and, now Sara noticed, into her hair as well. Like a river of silken black, her hair wound its way down her back, and it was bound into her clothes with woven leaves and cord. The sleeves of her strange garment spun into woven gloves when they reached her hands, and they wrapped themselves around each finger like a cocoon. A few of her bats periodically hung themselves from the sides of her long coat as transient decorations themselves and her fingernails were stained black to match her raven-like eyebrows. Inevitably, however, Sara was drawn back to her eyes, glimmering from the reflections in the flames, like gemstones. She watched them with a piercing gaze as an apprehensive silence stretched out inside the cave.

"Who are you to intrude in my land?" The woman finally spoke evenly. "I know from your garb that you do not belong in Boctor."

"We're travellers." Shumuti answered carefully.

"It has been many years since travellers have come to Boctor. Why I wonder, are you here? You do know where you are, do you not? What is your purpose here? Tell me."

Her questions had an underlying, enticing authority to them that almost made Sara want to reveal everything about what Seaglen had sent them to do. With a strong will, she forced herself to keep silent. Above them, the bats increased the speed of their fluttering.

"We did not know that this land belonged to anybody," Shumuti said, seeming to have trouble forming her words, "we are sorry for trespassing. Tell us, who are you? Why do you live high up here with these bats?"

The woman's face curled to reveal the points of her white teeth but she did not answer.

"What is your name?" Sara asked.

The full attention of the violet gaze turned on her.

"My name?" she repeated, "in exchange for yours, I will tell you mine."

"My name is Sara." She could not stop the words falling from her mouth. "This is Shumuti and Aurielle."

"Sara!" Aurielle glanced anxiously at her.

The woman considered each of them, looked from one of them to the next, before finally responding.

"I am Xeylia."

The bats on her coat fluttered their wings at the mention of her name.

"Who are you?" Aurielle asked, with a frown.

"I am simply a woman of some power. To some, though, I am known as a witch, and to you, I am known only as Xeylia."

Shumuti and Aurielle had become attentive.

"What do you mean by 'power'?" Shumuti asked.

Xeylia remained silent.

"Will you let us leave?" Sara asked.

"I think not."

"Why?" Aurielle asked.

"Because you have not answered my questions even though I answered yours. I know nothing about you or what you are planning to do here. I will leave you until you decide whether you will tell me. If I am satisfied, perhaps I will let you go."

Xeylia turned to leave. There was a gentle boom as the door was shut, and they were all still for a breath or two.

"Who is she?" Shumuti asked. She spoke to the closed door that Xeylia had just left from and almost made a move to try to follow the mysterious woman.

"We're in such a mess," Aurielle said, "we ought to be sailing Stannair down the Winterburn, but instead we crashed the boat, wrecked the sail, travelled for a day into the enemy's country."

"It's not all bad," Sara said, "at least we're still together."

"Where were attacked by a horde of bats, taken captive, locked in a cell for who knows how long and are nowhere near close to what we came looking for," Aurielle finished.

Shumuti did not turn away from the door. It was as if she had not even heard Aurielle. Sara pushed back her sleeves, wincing as she did so, to check on her numerous scars. The bats had made their mark on her arms and face.

"The only way out of this is to decide what to tell her," Sara said.

"Why did we even follow her here?" Aurielle rounded on Shumuti, so she could not be ignored.

"There is something about her, can't you see it?" Shumuti said.

"All I know is I don't trust her. On the hill, you said we turn away the moment we feel we're in danger, and yet you let her walk us here."

Sara was struck by an unnerving thought. "What if she can control other animals the same way as the bats, like vultures, for instance?"

"She could have set up the attack on the boat to lead us here," Aurielle voiced what Sara had been thinking.

"But she was surprised to find us in Boctor," Shumuti said, "she accused us of trespassing. I don't think she is connected to them."

"How did she find us then?" Aurielle asked.

"I don't know," Shumuti muttered.

"Can she use Magic, the same as you two?" Sara asked.

"There is something strange about her," Shumuti said, "it isn't the Magic I recognise but almost as if something about her is being suppressed. She has strange abilities, like this power of persuasion and commanding the bats. Nothing like we've ever been able to do."

Sara found herself wondering who Xeylia could be, and an idea crept into her head that she was reluctant to voice aloud.

"Have you noticed how little Magic there is in this cave too?" Aurielle asked Shumuti, "as soon as we got to Boctor, I noticed it was bad, but here I think it is worse."

Shumuti nodded, with a slight grimace. "I'm not used to it."

Looking at the pair of them, Sara was surprised to notice they did look paler than usual, almost ill. She had not realised how closely linked they were with Magic before, and neither had she been aware that the absence of it could make them feel physically unwell.

"She mentioned some people call her a witch," Sara said, "that's what people used to call my mother in Silverspring."

"I would like to find out more about her," Shumuti said, "but it would be unwise to bring up Magic to anyone, not just her."

"Regardless of what she is, we need to figure out what we can possibly tell her to make her let us go," Aurielle said.

Aurielle wandered over to the door to try to find a way to break open the lock and Sara took the opportunity to turn to Shumuti.

"Seaglen said that Aurielle's mother disappeared into Boctor and she was never heard from again," Sara murmured, "could this woman be somehow linked to her?"

Shumuti glanced over at Aurielle in surprise.

"Lyria?" she answered in a low tone, "you think they might be one and the same?"

"Is it possible?" Sara asked.

"I don't know," Shumuti answered, "she bears no resemblance to Aurielle that I can see, but at the same time, I know of nobody else linked to Magic except for those original six. I don't think Xeylia is like us though. She is a paradox to me, and I don't know if I'll get the chance to understand who or what she is."

They fell silent as Aurielle wandered back over to them.

"Can we get out?" Sara asked.

Aurielle shook her head. "Perhaps talking is truly our best option for the moment. If that fails, then we shall see."

"We could tell her what happened to us," Sara said, "just about the sail I mean, and maybe we might be able to find out where to get a new one. It's perfectly reasonable we were sailing to Attaching or Elmdale and did not mean to end up on this side of the river."

"Don't forget that she comes from Boctor," Aurielle said, "I wouldn't count on her help."

"Not everybody in Boctor supports Nimaz," Shumuti reminded her.

"It's still foolish to blindly trust her," Aurielle answered.

"She dœsn't look like she is going to return any time soon." Shumuti eyed the firmly shut door. "We should rest and stick to our story largely as it happened, except the reason for our travels. Hopefully, that will be enough."

It barely felt like a sleep at all when the sound of the door creaking open awoke all of them instantaneously. The black figure of Xeylia swept in through the doorway. She approached the three of them and sat down opposite, with a steady gaze.

"Will you speak?" she asked.

"We will tell you how we ended up in the north of Boctor," Shumuti slowly, "will that be enough?"

"I will have to decide on that later," she answered.

Shumuti took a breath. "All right. Well, we were sailing up the Winterburn River to visit some friends of ours in Attaching. Yesterday, a creature attacked us. The sail of our boat got torn apart, and we ended up on the Boctor side of the river. We needed to get a new sail and saw the village below, hoping that someone would be able to help us."

"I would not venture into the valley village for aid," Xeylia said, "they would offer more damage than help to you."

"But we need to get our sail fixed," Shumuti said.

"Do you have it here with you?" she asked.

Shumuti brought it out from her pack in its several pieces. Xeylia took it and examined it for a few minutes.

"I may be able to remake this," she said finally, "for repayment of what my bats have done to you, but also for another price."

"You would?" Shumuti asked in surprise, "what is the price?"

"For your entire story. You are keeping a lot hidden from me and what you have said is not enough for me to allow you to walk out of here freely. More than you have said, I believe I have guessed, but I wish to hear it directly from you."

"Why do you want to know about us?" Aurielle asked.

"To tie in with knowledge I have gleaned from elsewhere," she replied, "give me this sail and I will have a new one made to take its place. It will take a while, and that will give us all time to think, and talk."

"How will you make it?" Sara asked.

"It is my bats that will be the makers."

"Your bats?"

"This sail will be one of a kind," Xeylia said, "that is guaranteed. You should hope that your information is valuable enough to pay for it. I will permit you to leave this cave but be careful where you walk. I would suggest not wandering too deep into the darkness of the tunnels. Remember, I can help you continue on your journey."

She glanced meaningfully between each of them in turn.

"Who are you?" Shumuti asked her again.

"Tell me who you are, and perhaps you will learn," she said to Shumuti.

Xeylia gathered the old sail up in her hands and once more moved silently out of the cave, leaving the door open behind her.

"What now?" Sara asked.

"We wait," Shumuti answered, "we wait for our sail and try to figure out whether or not we can trust her. If we can't, we figure out how to escape from Boctor as quickly as possible."

CHAPTER 13
THE WORK OF BATS

Aurielle was worried about Shumuti. Her friend was usually so calm and focused on the job at hand, but around Xeylia, she was different, distracted. Aurielle sensed the unfamiliar connection to Magic with Xeylia too, but whereas Shumuti seemed drawn to it, Aurielle felt like it was something to fear. There could well be a plausible link between Xeylia and the vulture that had attacked them just before they had met her. They had only the word of Xeylia that the village nearby would be of no help, and Aurielle believed she was prepared to take the risk to trust them instead. Things could not get much worse for them anyway, Aurielle thought.

She suggested to the other two that they leave the cave for a small while, hoping that persuading them to go would be much easier once they were outside. Sara eagerly agreed and Shumuti more reluctantly. Aurielle led the way as they slowly edged their way back down the tunnel they had entered. Aurielle winced as they rounded the corner into a large, open cavern, where Xeylia stood at the centre. She was facing away from them but any hope Au-

"""

rielle had that she had failed to notice them yet was doused, as she called out to them.

"You are just in time," she said.

She lifted her arms and raised them high above her head, revealing the fabric of the sail draped across them. Thousands of bats flurried in and out of the dim light, and slowly Aurielle noticed that they were grouping and forming a single cloud. She could only see the few closest to them, as the roof of the cavern appeared almost endless and drifted into nothing but darkness at the top.

"What is happening?" Aurielle dared a question.

"I have to give them the old sail," she replied, gazing upward. At her words, the giant cloud of bats descended through the air to collect the tattered piece of material that had been sewn roughly back together into one piece as much as was possible. The noise of the bats became more frenzied as they came down and took the sail, tiny claws gripping every section of the fabric before soaring upwards in a spiral again, eventually fading into darkness and quiet.

"I will spend the day with it," Xeylia said, "I will find you when it is complete, so long as you are within the caves. There is only one day a year when I may wander freely outside under the gaze of the sun."

"One day a year?" Aurielle questioned, "why?"

"It is a curse, of sorts," Xeylia answered.

"When is that day?" Shumuti asked.

"The day that summer turns to winter." She turned ever so slightly back in their direction.

For a second, Aurielle thought she saw a glint of scarlet mixed in with her lilac eyes, a strange trick of the light. Even so, Aurielle felt herself shudder slightly.

"Let's go outside," she urged the other two.

Sara turned instantly to walk away, but Shumuti was transfixed, staring at Xeylia as though she wanted to ask more, until Aurielle physically grabbed her arm and escorted her away. After giving her a tug, Shumuti cooperated, and giving Xeylia a wide berth, Aurielle led the way in pacing slowly out of the cavern. Xeylia seemed to glitter in the darkness behind them.

Turning a corner of the tunnel, Aurielle forced Shumuti into a jog as they passed the rows of lit torches that led the way out into the light. Aurielle, Shumuti and Sara broke out of the tunnel and scrambled their way up the mountain slope until they were a safe distance from the cave entrance, where they finally stopped. The wilderness stretched out before them, rolling on forever, but to the east, the bright blue band of the Winterburn River stretched out enticingly, and Aurielle wanted nothing more than to start running and not stop until she hit fresh water. They sat down on a small plateau halfway up the side of the rise, with their legs dangling into nothing and the cave entrance still clearly visible below them.

"Did you see her eyes?" Sara asked eventually.

Aurielle nodded.

"She's not...human is she?"

Aurielle shifted uncomfortably. "Not completely, I don't think."

"What is she?" Sara asked.

"It's hard to say," Aurielle said, "nothing Seaglen has ever taught me can explain her. She hasn't killed us yet, but perhaps she is waiting for us to give her more information first."

"She's mending our sail."

"Says she's mending our sail."

"Why does she want to know everything about us?"

"I don't know, but I don't trust her one bit. We ought to run while we have the chance."

"What?"

"Now. We run. Let's get as far away as possible before nightfall. Whether she can come outside in the day or not, we know she definitely can at night."

"But what about the sail?"

"We'll try the village. If not we'll get back to Stannair, I can get us back across to the Merrywater bank with Magic, somehow."

She failed to add to Sara how much damage she would cause by attempting to do that, but did believe she could manage the task.

"All right," Sara nodded, finally taking her side.

Aurielle turned to Shumuti, who had not said a word, with her eyes remaining fixed on the cave entrance.

"Shumuti." Aurielle shook her. "We have to go."

Her friend did not turn her eyes from the cave.

"No."

"What?"

"I said no."

"Shumuti, listen to me." Aurielle put one hand on Shumuti's arm. "We need to run."

"And how far do you think we would get?" Shumuti asked, finally turning and acknowledging her. "We would have a good few hours before dusk, yes, but then the speed of her bats would mean she would catch up to us fast. We will not make it to the river before then, so we are confined to Boctor. Her territory. It would not be long before she found us and I don't think this time she would so willingly call her bats off."

Sara rubbed her wounded arms uneasily.

"Dœsn't she frighten you?" Aurielle asked.

"No," Shumuti answered, "she intrigues me, and if we stay, we can find out more about her. I want to know more about her story the same as she dœs about ours. Aren't you the least bit curious, Aurielle?"

Aurielle shook her head in firm disagreement.

"Not that I'm saying it would come to it, but could you fight her, if you had to, with Magic?" Sara asked, "are you stronger?"

Aurielle shared a glance with Shumuti. Typically, she would have been confident against almost any opponent with Magic to hand, but here she felt unsure for the first time. Coupled with the general lack of Magic to draw on in their surroundings, she was honestly not confident how a fight would go. Especially since they had no idea what Xeylia was capable of.

"I still think we should leave," Aurielle said eventually, "we have time to collect our things and reach the Winterburn before night. Then I'll use the water to get us across to the other side. I'll have the whole Winterburn as a source if needs be. I can fight her bats then. You can't tell me that if Seaglen were here, he would allow us to trust in somebody from Boctor?"

"Aurielle," Shumuti said, "you know we wouldn't make it. Besides, don't you know what day it is?"

"What do you mean?" Aurielle asked.

"The turning from summer to winter," Shumuti explained, "this year, that day falls tonight. They will be celebrating getting the last of the harvest in, back in Thayll. It marks the beginning of the transition into the darker half of the year."

Aurielle sat back, working out how long they had been away and realising that she was right.

"Does that mean she will be stronger?" Sara asked.

"All she said was that she would be able to go out under the sun," Shumuti said.

"There has to be more to it than that," Aurielle said, "Seaglen never mentioned anybody being subject to a curse as a result of Magic."

"Maybe we should let her explain it to us?" Shumuti suggested, "all we have to do is offer up our story in return."

"You want to go back in there?" Aurielle said to her.

"You two stay here," Shumuti said, standing up, "I'm going to go talk to her. I'll exchange some portion of our story for the sail, and then we'll be on our way."

Aurielle opened her mouth in protest, but Shumuti's expression silenced her.

"This solves your problem, does it not?"

"I don't think we can trust her."

"I have decided to. It's time to go and find out if I was wrong."

Shumuti scrambled over the rocks and down on to the path before they could stop her. Aurielle made a move to go after and faltered, conflicted with worry. Was she being too mistrustful of Xeylia? So lost in thoughts of her own, it took a while before Aurielle realised Sara was trying to get her attention.

"You're just going to let her walk in there alone?" Sara asked in disbelief.

"You don't trust Xeylia either?"

"No, not the last time we saw her. We can't let Shumuti go in there by herself."

"You're right." Aurielle nodded, composing herself. "Come on."

They vaulted their way across the rocks, almost running back the way they had come and landed in a cloud of dust by the opening to Xeylia's lair. Beside her, Sara crept forward into the darkness. Aurielle shut her eyes for a moment to let them adjust and then quickly opened them, before slipping inside. Aurielle and Sara promptly sank into the shadows at the side of the entrance. All the while she strained her ears for any sound, but there was nothing except for the constant fluttering of bat's wings.

"She's not here," Sara whispered.

"No," Aurielle replied, gazing into the dark corridor ahead, "but then where is she?"

Chapter 14
Unlucky for Some

As Shumuti tiptœd forwards, a small movement out of the corner of her eye distracted her in the inky blackness. She had been heading down the tunnel back to the main cave but a small side tunnel she had not noticed before, drew her inexplicably towards it. She had thought that something had moved in the darkness.

"Xeylia?" she called.

There was no response. Undecided, Shumuti gradually took a few tentative steps forward. Suddenly decided, but not sure what she was doing, she inched forward, her senses alert to any possible sound. She turned to look for torchlight inside the central tunnel behind her, but all around was complete darkness. Disorientated, a small noise further into the cave alerted her senses again, echoing around her and amplifying. Her hand found the slimy wall of the cave as she stumbled forward.

Shumuti crept forward keeping one hand on the side of the wall next to her. After a few seconds, she realised she was heading downhill, and the wrong way. Xeylia's words from before sprung unbidden into her mind, her warning against wandering too far into the tunnels. She turned around, confident she could retrace her steps back out. Where sight was failing her, she strained to hear anything beyond the quickening beat of her own heart.

There was another echo of movement in the blackness.

"Hello?" she called out.

Shumuti waited for a reply. None came.

A hand clamped down on her wrist. A grip that clung as firmly as freshly wrought iron. Shumuti screamed and writhed to break free, but the restraint was unbreakable. A voice groaned in her ear, electrifying the hairs on the back of her neck.

"You should have listened to your friend and fled when you had the chance."

Crimson eyes glowered out of the darkness near her face.

"No! Xeylia, why are you doing this?"

Xeylia's grip tightened.

Shumuti tried to twist, but she couldn't move. A fierce burning pain shot through her forearm where Xeylia gripped her, and she cried out again. Her instincts naturally reached for Magic, but instead of the usual energy, she felt as though she had slammed into a brick wall. Where it had been lacking before, the presence of Magic was suddenly non-existent. Winded, she was finding it hard even to remain standing. She stopped fighting and gently, bit-by-bit the pain receded.

"Do not challenge me," the voice said, satisfied she had stopped trying to resist, "you are already too weak, and soon, my strength will be even greater."

"What are you?" Shumuti choked.

"It's far too late for that," Xeylia hissed, "you had your chance to ask questions."

"Shumuti?"

"Shumuti!"

Two cries echœd down the tunnel in their direction. She turned frantically in Xeylia grip and summoned all her strength.

"Help!" she exclaimed.

Everything was silent for a moment, then suddenly liquid blue veins streamed their way through the rocks of the tunnel, following the water droplets that clung to the moss on the walls, illuminating the chasm like a blue grotto. A roar of Magic came with the new light, and suddenly Aurielle and Sara were illuminated in the centre of the tunnel, carrying all of their gear in hand.

In the distraction, Shumuti wrenched herself free of Xeylia's grip and forced herself to run back to her friends. Sara grabbed Shumuti's arm and stopped her from falling. They faced the shadowy figure across the cave and hardly recognised her. Bathed now in blue light and twice as large, Xeylia's form was distorted and fuzzy, while the only areas of sharp focus were her bright eyes. Her body was no longer humanoid-shaped and took up most of the space within the tunnel around them. Shumuti shied away in fear.

"Run, now!" she cried to the others.

They turned as a unit and broke out of the dark passageway. The fluttering of bats rose to a crescendo in the cavern air above them, Aurielle's Magic lighting the way ahead. There was a rush of wind behind them as they threw themselves out into the fading sunlight. Not stopping to look back, they sprinted downwards to the base of the mountain, leaping recklessly from one rock to the next.

After throwing themselves down the final slopes, the trio collapsed at the base of the cliff in exhaustion. The evening was now beginning to fall, and turning to the sun, Shumuti saw that it was now nothing more than a blood-red disk suspended a few feet above the horizon, wreathed in red mist. Still shaken, Shumuti was unable to prevent herself from tripping and sprawled over the path. The other two came to a halt ahead of her.

"Are you all right?" Sara asked, kneeling beside her.

Realising she was trembling, Shumuti managed to sit up, the adrenaline beginning to fade away slowly. Aurielle regarded her from above.

"What happened to you?" she asked.

"I heard her when we went into the cave," Shumuti gasped, "I had no idea...she would be like that. What happened to her?"

"Did she say anything to you?"

"I...yes," Shumuti stopped. "She said she was getting stronger, and I was already too weak to stop her. She said we had missed our chance to ask questions."

"It will be dark in a few hours," Aurielle commented, "this isn't a safe place to stop."

Shumuti looked up at the sky to find the sun was setting in deep purples. Within a wink, it would vanish. A trill of fear sparked inside her, and she jumped up.

"There is no time to make it to the river," Shumuti said.

"We have to get out of the open," Sara said.

"The village!" Aurielle exclaimed, "it's the only place with cover."

She stood up and offered Shumuti a hand. With a grimace, Shumuti forced herself upright once more as they set off at a fast pace.

"What if it won't do any good?" Sara shouted as they ran, "Xeylia's freedom lasts tomorrow as well, until the setting of the sun!"

"I know," Shumuti panted, "but if the villagers have survived all these years..."

"We just have to hope we're not running into even more danger," Aurielle added.

Shumuti had no answer to that and could only manage to pound her legs even harder into a sprint across the open plain. The village grew tantalisingly closer as they sped forward. She took a glance back at the mountain and ran faster than she could ever remember doing before in her life. They had to get there on time.

All Shumuti could hear was their rapid footfalls as she pushed on and the terrain turned into a long dirt track leading straight to the village. With a sense of formidable dread, she chanced a look behind them, now that night was transforming the skies completely. The view made her let out an involuntary gasp that alerted Aurielle and Sara to what she was seeing.

A colossal spiral of bats wove their way upwards towards the moon over the mountain like burnt scraps of parchment lifted on the breeze. Several hundred more were making their way across the plains almost hidden in the darkness, travelling at an alarmingly swift speed in their direction.

"Faster! RUN!" Shumuti yelled.

She pushed Sara forwards, and they took up the sprint once more. Her heart pounded against her chest, and soon she could hear her breathing becoming ragged. A small wind whipped up, and it flurried the sand around their feet. It was an icy cold blast, but it kept Shumuti going. They had almost reached the village.

Shumuti felt relief as the first buildings rose up on either side. They thundered into the deserted village and stared wildly for a place to hide. Every light from each window was cut off, and the town held an eerie silence to it, as though it was holding its breath in anticipation.

"Over there!" Aurielle pointed.

It was a small, stone inn, and the nameplate swung gently in the breeze. They ran over to it and just as they reached the door, it swung open.

A man with wide, sunken eyes stood in the shadows holding a hatchet.

"Please," Shumuti begged.

There was a moment where she thought he was going to shut the door on them before he nodded.

"Inside."

They hurried into the inn, and the door creaked shut behind them. The room was dark, but gradually Shumuti noticed lots of shapes shifting at their arrival. Faint beams of moonlight illuminated individual faces, all which were silent and grim.

"Here, sit here." The man who had let them in showed them an empty table next to the window. They sat, and as Shumuti looked around, she noticed that everybody else was as far back into the shadows as possible. They were the only ones anywhere close to a window.

The man who had let them in came and wordlessly sat by them with a jug of amber liquid.

"You look like you need this."

Out of the corner of her eye, Shumuti spotted a figure outside running towards the door of the pub.

"The scout's back. Open the door!" The man stood up to let the scout in, and it was then that Shumuti curiously noticed several carved talismans that had been hung up to adorn the windows, and what looked to be offerings of wheat and other crops. There was also a strange scent in the air that she believed to originate from the ornaments. She grimaced, thinking that whatever they had attempted, it would do little good.

The scout hurried inside, breathing heavily. The silent crowd in the pub became, if possible, even quieter as they waited for the man's report.

"There is a crowd of bats almost over the village," he panted, "and a larger shape with them."

Shumuti chanced a worried glance at Aurielle and Sara.

The two men whispered together and nodded in their direction. The scout eyed them suspiciously, and they approached slowly.

"Come with us," he ordered. They rose nervously and walked with the two villagers, under the gaze of the crowd in the inn.

Shumuti, Aurielle and Sara were led down a flight of stairs into the cellar of the inn. There was just room amongst the barrels to stand. A flint struck up a lantern that emitted a pale glow around the room, where they waited silently.

"We'd like to know who you are and what your business is here." Both men regarded them carefully, and Shumuti only watched them back, while Aurielle opened her mouth to speak.

"We're travellers," she said gruffly.

"Travellers to where?" The man's tone had altered.

"A long way from here." Aurielle was losing her confidence. She felt the same way, and they needed to get out of this interrogation as soon as possible.

"You provide us with a straight answer or-"

"We're going to Attaching," Shumuti spoke up. Resting on the wood of a nearby barrel, Shumuti felt her hands shake.

"We lost our way, and then we saw that thing outside."

The two men leant back in their chairs and exchanged a glance. A thud shattered the silence. A scream followed it. The men leapt up and turned to each other in fear.

"Alf, she's trying to break in!"

The man hesitated.

"Come on, Russ."

The scout opened the door, and the two men pushed through. Aurielle sprang to her feet in objection.

"Wait! We can help you! We can fight!"

The men eyed them with a mixture of distrust and fear. The door banged shut with a heavy thump. Aurielle ran up the stairs and yanked at the handle, but it felt bolted fast.

"They've locked us in!" she cried in disbelief, ramming her fist on the door.

"Use Magic!" Sara blurted, "get us out!"

"Shumuti, I need your help," Aurielle said, "I can't manage it alone."

Steeling herself, Shumuti felt out for Magic in the surrounding air. Out of nowhere, her arm flared in pain, and she almost blacked out.

"I can't," Shumuti said in disbelief, as she fell to her knees, shivering.

"What's wrong?" Aurielle asked with concern.

"Xeylia." Her voice shook. "Her power, whatever it is. It's everywhere..."

Shumuti could not stop shaking. She slunk down against the barrel and pulled her coat tight around her, waiting for her head to clear.

"What did she do to you?" she heard Aurielle whisper angrily.

"This is her night," Shumuti managed to say, closing her eyes against the pain, "and she's too strong. We're trapped here."

Sara sank back down into her chair. "Can you hear something?"

Aurielle pressed her ear to the trapdoor.

"Glass. Breaking glass."

"What are we going to do now?" Sara asked.

"There is little we can do. We shall have to wait to see if she finds us."

They sat in silence as the night around them filled with unearthly noises and more disturbingly, sounds of screaming far into the night. Shumuti heard it all from afar as though she was listening from far away. It was getting harder to struggle to stay awake, and her strength had finally run out. Before she realised it, she had slipped into unconsciousness.

CHAPTER 15
THE FIRST DAY OF WINTER

The sound of voices brought Sara to her senses. She jolted up from where she had been on the border of consciousness, and her hearing sharpened as the source of the sound became apparent above them. Next to her, Aurielle was still watching over Shumuti, who had passed out several hours ago. None of them knew how many hours had passed. Sara jumped over to the door and hammered on it frenziedly.

"Hey! Hey! HELP!"

The conversation above her went silent, so she took the opportunity to intensify her knocking. After a few seconds, whœver it was upstairs, detected the location of her distress signal and she heard the sound of objects being hurriedly cast aside as those above attempted to answer her call for rescue. All the commotion finally woke Shumuti. After what felt like an age, Sara heard the sound of a bolt lock pulling back, and the trapdoor creaked upwards. Three men's faces stared down at her in astonishment, their faces covered in a mixture of blood and dirt, contrasting with the whites of their terrified eyes.

Aurielle and Shumuti appeared beside her, and the men stood solidly for a second, taking in their discovery. A second later, arms reached down and helped them up the stairs. Supporting Shumuti, they exited the cellar as fast as they could. Sara glanced back to notice one of the men vanish back down the steps.

The inn was now missing half of its roof. The bar still smouldered, with charred beams littering the floor and the smell of smoke still heavy in the air. Striding through the remains of the inn, they sat Shumuti down on a splintered bench just outside the door, to discover that most of the village had gathered in the square outside. The third man emerged from the doorway, at last, carrying a full cask of ale in his arms, giving a shrug in response to his friend's criticism.

"Are these the only three?" an older man came to ask their rescuers.

"The only three left alive inside."

"Half the village has been destroyed this time. This time was the worst year we've known yet. Still, the tavern seemed to bear the worst brunt of it, almost as though she was looking for something."

The older man eyed Sara suspiciously but had no chance to say anything further as another voice cut across the crowd.

"That witch has ruled over our village long enough! I say it's high time we did something."

"Aye!" a man affirmed from nearby.

More villagers added their voice to the crowd, and the volume of the discussion grew steadily.

"You say this every year, and every year I have to point out that we have no way to fight her. The only thing we can do is leave the village and find somewhere else."

"And go into Boctor proper? Only death waits for us there."

"And this is a better life?"

"At least death only comes once a year here."

The crowd fell into a murmuring bicker as the arguments flew back and forth, making no real progress.

"Thank you for saving us." Sara turned to the man with the barrel. "At least you've had some reward."

"Not a worry," he replied, with a sly smile at her, "if you'd like, the three of you can come back to our home? We'll take care of you there."

"Perhaps then you can reward us for saving you," the second man added with a wink.

"I think you've had plenty reward already," Aurielle said.

"Apologies!" The three men backed off with a grin and walked away laughing between themselves, casting one final look back at Sara. The talk in the square had increased in volume again.

"We can't let her continue to ruin our village!"

"There is nothing we can do!"

"What do you mean she was searching for something? What was inside the inn?"

"Dœs anybody recognise the girls who were pulled out of the inn?"

"I have never seen them before..."

"Over by the door!"

The talk had finally begun to turn to discuss the few strangers within the crowd. The older man who had scrutinised Sara earlier pushed his way back through the mass of bodies to the front of the inn again. But the three rescued figures by the broken remains of the door had vanished, and only the splintered piles of wood and glass remained.

"Do you think they will search for us?" Sara asked, casting a glance back at the silhouette of the village in the distance.

They had been walking most of the day and it was near-ly evening again now. Almost a full day had passed since being trapped under the inn.

"I'd rather the villagers find us than Xeylia does," Aurielle said.

"Hopefully, she thinks we're dead," Shumuti said, "whatever she did to me is finally wearing off."

They had covered a fair amount of ground since escap-ing from the square and rediscovered their original route from the Winterburn River.

"Where do you think she is now?" Sara asked.

"Terrorising some far away village most likely," Aurielle said.

"I know what you're going to say, but I am still curious about her," Shumuti said, "there is some link to Magic there in her past, I know it."

"Still?" Aurielle asked, "after all this and everything you've seen her do, you want her to be a friend?"

"Not a friend, but I want to know more about her. Doesn't she interest you at all, Aurielle?"

"She would if I didn't think she would kill me before talking to me."

"Perhaps this day under the sun changes who she is. You saw how different she looked in the tunnel. I would talk to her on any other day that wasn't today."

"She has you fooled."

"Perhaps."

"We are not returning to that cave. I am not pulling you out of there a second time. We'll make our way somehow across the river."

"Agreed, and thank you again for that."

Sara suddenly laid a hand on both Shumuti and Au-rielle's shoulders, slowing them both down to a halt.

"We don't need to return to the cave. Look! She has found us."

Aurielle drew her sword immediately. Down the slope ahead, the black figure of Xeylia stood before them, watching silently. She looked the same as when they had first talked to her in the cave, calmer and more human. Bats fluttered around her clothes once more, eager to escape even the soft light of the approaching evening.

Shumuti made a move to walk down the hill before Aurielle could hold her back. Sara saw Shumuti wince slightly as the movement came into contact with her injured forearm.

"No," Aurielle said.

"You stay here then," Shumuti answered.

Shumuti moved tentatively down the slope, and after a momentary hesitation, Sara followed her, surprised to notice Aurielle had actually stayed behind on the hilltop, the tip of her sword resting against one of the stones at her feet. Xeylia pulled something out of her robes as Shumuti and Sara approached. It was a jet-black bundle draped across her arms, which she laid on the floor and partially spread it out.

"It is finished," Xeylia said.

"What is it?" Sara asked.

"This," she proclaimed, "is your new sail."

It was incredible. They went forward to have a closer look and Sara touched the cloth. It was unlike anything she had seen before. Glimmering silver threads cut through the black sheen as she held it between her fingers. The sail resembled a black wave that rippled and glimmered under the slightest wind.

"What is it made from?" she asked.

"I will not give away my secrets so easily. But I guarantee you will not find this fabric anywhere else in Meteorath."

The sail glided underneath Sara's fingers, and she could not help wondering whether or not it would be strong enough. Shumuti voiced her thoughts.

"I should not worry," Xeylia said. "This fabric has unusual qualities. I should know. I have worn the same garb for as far back as I can remember."

She was right. Xeylia's dress matched the fabric of the sail perfectly.

"Thank you," Sara said.

"You are giving this to us even after what you said?" Shumuti asked.

"In light of my most recent actions, I feel I owe it to you." She glanced regretfully at Shumuti's arm. "This one day I am given comes at quite a high cost. In the last hour, I have become myself again, but I have little time to enjoy it before I have to prepare for another year of becoming nocturnal. I will not make you exchange information for the sail. I saw the display of Aurielle in the tunnel, and it confirmed to me most of your story. You are who I suspected you to be. If I may, I would give you a small portion of advice. Do not be tempted by any darker Magic. I am living proof that you will regret it if you do."

"Darker Magic?" Shumuti questioned her.

"Trust me. You will know if you come across it," Xeylia answered.

"I would ask you a little more if I may?" Shumuti began.

"My history is my own," Xeylia said, "there are many mysteries to Magic that have become lost. Perhaps if we meet again, you may ask me more, but for now, I would ask that you let me enjoy the last few hours of daylight that remain to me. When you return from Attaching, if you have time to return to Boctor then, I will answer all the questions you have Shumuti. I promise."

"I hope we do meet again," Shumuti said.

"Hopefully in the dead of summer though," Sara muttered.

"Xeylia, have you ever had another name?" Shumuti asked.

Sara thought she noticed Xeylia tense slightly as she reacted, but it was quickly hidden.

"Once."

"Was it Lyria?" Sara asked.

"No. No, it was not that."

"Oh," Sara said, sure that she had been right.

"I apologise again," Xeylia said, "even I cannot control the strength and power inside me. Keep in mind that I could be a dangerous friend, and I would warn you of that now. Be careful of how you go from here. Walking into Boctor was not the safest move to make, and I would not do so lightly again. I never thought I would see Magic again and now there are things which I dare to dream that never entered my mind before. I must think long about what this means. Go quickly back to the river and keep your senses alert. Also, offer my apologies to Aurielle. She was right not to have trusted me."

"I would maybe remain cautious of the villagers," Sara added, remembering, "we heard them threatening to come and remove you from the mountain."

"Ah," Xeylia said, "an old threat. One I can certainly handle. Thank you, Sara. Now I will wish you luck on your journey and leave you. Here would be a safe camp for the night if you wanted to rest, I feel. There is nothing dangerous roaming nearby tonight."

"Are you sure you will not stay?" Shumuti asked, "you are quite welcome, however it might appear."

"You must understand, Shumuti. This is the only day I have a year to see Boctor. Even then, I am prevented from crossing over its borders and travelling further, but for now, seeing this region is more than enough."

"Why can't you cross the river?"

"The Winterburn is more than a natural boundary between regions. It is also a magical one, one that I cannot cross. I am bound to Boctor, always."

"Why?"

"Perhaps one day if you return I will share my story with you."

Shumuti dropped her questioning.

"I have one final thing I must do before nightfall," Xeylia added, with longing in her voice, "I cannot miss the sunset flight I take once a year to the western coast. It is the thing I miss seeing most of all in the daylight. So, I must bid you farewell."

With that Xeylia took a step backwards and the colony of bats detached from her cloak and dress. The fabric transformed itself into a pair of ragged wings as she widened her arms, and both bats and woman took to the skies high above Boctor. The bats encircled her in a swirling cloud until they could no longer distinguish her from the colony. Sara and Shumuti watched her go as Aurielle finally strode up beside them, her sword now sheathed, and they began to prepare their camp for the evening.

CHAPTER 16
RETURN TO THE BOAT

~SHUMUTI~

The north wind blew across their faces and whipped through their hair. Six brown, hooded figures matched each other's pace as they strode evenly across the sandy beach, heading towards the grassy bank beyond.

A bell tolled in the distance, ringing out six times. The figures increased their pace as the sand ran out beneath their feet, and they ascended the gentle slope of the hill to their destination.

A small abbey rose over the crest of the hill, and the voice of the bell's call rose, summoning the figures onwards.

High above, a warm sun warmed the ground from a cloudless sky. A dark shadow rippled over the sapphire sea, coming closer at a frightening speed. One of the figures halted, alert. The shadow drove forwards high in the sky and cast a shadow over the sun. The figures looked up as the shadow dropped nearer and a shadow blocked out the light. A roar thundered in their ears...

Shumuti shot up out of sleep.

"What is it?" Aurielle questioned her, blinking sleepily from the last few hours of being on watch.

"Nothing." Shumuti waved her friend's concern aside. "Just a dream."

It took a moment for Shumuti to adjust to the real world. She also realised she felt weaker than usual and her right arm still burned as if it had been on fire. Shumuti pushed herself upright.

"Time to get up," she said, wincing and rising to her feet.

She got up before Aurielle could ask anything more about that dream that had seemed too real. Sara got up after her with a yawn.

"Will we reach Stannair today, do you think?"

"Today or the next," Shumuti replied.

"Early start then?" Sara said, cheerfully shouldering her pack.

Shumuti nodded absently, her mind elsewhere. They searched through their packs to find the last scraps of food to eat as they began to walk.

When they had looked south from Xeylia's mountain, all that was visible were rolling plains and a desert wasteland. But here, the land was closer to the river, and there were traces of green in the earth as grass finally began to grow close to the water's edge. Winter was undoubtedly now approaching, though. The winds that were blowing from the west carried a chill with them, and soon, the weather would become harsh and bitter. Shumuti knew they needed to reach Attaching before then, or else they would fall into more trouble.

The day was uneventful, which was a relief, considering the wild events of the days before. Birds swooped and dived in the sky alongside the bees and other insects. More distant hawks were gliding in the air currents above that, judging the location of where to attempt breakfast.

Sara was leading the three of them and had been doing so ever since the morning. Shumuti guessed from this that Sara was eager to reach Stannair and get out onto the river again. As much as she tried to avoid it, Shumuti found her thoughts unconsciously returning to Xeylia. Despite all of Seaglen's training, there was so much more to Magic that remained unknown to her. Seaglen had never mentioned anything like Xeylia to her. She wondered if he would even have been able to tell her who Xeylia was. What had happened to her in the past that trapped her in that mountain?

Perhaps when they had finished in Attaching, she could return and talk properly with the mysterious woman, but for now, it seemed she would have to be content with wondering. There were more urgent problems for them to deal with right now. She readjusted the pack on her shoulders and tried to focus on planning ahead instead.

The midday sun burnt through just enough for Shumuti to feel her pack sticking and digging into her back. She looked up to check their progress. Boctor was remarkably barren and desolate. Shumuti had been staring at the ground for the last hour, so much that she began to believe she was walking the same stretch repeatedly, over and over.

"Can either of you two remember coming this way?" Shumuti asked.

Silence descended between them. Shumuti cast a glance at Aurielle, who was now scanning the terrain around them for a sign of something familiar. Then Sara pointed.

"There's a hill in the distance over there. If we can get a bearing to the river, then we'll be fine."

"When we were coming this way," Aurielle said, "I think I remember that we had the sun on our right." She rotated. "So, we need to head in that direction."

She now faced the east of the hill and let slip one uncertain glance between her two companions.

"Let's just get to the top," Shumuti said quickly.

Aurielle had not been unknown for getting lost before and right now, what with the weight of the pack, Shumuti was not willing to walk any further than she had to. They set off with eyes fixed on the distant hill. Behind them, the sun was sliding steadily down in the sky to show that mid-afternoon was now approaching.

"Can you see the river?" Shumuti shielded her eyes.

"Yes!" Sara exclaimed, "there!"

"Really?" Shumuti looked up and saw without a doubt, to her delight, the silver spun thread of the Winterburn River.

"Well, what do you know?" Aurielle said, "I can see Stannair."

"Where?" Sara asked.

Aurielle pointed, and they followed her arm down to a steep meander in the flowing current. There sat their broken little boat, cushioned by the riverside brambles, awaiting their return. Shumuti's heart went out to their small vessel, mingled with joy at seeing it once more.

"Do you think we'll make it by dark?" Sara asked.

"I plan to," Shumuti replied.

"I'd like a proper bed to sleep in tonight," Aurielle said.

Renewed with energy, they almost ran down the hill in the direction of the boat. Shumuti took a final look back the way they had come. Xeylia's mountain was barely visible, looming out of the distant horizon, but it was there. What was more, rising above and behind it was a spiral of thick, thunderous black clouds. There was a storm coming.

Soon after they had run over the rocky terrain of the hill, it transformed into rough grassland. Energised by the proximity of their destination, they picked up speed. A new determination and focus to get to the river dulled the pain of Shumuti's feet, her shoulders, her legs, arms and back.

A crack of thunder rolled out from behind them as they closed in on half a mile from the river. Shumuti slowed to a walk and let the others go on ahead, still feeling weakened from her encounter with Xeylia. Pulling out her waterskin, she finished the remaining water she had and listened as she walked.

A hushed rumble gently echœd out behind her. Remembering the old trick she had learnt, she counted out the seconds, until the crash of distant lightning flashed in the distance. Ten, Shumuti had reached. The storm was still a long way away.

She broke into a small jog that was little more than an amble so that she was slowly diminishing the distance towards the boat and the river. Stannair sprang into view as she broke the crest of a bank to meet the rushing Winterburn River. Speeding up once more, Shumuti arrived at the boat and hauled herself up onto the deck.

"We were just coming back to find you," Sara said, popping her head up from the cabin below, "here, give me your pack."

Shumuti yanked the pack gratefully from her shoulders, before weakly tossing it at Sara and watching it land a few inches from where Shumuti lay. Sara gave it a pitiful glance before retrieving the bag and throwing it below.

"Sara!" Shumuti called down.

Her head reappeared out of the boat.

"Have you heard the storm?"

"Storm?"

"Coming from the north, over Boctor."

"From the mountains?"

Shumuti nodded.

"Well, all right, I'll tell Aurielle."

With a final check of the oncoming storm, Shumuti hurried towards the steps to the cabin below. They secured the boat from any damage the thunderstorm might cause and retreated down into the cabin. All three of them slipped into sleep uncaring that night and slept right through the wind and rain, all the way on till morning. Shumuti found that no more strange dreams came to her that night. None at all did in fact, or at least not that she could remember.

Chapter 17
Sailing on the Winterburn

By the time the three of them went out on deck the next morning, any signs of the weather front that had battered the boat last night had now passed. The morning was as clear and bright as ever, but it was also cold. There was a soft winter chill in the air.

"Here." Sara tossed Aurielle a cloak.

Aurielle gratefully accepted the layer and the three of them wrapped themselves in the warmth of the long cloaks.

"Well," Shumuti said, "shall we get our new sail out?"

Aurielle smiled and waited as Shumuti ducked down below to retrieve the wrapping from where she had locked it away last night. The sail was unrolled carefully because the fabric seemed to slither and glide in their hands as they laid it out. They held it flat and under control and then each of them attached it section by section to the mast. It took less time than Aurielle would have first thought and then slowly they began to haul it up the pole to the very top. The wind caught the fabric as it billowed in the breeze and gently the boat rocked.

"Here," Sara said, coming forward. She held up two long poles, tipped with hooks.

"Right," Shumuti said, "Aurielle, could you cut away the tangle of branches from the bush? Sara, we'll use these to push off from the banks."

Aurielle swiftly jogged down the side of Stannair to a compartment by the helm specifically designed for weapon storage. She drew out her blade, before returning to the bow of the boat and began to hack away at the barbs that held their craft tightly. She worked for a few hard minutes and eventually, the mass started to thin out.

"Try it now!" she called.

The other two obediently turned to the bank with the long poles and placed the hooked ends on the grass bank, before using the poles to push off from the side. Stannair would not move at first, but then gradually as Aurielle went back to chopping, the boat gently began to edge back through the water.

"Sara!" Aurielle exclaimed, "get to the tiller!"

Aurielle ran forwards and took Sara's place as she raced to the back of the boat, and their new sail billowed out around the captured breeze. She steered Stannair round to face upstream. Safely back into open water, they stood up and brought the poles back from over the side of the boat. Sara told them where to store them, and then they congratulated each other for a moment. The tailwind was blowing correctly to fill Stannair's sail, and speed was gathered quickly as the chill wind wove around them, creating small, white waves along both port and starboard sides. The sail fluttered mesmerisingly in the gathering breeze.

"Do you know how close we are to Attaching?" Aurielle turned and asked Shumuti.

"No," she replied, "first we need to traverse the length of Elmdale."

"We'll know when we're near each new region, won't we?" Sara said, "because there is a tributary river that cuts along the top border of Merrywater, and the same for Elmdale."

"We ought to be close to the Merrywater and Elmdale border," Shumuti said.

"Attaching won't be for a while yet then," Aurielle said, looking out ahead. There was no other river but the Winterburn, spread out as far as the horizon. "There's also the border river of Boctor and Nimaz on the west side to look out for."

"Well, if we keep travelling at this speed, we'll be there in no time," Sara said.

Almost predictably, at that moment a drop of rain fell on the decking at their feet. Aurielle exchanged a look with Shumuti, and they both turned to Sara as though it was her fault. The rain fell slowly from that moment on through the morning, but the high wind still kept up, and they did not fall to a halt. Hoods were drawn up, and they pressed on in silence, through the grey world that the river had become. Very soon, their cloaks became little more than wet rags, and the wooden decking of Stannair had turned deadly slippery, so they moved around as minimally as possible as Stannair tacked her way down the river.

They halted for a break in the afternoon. The rain had thankfully died down and eventually fizzled out altogether, but the cold still bit through Aurielle's sodden clothes.

"Ugh," Shumuti uttered in disgust, sliding off her cloak. She glanced at Sara and Aurielle before walking to the side of the boat. Holding the coat over the edge, she wrung out the material, and a torrent of water gushed out from the folds of the fabric. When she was satisfied, Shumuti shook the cloak and brought it back over into the boat. Sara stood up and went to the starboard side of Stannair, leaning out over the edge.

"Can you see anything?" Aurielle called out to her.

"Nothing yet," Sara said.

They went and joined her at the side, shivering in their damp clothes.

For a few more days, the trio sailed on up the river until eventually, Sara was the one who spotted the dual tributary watercourses that flowed into the Winterburn from the east and west. They passed the large opening and left the presence of Boctor behind them. Soon though, another landmass took over the view on the western bank, and this one was even more foreboding than the last. Nimaz could now be seen stretching out into the distance, even more significant than Boctor. The trio looked out silently as they sailed by and Aurielle gulped. The stripped and bare landscape that they saw at the edge of this nightmarish region made the desert stretch of Boctor seem pale in comparison. The inhospitable view of bedrock and cut ravines that struck out at them was enough to make them recoil and turn their heads the other way.

That night they moored on the eastern side of the river that belonged to Elmdale. Sara was quite quiet, and occasionally Aurielle caught her glancing out over to the horizon, lost in thought. Aurielle was about to speak up, when Sara left the deck of the boat and disappeared down into the cabin.

While Shumuti was tidying up on deck, Aurielle went down below and found Sara sitting on her bed, staring at the floor. She had not noticed Aurielle come down yet and Aurielle hovered on the bottom step, wondering whether to go forward.

"Hey," she said, "is something on your mind?"

"I was just thinking," Sara answered quietly.

"What about?"

"You know, we're no more than a few days walk from my village."

Aurielle felt her eyebrows rise. "Do you want to go back there?"

"The thought keeps tempting me," Sara admitted.

"Why? Is something there for you?"

"My friend. His name is Stephan, and he helped Astrid and I get out of Silverspring. We left him when we fled, and that was the last time I saw him."

"Maybe we could stop by on the way back from Attaching?"

"What if I don't make it back?" Sara asked in a hushed voice.

"Are you worried about the danger? Shumuti and I are here to protect you, just like you do the same for us."

"I didn't know we'd be running into things like Xeylia, things that I don't have a hope of defending myself against. I can't help worrying I'm just going to be a burden to you."

Aurielle wasn't sure what to say.

"I suppose you're not bound to this task the same way as Shumuti and me. Because someone is misusing Magic up in Attaching, it's our job to deal with it. You've joined us of your own free will. So I suppose what I am trying to say is that you could go now and find your friend if it's so important to you. But the last thing I want is for you to leave, Sara. Shumuti and I are always here if you want to talk. Promise me you won't do anything rash."

Sara nodded, deep in thought. "I promise."

Aurielle took out some dry clothes and went back outside. She felt troubled all of a sudden but decided against mentioning anything to Shumuti just yet. Instead, Aurielle set about clearing the deck for the night in silence.

CHAPTER 18
CHANA

Ever since Sara had mentioned the possibility aloud to Aurielle that she could abandon the journey and take the chance to return to Elmdale, the idea had been growing inside her head. It made her uncomfortable to think that she was so readily willing to leave her friends, but there were a few strong arguments that made a case for her departure.

She was no Magic user, after all. She did not belong here, only invited along because she happened to be with the other two. She was useless against whatever magical foes they may encounter, just another thing for Shumuti and Aurielle to think about and protect. They had already needed to save her from the attack on the boat. That feeling was only going to get worse once they found the source of Magic they were searching for and she became more and more out of place.

Sara knew if she mentioned her troubles to Shumuti, her cousin would inevitably try to stop her from leaving. But most of all, Sara knew deep down the main reason she wanted to return to Elmdale was to see Stephan again. Selfishly, she also knew her motivation was that she wanted to be around somebody who was like her, somebody who could not use Magic.

"Sara!" Her name was called from on deck above. "Come and help me with the sail, will you?"

She quickly leapt up the stairs from where she had been sat alone inside the cabin and went over to help Shumuti.

"I thought we weren't going to sail any more today?" Sara asked Shumuti.

"Well, we weren't," Shumuti answered, looking out over the water, "but there's a strange mist that came out of nowhere over the river. It has grown since yesterday, and there is something about it that unsettles me. Maybe I'm just overly cautious, but I'd quite like to outrun it if possible before nightfall. There is a good wind behind us, and it seems foolish not to make use of it."

Sara took in their surroundings as well and saw nothing especially menacing in the early evening fog, except perhaps a more noticeably significant chill in the air, but nothing unnatural for the time of year. She kept quiet though and set about preparing Stannair for sailing. Once they were underway, Sara took over the tiller. She hoped they would not have to travel too far this evening. Their current mooring had been on a direct level with home and any further north they journeyed from here would take her further and further away from Silver-spring.

"Sara, watch where you're going!"

Sara jumped out of her trail of thoughts in embarrassment as she quickly swung Stannair round back to face the centre of the river. The boat had veered a little too close to the western bank for comfort then, and it was clear Shumuti did not want to stop so soon.

As night took over and the sun sank below the horizon, it became clear that they were not going to escape the murky weather. A low mist had descended across most of the water surface, engulfing the way ahead and making Sara uncomfortable to travel on when her vision upstream was limited.

They moored on the right side of the river, by Sara's decision. The fog had caught up with them, and it had become too misty to see where they were going. The translucent film settled over the boat and portions of the sail and rope began to accumulate with drops of dew from the fog.

"I think I'll go and scout out ahead up the riverbank," Shumuti said, "to see if there is anything nearby. I'll be back soon."

She hopped off the boat and onto the shore. Stannair swayed gently at the shift of her weight and sent ripples out along the river, echoing across the surface of the water. Aurielle went to the front of the boat, and Sara settled cosily in her cloak at the back.

A few minutes later, Shumuti returned with a restless expression.

"Everything looks normal to me," she reported, "if a little foggy."

"It's getting dark," Sara said.

"I suppose we should get some rest," Shumuti agreed, "but I think we should set a watch if both of you don't mind. I'll go first."

"If you like," Sara said, "wake me after then."

"If any of us spot anything, don't leave the boat," Aurielle said, "wake up the others first of all."

Sara sensed Aurielle's suggestion was aimed more at her than Shumuti and could not help feeling like Aurielle believed that she was unable to look after herself. After agreeing, Sara and Aurielle went down below to get some sleep, leaving Shumuti on guard up above. Sara could not manage to fall asleep though, and eventually she climbed back out of bed and went out to offer Shumuti a swap.

From the look on her face, Sara could tell that Shumuti, while troubled still, was also very much in need of sleep, so it did not take much persuading to exchange places.

Shumuti had reported nothing of interest in her few hours of watch and Sara had much the same experience as the hours began to tick by. She thought the idea of a watch had been a little extreme and was not particularly nervous sat amongst the silence of the river.

Her mind was occupied by something else entirely. She had roughly calculated in her head that they were only a few days walk away from Silverspring. If she left, she could check on Stephan and maybe even persuade him to accompany them. The pair of them could catch back up to Shumuti and Aurielle in Lyria, perhaps. He had always talked about wanting to travel Meteorath. Even if he didn't, it would be nice to get the chance to speak to him again and make sure nothing had happened to him.

She sat up from inside the folds of her cloak and shook off the cumbersome layer, then strode to the side of the boat and leant out over the edge. Part of her wondered why she was suddenly so set on leaving, but that was a quick thought that she hurriedly brushed aside.

With her hands on the rail, she debated what she was planning on doing. Shumuti and Aurielle would not know she had gone, she told herself, but it seemed a shame to be so close and miss out on the opportunity. Aurielle would be able to guess at what had happened. With a small creak, Sara leapt over the edge of Stannair and cringed as the boat rocked unsteadily under her shifting weight. Looking back, all was still, and the boat settled into a balanced position once more.

Pushing back a thought that she was doing something stupid, Sara began to stroll forward confidently. Perhaps she would just walk for a few minutes to try to find the main track that led to Silverspring. Then she could leave properly tomorrow. Out in the darkness, the mist pressed in more tightly, and Sara took a moment to locate a path, before heading forwards once more. It was her casualness that meant it took her longer than it should have to detect the rustling.

Suddenly alert, she listened out for the noise again to try to detect where it had originated from, but all was silent in the fog once more. The only anomaly she noted was one patch of slightly darker mist a few hundred metres inland, just at the limit of her vision. A brief flicker of uncertainty ran through Sara's mind, and uneasily she ignored it, drawing her sword instead. It flashed with a comforting silver light for a second before the dark, murky grey filled her vision once more. The inky blur seemed to fall back with every step she took forward. Pausing, she realised how easily she could get lost and turned to check on the position of Stannair. The boat was no longer visible. Sara tried looked down at the path before her feet and retraced her steps a little. Under her boots, the worn down trail she had been following had ended and became grass. She had become completely disorientated.

Sara froze, and then suddenly her mind cleared, and it hit her how big the mistake was that she had just made. Now she was utterly alone, lost in the fog, not wanting to seem like a burden but having just made herself more vulnerable than she ever had before.

The best thing to do would be to stay where she was, Sara thought desperately. If she yelled, she might attract the wrong kind of attention. She could attempt to find her way back to the boat, but that was one correct direction out of dozens of wrong ones. She tried to peer through the fog for any landmark at all but her view was completely cut off in every direction, except for the darker blur that still remained distinct from the surrounding fog.

A weird, unnatural sound, yet an oddly familiar one, reached her ears over the pressing silence of the night, though Sara could not place it. Then it was replaced by lots of voices coming from every direction. Some were laughing. Others were hissing.

Move, Sara heard her brain shout.

Now they seemed to be saying something. Sara strained to hear what, but it was just out of reach.

Move!

They were on her left. She turned. No, wait. Now they were on her right. Sara turned again. Back on her left. Even above her, the whispers were everywhere. There was a chance that the distinct shape in the fog was Stannair, but the possibility felt too slim to her, so Sara turned and fled in the opposite direction.

The second she came to her decision whatever was here in the mist with her also began to make their move. Sara's boots thudded out a quick rhythm on the grass, and on either side, she felt the sickening presence of unseen figures. Every now and again, she noticed a dark silhouette shoot past. She had no idea where she was heading but only felt herself hoping she would reach the river or any landmark.

Something came so close to her that she had to contort wildly to duck out of the way. She slowed to a halt and swerved back around in the other direction, back where she had come from, or so she hoped. But it was not long before her pursuers were once again, back on her tail.

With a sudden cry, Sara swung round and slashed with her blade. It cut through thin air, and a jubilant shriek sliced the fog, filling her with rage and fear.

"Why are you hiding?" Sara called, "if you want to fight, then show yourselves!"

Her words were nothing more than an enormous bluff. The last thing Sara wanted to do was die, but seeing as how that was becoming frighteningly possible, she preferred to go out fighting. Unconsciously, her fingers grasped the cold, bronze amulet at her throat. She had almost forgotten about the charm her father had given her. The familiar feel of it and the memories warmed her heart the tiniest bit. It gave her the courage to take a few steps backwards and face the direction of the noise.

There was a figure in the mist ahead now, and she could make out a tall form. Then she heard the sound of a bow being drawn back from behind her and Sara feared she was as good as dead.

"Well, well," a voice whispered, "looks like we caught one on their own. Let's see what powers you have acquired since you met your friends."

Slowly Sara turned, dreading what she might see and yet knowing what she would, all the same. Facing her through the half-lifted fog were two more thin, tall, black figures. They had hunched-up shoulders and wore long black capes. Seemingly human apart from their faces, where scarring had spread across pale pink, wrinkled skin, twisting noses into long hooked beaks and their eyes into two black, cavernous pits. Sara shivered in recognition at the vultures.

This time there were three of them. The one on the left had a bow aimed at her heart, the weapon held by a hand composed of a fusion of claws and fingers. Sara gulped and subtly moved her sword into the shadows behind her, in a vain attempt to delay the fight.

"Shall I shoot?"

The tallest vulture held out a hand to wait.

"What do you want?" Sara heard the pitch of her voice rise ever so slightly.

"What do we want?"

Sara backed away at the sound of the voice, also guessing from the difference in tone that one was male and the second was a female.

"We want you."

With that, the third figure behind her shrieked and took off into the air, its claws outstretched to attack and grab hold of her. As the creature flew towards Sara, all the training Seaglen had given her burned through her mind like wildfire. Revealing her sword as if from nowhere, she swung to the left, felt the breeze from the creature's speed and lashed out, clipping the creature's wings on one side.

There was a second scream as the vulture hit the ground. Sara's sword hacked down to meet her target, but the creature rolled away in time, disappearing back into the fog. Defiantly, she held the gaze of the female vulture who glared stonily back, all the while scanning the mist.

"Shoot her," she spat.

Sara's face fell. She could not parry an arrow.

"Oh no, you don't!" a voice cried through the night.

A fierce gust of air whipped around Sara's hair and cloak and buffeted the vultures. Hardly daring to hope, her heart leapt as the wind only strengthened and cut beneath the fog, lifting it from the ground. The smoke billowed away into nothing and revealed a calm black sky above them, sprinkled with stars and a silver moon. Shumuti and Aurielle walked calmly forward through the lifting fog. They met Sara and stood on either side. She felt the anger radiating off them so fiercely that it made her nervous, but also suddenly privileged to be their companion.

The vulture that had tried to attack Sara was now visible once more and had scrambled back upright with a look of vengeance in both cold eyes. Tattered black wings spread out menacingly, in preparation to lunge.

"Let me correct my earlier mistake, Chana," he hissed and leapt forward once again.

"No! Wait, you fool!"

Aiming at Aurielle, who was closest, he ran with fierce speed and simultaneously drew a grisly, longsword from his side. Aurielle unsheathed her own and faced her attacker head-on. With a yell, she parried the first flurry of blows and exposed the left side of the creature. The vulture's eyes widened before the expression altered to shock, as Aurielle calmly and swiftly dispatched it with a single stroke embedded in her enemy's chest, knocking it over and spearing it to the ground. Sara turned to face Shumuti with her mouth open, but her cousin's attention, like Aurielle's, was fixed on the remaining vultures.

"You don't have the fog to rely on anymore, Chana," Aurielle said. Her tone was cold and sharp. "You might want to rethink fighting the three of us in the open."

The vulture twitched at the use of her name. Chana forced her face into a sneer.

"We shall see. Rix, get the girl!"

Sara was taken by surprise as the second vulture flew at her, but then Shumuti stood between them and raised an arm as if to direct Magic at their attacker. Rix screeched and pivoted back towards Chana to avoid whatever was coming, but Shumuti hacked out with her sword instead, her blade coming into contact with a retreating clawed foot. A scream of pain tore through the night.

Rix turned and circled high above them, debating the next move. An arrow whistled out towards them, and suddenly Aurielle was throwing Sara to the ground as the shaft flew just over them. Sara rolled in panic towards the sword that she had dropped. She rotated onto her back, and black claws and a razor beak slashed towards her, filling her vision. Flinching to avoid them, she grasped the pommel of her blade and slashed Rix across the chest. He screamed in agony and retreated once more towards Chana.

"You all right?" Aurielle crawled over to Sara.

She nodded, feeling decisively sick.

Chana fixed an arrow to her bow and drew it back, aimed at Sara once again.

"Wait..." Aurielle began.

"Now who's pleading?" Chana said.

The bow was fired and Sara closed her eyes. Surely this was it. She heard the snap of a bowstring as an arrow shot through the air and a thud as it hit. The cry of pain was unnaturally inhuman. Sara's eyes shot open. Shumuti stood with one arm outstretched towards her, as though she was clutching at something invisible in front of her, with concentration etched on her face. Chana's arrow had frozen in mid-air, inches from Sara's nose. Instead, she had Shumuti's sword protruding from her shoulder. Chana yanked it out and dropped it like it was poisonous to her touch. With a flash of anger, she launched forward, wings widespread and charged Shumuti. The arrow fell harmlessly to the grass in front of Sara.

"Aurielle! Sword!" Shumuti said, as Chana prepared to take off.

She caught Aurielle's flung weapon by the hilt and dodged under Chana's airborne attack, receiving a deep scrape to her upper right arm from a large talon. Shumuti cried in pain and twisted, slashing up with the sword at the same time and brought Aurielle's blade into contact with Chana's retreating back, severing both wings from the back in one clean manœuvre. Chana crumpled unnaturally to the ground, and a second later Rix was there, bowling Shumuti over and gathering up his wounded leader.

He clutched her close and took off, struggling to gain height, but before long they were indistinct from their backdrop. Nothing was left but a pair of large withered wings, cast unceremoniously on the ground.

Chapter 19
The North Border

Shumuti gritted her teeth as a searing pain ran down her right arm again. This particular limb was not faring well in their travels so far. Sara dabbed a mixture she had concocted onto the bare skin where the vulture claw had sliced through her arm. Shumuti drank in the herbal scent that filled her nose from the poultice and felt a little better.

They sat on the grass just in front of where Stannair was docked, as the early glimmer of dawn flickered above the horizon. Shumuti did not particularly want to look at her wound, but she could still feel the dry blood that was crusting there. The tear cut deep into her arm and caused repeated, sharp bursts of pain. It didn't feel like a clean sword cut. It felt infected or dirty.

Shumuti turned her head away from her wound and looked over towards the Winterburn River, searching for a distraction. Stannair bobbed gently on the surface of the water, with the midnight sail dancing in the early morning breeze. Aurielle must have put the sail up, Shumuti thought, probably eager that they move off soon.

Casting her eye around the riverbank, she felt a surge of guilt. The grass around them stretching out in either direction had withered to a pale brown, cracking and dry, as though it had spent months under a hot, summer sun. Sara noticed what had caught her eye.

"I can't believe I used so much," Shumuti said, "but we had to find you, Sara."

"So this is what happens?" Sara asked. She ran a hand curiously over the wilted grass and the blades disintegrated under her touch.

"If you overuse Magic something will pay the price. I've upset the order of things here. The land here will recover in time, but it will take a while. I don't know if anything will even grow here next year."

Sara bound her arm with a clean cloth and stood up. She offered Shumuti a hand to get up and clumsily she accepted, her wounded arm feeling stiff and heavy. Aurielle emerged from the side of Stannair.

"We're ready to set sail," she said.

"I'm ready," Shumuti said.

"I don't like it here," Aurielle said, "do you think we should leave that body?"

"What body?" Shumuti asked, before suddenly remembering what had happened last night. The vulture that Aurielle had stabbed must still be spread out on the wilting grass back at the site of the attack.

"Where is it?" Sara asked.

"Just over to the left side of the bank," Aurielle replied, "I could just make it out from the boat before."

"There's nothing there," Sara said, looking where she pointed.

"What?"

Aurielle swung over the side of the boat and headed in the direction of where they had fought last night. Shumuti and Sara followed close behind. They reached the site soon enough, easily recognisable from the small splatters of blood strewn around the area and the remains of one of Chana's arrow shafts. But there was nobody present.

"He can't have still been alive?" Aurielle asked.

"Perhaps these creatures are harder to kill than we first thought," Shumuti said.

"You mean he got away?" Sara asked.

Aurielle huffed and turned back towards the boat. They walked back slowly, over the beaten earth, each of them lost in their thoughts. Getting over the side of Stannair with only one useful arm was trickier than Shumuti had imagined. Once everybody was on board, Aurielle pushed the boat off, and Sara took her place at the tiller.

The next section of their journey passed thankfully without any kind of incident at all. The three of them began to relax fully into life on the water and their confidence in the tasks surrounding taking care and running the boat grew each day. They planned to pull into the docks at Harland Point, just on the border of Attaching, to refill their slowly dwindling stock of food and supplies. The mood was still quiet aboard the boat as the lands of Elmdale rolled by, and the sun rose higher in the sky.

"You know, Shumuti," Aurielle said eventually, "I've never seen you display a level of control with your Magic like you did in that fight the other night. You've never stopped an arrow mid-flight before have you, right?"

"No," Shumuti said, feeling a little proud, "I've been trying for a while now. I guess the danger was the added factor I needed. It's a whole new side to air Magic that I have never had a chance to explore before. I've never considered the possibilities of controlling the air around objects, altering what is expected to happen. It is much harder though, and it's not without consequences."

"Thank you again for saving me then," Sara said, "you should probably know though, before you arrived the vultures said they wanted to see what 'powers' I had gained since meeting you. I think they thought I could use Magic as well."

"They did?" Shumuti asked.

"I guess they must have just assumed that I would be like you," Sara shrugged.

"That's interesting."

"Better the vultures think I might be more of a threat, than helpless."

"Sara, you're far from helpless," Shumuti said firmly.

"Sorry." Sara sighed. "I'm just annoyed at myself. It's my fault you two were even dragged off the boat in the first place. I don't know what got into my head. Do you know I was even considering leaving you both altogether in the fog? I nearly left to go back to Silverspring."

"That weather felt entirely unnatural," Aurielle said, "you're not thinking the same in the morning now, right? I wouldn't overthink it."

"No," Sara agreed. She looked away, seeming comforted.

"But sometimes circumstances only exaggerate thoughts that are already in our heads," Shumuti said, "Sara, have you been thinking about leaving us?"

"Only because we had been so close to my home recently," Sara answered, "truthfully, I have been trying to debate whether you would be better off without me. I felt as though I was little use on a magical quest, but now I've realised that perhaps I still have skills that can be of use. I can heal and still fight with you."

"Sara, we do need you," Shumuti said, "we make a good team."

"I know. Besides, if I leave, who else is going to steer Stannair?"

Shumuti laughed.

"But do you know something else?" Aurielle said.

"What?" Shumuti asked.

"Look out ahead."

They looked to the front of Stannair, and Shumuti smiled. Snaking its way along the horizon was a band of silver-blue, a tributary of the Winterburn River, which marked the northern border of Elmdale. They had finally reached Attaching.

Chapter 20
Arrival in Attaching

~AURIELLE~

Long, soft, draping willows brushed the surface on the shaded water. They lightly swept across Stannair as the boat drifted gently alongside. The dark hue of the trees partly obscured the sunlight, causing cool green shadows to dance over the water, the vessel and its three companions. They floated silently along the avenue of willows, trying to catch a fleeting glimpse of the city that lay just tantalisingly beyond. This waterway was one of a few paths leading to the centre of Lyria, and now that they were here, the three of them were enthusiastic about reaching their final destination.

Stannair turned a corner, and all of a sudden, the obscurity of the trees lifted as they glided out towards the light once more. A cold wind rose up, buffeting them now they were more exposed, and Aurielle huddled more tightly inside her cloak. The port was now clearly visible ahead, a forest of its own, comprised of rows of bobbing masts and craft of all sizes. She raised a hand to shield her eyes and heard a gasp escape from Sara's mouth as Stannair broke out entirely into the light.

Spread out high above them and built into the curved mound that formed the base of the city, were buildings of a craftsmanship Aurielle had never seen the like of before. Colourful buildings clung to the foundations beneath them, almost appearing to be stacked on top of each other from this angle, every structure built from a thick red stone that shone throughout the city, reflecting in the water and resonating with a vibrant glow. Thick walls encircled the whole city and towered high above Aurielle as they sailed into port at last. The difference of this city compared to the life they knew out in the wilderness was stark. The life and noise that oozed out of the city walls seemed almost threatening. Aurielle had never seen a city as large as this one and suddenly felt intimidated.

"Have you ever seen anything like this?" she asked.

"There are so many people here," Sara said, "It feels like there's the opportunity to have any life you wanted to here."

"And many dangers, if we're not careful," Shumuti added, "look."

Aurielle and Sara followed where she was pointing into the distance. Rising high above the great mass of the city, at its crest shone a bright stronghold of red and white. From the central and grandest tower rose two fluttering, vivid red and white banners symbolising, if they somehow had not yet realised, that they were now in the heart of Attaching.

"That's the Lyrian Citadel, isn't it?" Aurielle asked, "the home of the King."

"Yes, there it is," Shumuti said, "somewhere we should try to avoid."

"Wait," Sara said, "what is that even larger landmark? Beyond the city?"

"What do you...? Oh!"

How could she have missed that? Aurielle thought to herself. Behind the city was a second notable breach in the flat landscape that stood out more prominently because it was a single inselberg. Although maybe slightly shorter than the mountain ranges surrounding Thayll or the peaks in Boctor, this isolated landmass dominated the landscape more effectively than either of them. As Aurielle stared, she remembered hearing that this was not an ordinary mountain.

"Is that the volcano?" Sara asked, "I wasn't sure it existed."

"The only one in the whole of Meteorath," Auriclle said.

"The Ember Mountain," Shumuti said.

"It erupts fire and rocks?" Sara asked.

"It has not been active for years, according to what Seaglen told me," Shumuti said.

"Which is a good thing, considering the number of people living here," Aurielle said, "and speaking of this enormous city, where in it are we going to begin our search for information? We don't know if whœver we're searching for is anywhere near here."

"No," Shumuti agreed, "but it is a good starting point, even if what we seek is elsewhere. I think we might at least be able to start to gather some information here."

Stannair edged in between the other boats moored in the harbour under Shumuti's navigation. The silky, dark blue-black material of the sail fluttered as it caught the wind, as well the attention of other boat owners idling close by in the port. Amidst several stares from the residents of Attaching, Shumuti found a place to dock their boat. Aurielle and Sara secured Stannair fast and lowered the sail hastily, before storing it underneath. For the first time on their journey, Aurielle felt an inkling of distrustfulness towards the people around them and wondered whether their boat would be safe here, in such a large city.

However, most of the people had forgotten them just as quickly as they had first taken an interest.

It was midday by the time they finally came to a halt. Even here, on the outskirts of Lyria, their surroundings were quite stylish and grand. Stannair was recorded down in a logbook to prove they had officially entered the port. After that, Aurielle, Shumuti and Sara gathered a few things to take with them as they took a look around. They debated over weapons for a moment, but nobody else in the port seemed to be armed, so their swords and armour were left locked inside the boat.

Making sure everything was secure, Shumuti took the keys, as they climbed over the side and onto the wooden jetty. The solidarity of the terrain unnerved Aurielle for a moment, and she noted Shumuti and Sara wobble momentarily, before correcting themselves and walking forwards in a slightly unstable straight line towards the first line of buildings in the city.

They wandered into the outskirts, and Aurielle was once again dumbstruck by the size and enormity of everything here. The buildings in the port looked old, and ageing in places, when viewed up close. As the three of them ventured up the winding streets, the buildings closed in around them, making it almost impossible to keep track of where they were within the city.

Each corner led to a new surprise, from market stalls dealing goods of the like that none of them had ever seen before, to sculptured fountains and decorated gardens. Lyria was unlike any other place they had ever been. The streets seemed alive with energy and activity. As the three moved on, Aurielle tried to remember the way that they had come and kept glancing back, but soon all she could see was a glimpse was a sparkle of the water behind her. Eventually, even that vanished altogether.

Further into the city, the quality of the buildings continued to improve, and the houses appeared to take on a rustic style. The buildings at the port seemed dull now in comparison. The colours of the walls and roofs were unanimously rich reds and browns. In this part of the city, many taverns and inns emerged, scattered around and quickly identifiable by ornate posts and signs.

Suddenly though, there rose one building that overshadowed them all. Turning a corner, Aurielle saw the Citadel up close in perfect sight, centred high above the rest of the city on a grassy hill. The Lyrian Citadel was somehow still even more so impressive than the rest of the town, and it seemed to almost sparkle and glitter in the sunlight.

The Citadel itself was an enormous, complicated structure of high walls and towers, with rich, red banners draped from the walls and balconies. It was a cross between a castle and a palace, a fortress and a home. The beauty of it left the three of them stunned into silence for a minute or two while they stood on a corner, attempting to take it all in.

"King Pala is the King's name, isn't it?" Sara asked.

Aurielle nodded. Slowly the three friends took an oval-shaped circuit around the Citadel walls. Their eyes were drawn to the building the whole time, and they barely checked the path they were walking. The Citadel looked equally grand from an angle, surrounded by a high white wall, with the exception of the front entrance.

"Aurielle." Shumuti whispered in her ear. "Have you identified anyone with Magic so far in the city?"

Aurielle noticed Sara also listening inquisitively. She instinctively searched around, her senses alert for any sign of that familiar touch that might indicate another Guardian, but there was nothing. She shook her head sadly in answer.

"There's nothing here."

"That's what I thought," Shumuti said, "the Citadel is big, so I might be wrong, but I don't think there's anyone inside who can use it, or immediately nearby."

"Which is perhaps a good thing," Aurielle said.

"It dœs makes things less complicated," Shumuti said.

"Imagine if the King could wield Magic though," Sara commented quietly.

"In my head, I prefer the idea that there isn't meant to be anybody as a Guardian who has power or status," Shumuti said, "and to think that all Guardians just ordinary people."

"Should we have a look around here then?" Sara asked, as they circled around to the front of the Citadel once more.

"Seaglen said that the Magic he felt ought to have been accompanied by a noticeable event," Shumuti said, "let's ask around a little first to see if anything out of the ordinary has happened recently."

There were several inns located around and just off the square they were in. One nearby had a name that Aurielle thought she recognised. The swinging sign above the door read, the Sickle Inn, and Aurielle dimly remembered where she knew the name. The same name had been on the tavern in Boctor that they had sprinted towards in terror, a few weeks ago. She followed Shumuti towards the door, hoping this tavern would be an improvement on its predecessor.

The inn was reasonably quiet, as it was still only mid afternoon. Not many people had cause to drink, yet today it seemed, so the three of them bought something and selected seats at the bar, close to where most of the conversation was taking place. The barman was a fairly short man, with a balding head and an apron tied across his front. He regarded the three girls curiously.

"You look as though you've been on the road for a while."

"For a short time," Shumuti said.

"Strange to see three young ladies travelling alone," he remarked, apparently hoping for an explanation.

"Is it?" Shumuti answered, unable to hide a trace of indigence, "why?"

They had better be careful, Aurielle thought, or they might accidentally become the talk of the city.

"We are waiting for a friend to meet us in the city," Aurielle said loudly, rolling her eyes at the barman, "he always takes forever."

"Ah, then let me know if you need another drink." He winked and wandered off to serve someone else.

"Shumuti!" Aurielle hissed, "perhaps we shouldn't draw too much attention to ourselves?"

"I know, but-"

"I know," Aurielle said, "but now is not the time."

They sat and listened, making a little conversation themselves while they decided if there was anybody they should approach. It took a while before hearing something of interest.

"...infuriating bloke he is, to be sure. He was playing music loudly outside my shop twice last week. That was until I chased him off of course!"

"They ought to ban singing in public altogether."

"He dœsn't even sing. He plays that fiddle from dawn until dusk."

Three big, burly men were speaking in low voices, and Aurielle casually pricked up her ears to listen, intrigued by their anger.

"I don't mind his tunes," another commented, falling silent as he received a withering glare from the first.

"It's not a proper use of his time. He ought to get a proper job like the rest of us."

"I spotted him the other day." A man with a greying moustache and a beard added. "He was lurking by the door of that glass chapel. I wouldn't be surprised if that's where he sleeps."

"They say that chapel be haunted."

"What by? It's deserted. I'll bet there's nothing scarier up there than your grandmother's frilly nightgowns!"

"How would ye be knowing about them?"

"Hey." The second man softly nudged the other two, breaking up their conversation and pointed over to the door.

"Speak o' the devil."

As inconspicuously as Aurielle could, curious to see for herself this person who had sparked so much outrage, she shifted her head towards the entrance where the man they were talking about was now standing. He was a figure garbed in a simple robe of brown fabric with a satchel slung over his back and a searching expression in his wide eyes, suggesting that he was looking for someone.

For a moment, Aurielle caught his eye and received such a steady pulse of Magic from him she was nearly knocked from her seat and clutched the edge of their small table in shock. Across from her, Aurielle heard Shumuti gasp as she reacted the same way. For a second, time seemed to stand still as Aurielle, Shumuti, and the stranger all stared at each other across the room, sharing such shock in a connection they did not expect. Then the men started to shout.

"Get out of here. You're not wanted!"

"Go back to your chapel and pray!"

"You'll need to if we catch up to you!"

The young man took a moment to process what was being shouted at him and wavered for a moment. In that instant, one of the men from the bar leapt forward as if to grab him.

"No!" Shumuti cried out.

Aurielle realised what was about to happen before it did as well and felt her stomach drop as she recognised the unmistakable feeling that Magic was about to be used. At the same time, the ground shook beneath them, and the attacking man was hurled into the air, straight over the bar and crashed directly into rows of spirits and ales stacked neatly behind the counter. A rift of broken earth marked his trail from the splintered bar to the feet of the stranger who had used Magic. Aurielle and Shumuti stared at him, aghast. He looked back at them, equally speechless. One of the men who had stood aside made another attempt to move forward and grab a second hold on the man.

Through the dust, he froze opposite them for a moment before turning on his heel and fleeing the building. A jingle of coin echœd from the satchel as the figure wheeled around and two of the men got up to actively chase him down. Aurielle and Shumuti pursued immediately. They could not afford to lose him now.

The pair charged outside and stared around the open square wildly for him. Their quarry was nowhere in sight and there were roughly ten different streets he could have taken. A small distance away, the men were also stood, looking equally confused. The stranger had not been much older than them, Aurielle was sure of it. In her head, she was desperately trying to memorise his face before it slipped away, his bright, blue eyes, brown hair and the beginnings of a beard growing on his face. Shumuti spun in a circle.

"He's gone!"

"How could he have got away so quickly?"

"Maybe he knows a secret way we don't."

Aurielle heard Shumuti almost scream in annoyance. "He was here, and we let him get away! Did you see what he did? Is he stupid?"

"What should we do?" Aurielle asked.

"We need to get out of here." Sara appeared out of the door, running up to them. "The people in the inn are talking, asking who you are. Let's go."

"Back to Stannair," Aurielle said, "we think it over and plan from there."

Aurielle could tell that her suggestion was making Shumuti angrier, but reluctantly she agreed, and they ran back downhill in the direction of the port to decide what to do. Aurielle's head tumbled with thoughts as they went. Was this the same person who had caused the event that Seaglen felt? The men in the inn had also mentioned seeing him in a chapel made of glass. Perhaps they did have a lead after all, Aurielle thought, maybe they could find him there.

They hurried back into the crowd of people going about their business in the city. Slowly, the streets darkened and all the while they hastened back to the harbour, Aurielle kept alert for the slightest traces of Magic, but there were none to be found.

CHAPTER 21
THE CHAPEL OF GLASS

Just like on the previous few days, Shumuti awoke at dawn and found herself sat up on deck watching the sunrise. Sara and Aurielle were both still asleep, but Shumuti had hardly slept at all. The face of the man in the inn kept swimming in front of her eyes. She had searched for that same face in every man who had set foot on the docks so far that morning. The sensible part of her knew he was nowhere near because she had checked for the presence of Magic. Several times.

They had been in the city for a week now, every day searching a new area for clues of the man, or word of a chapel made out of glass. So far, they had had little luck and met nobody who could help them. Most of the city had been searched, except for the north-eastern quarter, which they were going to attempt today.

Shumuti sat back against the mast and remembered the face again. Aurielle had thought that he had seemed to be looking for someone when he had burst through the door. She wondered if there was a possibility he had been searching for them, that he had sensed their Magic. If that had been the case, she had been hopeful that he might try to find them again. But if he had, he had not been successful, and neither had they.

They had thought if this man were playing music in the streets, he would be easy to find. But they had heard no music in the city and even after asking around after any street musicians in Lyria, a few people had pointed them to regular spots, but no musicians came. It seemed that their man was lying low.

She cast her mind back to the first night here and the conversation the men had had about a chapel made from glass. That was what they had said. But where could they find it? As far as the rest of the city was concerned, it was not real, or it existed under another name. Shumuti pulled her cloak closer around her as a sudden breeze curled around the harbour. Of all the people she had watched on the previous few days and this morning, Shumuti saw that not many wore weapons, except for the soldiers. She guessed these soldiers belonged to the King because of their red and white uniforms. Most wore swords or axes at their belts, but occasionally there were bows and even spears carried by hand. The residents who Shumuti saw pass them by eyed the soldiers with respect and fear.

She glanced back down the hatch at the other two, but there was no movement from below. Thinking had not helped her to reach any conclusions, so she decided action was a better course. After a second of hesitation, she went to wake the others, and despite their protesting, it was still relatively early by the time all three were ready. The other two had agreed to Shumuti's suggestion of going out with the specific aim of finding the glass chapel, rather than the man today.

Unlike the first day, all three of them brought their weapons along, concealed underneath their cloaks. Travelling in a different direction to yesterday, they covered the distance to the edge of the port, laden down by only a small lunch, as they aimed to be out all day if needed. For the beginning of winter, the day had grown surprisingly warm.

Shumuti's arm still flared occasionally from the attack on the river. She bit her lip with slight concern because the cut had been growing steadily more painful each day. Shumuti had kept this quiet from the others, but if the pain continued to increase, she might have to say something. She had kept the information to herself because she did not want them to have to remember that night. Everything had settled again, and now that they were safely inside the walls of Attaching where the King ruled, they were no longer in any immediate danger from the vultures. Sara was happy again and back to her usual self. But still, Shumuti was bothered by her wound.

"Can you sense anything, Shumuti?" Aurielle asked.

"What?"

"Any Magic?"

"No, there aren't any signs of it anywhere around."

"That's what I thought. Let's go and look somewhere else."

"Wait," Sara said, "there's a hill in this quarter of the city too. Why don't we head up to the top of it? We would be able to see most of Lyria from up there."

"Good idea," Aurielle said, "maybe we'll be able to see if there's anywhere we haven't checked yet."

Shumuti followed as they began to climb up. The road they were taking ran between various houses and small food shops. The potent smell of fish, cold meats and cheeses drifted through the area and lingered after them up to the hill. The scent made Shumuti's nose wrinkle and caused her to feel slightly light-headed as they progressed. After a long, hard climb, they broke out above the cluster of buildings and onto a broad, grassy plateau above. Standing above the concentrated atmosphere of the city, a brisk wind blew through their hair and to Shumuti's surprise and relief, the pain in her shoulder lessened.

Sara had been right. The hilltop view encompassed the whole of Lyria and laid the city out below them as though they were gazing down at a three-dimensional map. The small harbour was positioned almost directly beneath them, and Stannair could just be made out, arranged amongst the large crowd of other boats. To the right, the central plan of the city clustered around the central hill where the main road swept up to the Lyrian Citadel, which was raised high on a grassy mound, glinting in the sun.

Like the draw of gold, Shumuti's eyes slid further west, and the sight was no less impressive the second time. The volcano of Attaching was further away from Lyria than she had first thought. All grass and vegetation came to a halt about five miles from the base of the mountain, and its dark sloping sides were littered with giant rocks and sprinkled with dark grey ash.

An alarming stab of pain unexpectedly shot through her shoulder. Her hand shot out and clutched her right arm, and she winced.

"Shumuti?" Aurielle turned, concerned.

"I'm fine." She gasped. The pain had vanished just as quickly.

Sara hadn't noticed anything. She was busy marking down on a handmade map, the parts of the city that they had explored so far.

"Let's have something to eat," Aurielle said.

Shumuti agreed and sat down on the grass. She extended her arm experimentally but no more pain came, so Shumuti brought out her hunk of bread and chunk of cheese, and started eating. The other two sat down next to her, and they ate in silence for a while. Shumuti looked out again, past Attaching and back south where they had travelled. The streak of silver-blue water wound its way back through Elmdale to Merrywater, back to Seaglen and Astrid, and home.

On her right, Sara suddenly got up. She was staring at something much closer to their present location, at a wall a few feet to the right of where they sat.

"What is it?" Aurielle asked.

Alerted, Shumuti quickly checked for any Magic. A faint trace of something drifted by but before she could be sure, it had disappeared. Aurielle stood up, and Shumuti shadowed her.

"Over there," Sara said, "I thought I saw a glint of something behind the wall as the sun came out behind that cloud."

Aurielle and Sara slowly began to stalk towards the wall. Shumuti rested one hand on her sword hilt and followed them, each sense still alert for Magic. They reached the wall and looked around, but there was nothing of note to be seen. The sun had vanished back behind a group of clouds, and the temperature dropped slightly.

"I might have just imagined it," Sara said.

"Give it a minute," Shumuti said, holding out a hand and looking up at the sky.

After a few seconds, the sun broke through the clouds once more and shone on the wall. A sudden shimmer lit up something on the other side of the rocks, next to Aurielle and she turned in surprise.

"I was right!" Sara said.

Shumuti caught the faint scent of Magic, and from the look on Aurielle's face, she knew she had not imagined it.

"Is there a way over this wall, do you think?" Shumuti asked.

She scanned the length of the obstacle, both ways. It was quite high but not unscalable, if they were careful. Then she spotted what she had hoped to find, a few meters down from where they were stood, a diagonal row of stones jutted out from the bulk of the wall. They were almost invisible until you moved closer, but they protruded just enough to form a stile, and a way of crossing over to the other side.

Aurielle and Shumuti scrambled up the stile. Peering over the top, they saw what lay at the bottom of a small hollow surrounded by the stone enclosure. It was a small building of some kind, made out of a strange material that made every inch of it glimmer in the sunlight, like a rainbow-coloured gemstone.

Aurielle hopped over first, and Shumuti followed much more slowly, in front of an inpatient Sara. Most of the hollow was in the shade, except for the reflective building, which lit up as soon when the sun shone directly down on it. The light made it impossible to tell what the building was from here because it was so bright, so they walked into the shade by the wall to get a better look. The building was no larger than a small porch-sized space. It was quite tall but with a small doorway which meant the intruder had to bend almost double to enter inside. Even then, no more than three people could fit at once, unless the inside was a lot bigger than initially seemed.

The sun disappeared again, and the glow from the building was cut off. Without the shimmer of its walls, passers-by would never know that it was even there. With the sun gone again, it was clear now what material had been used in its construction. Sara reached the walls first and reached out a hand to touch them.

"It's glass!" she said, "fragments of glass set within the stone."

Aurielle clutched at Shumuti's injured arm, and she bit back a yelp of pain. "We found it! The chapel of glass."

Shumuti walked forward to examine thousands of small shards of glass set into what looked like clay walls, artistically arranged in an array of every colour and tint imaginable. Aurielle whistled softly.

"Wow," she said, "this place is amazing. Imagine how long it must have taken to build this."

"And how much care went into it," Shumuti added.

Shumuti walked around to the entrance, drawn by a curious feeling. Sara and Aurielle followed right behind her. The opening was small, and they stooped to get inside. Once Shumuti was in, she straightened up and looked around.

It was immediately cooler in here than outside. Although the building itself was short, its ceiling was relatively high, and it too was constructed from glass. Shumuti moved aside as Sara and Aurielle ducked under as well and stood inside the small building. The sun broke out of the clouds once more and illuminated the inside with a soft glow, causing the glass pieces to be reflected off one another in a prism of light. Except, she realised, for one place.

Opposite the doorway they had come in through was a slit of darkness the same height as the first door. Shumuti walked towards it, and her hand grasped a thin section of the back wall. Putting her left shoulder against it, she pushed, and the wall opened slightly, just enough to squeeze through.

Cautiously, Shumuti led the way and ducked passed the second doorway. The first thing she noticed, and just in time, was that she was standing at the top of a small flight of stairs. She warned the other two and then set off down them. From behind, she heard Aurielle and Sara follow closely and the soft pad of their boots following her down.

Shumuti reached the bottom and looked around. What little light reached this long underground chamber from above, illuminated the space in a pale green colour.

"There were some candles upstairs," Aurielle said, "hold on, I'll be right back."

She disappeared momentarily and returned holding two stubs of wax and small brass candlestick holders, as well as a piece of flint. She lit the first candle and used it to slightly melt the wax on the underside of the other so that it stuck to the holder, before handing the flame to Shumuti and repeating the process. Shumuti took the candle and went to examine the room further.

On the walls at either side were dark windows of more stained glass decorated with images of mountains, rivers, forests and deserts, each overlaid with a collection of unknown symbols. Some of the scenes, Shumuti thought she could place. They were Meteorath, but then again, there were places that she had never seen before in her life, and the symbols meant nothing to her. Only the odd sensation, which she had been feeling was still present. It was now firmly distinguishable as Magic, but a strange kind that was old and faded.

She turned back to Aurielle and could tell that her friend felt it here too. Energy flowed out of the walls and the glass, and it warmed Shumuti's heart, unconsciously making her stand up straighter. She could even tell that Sara was feeling something of the power that was residing here, even if she didn't know what it was. The atmosphere in the chapel reminded her of the training room in Merrywater. It was concentrated with Magic just the same, but the difference here was that the chapel was human made.

"He's not here," Aurielle said.

"No, not at the moment," Shumuti said, "it dœsn't look as though anybody has been in this place recently, but the door down here was slightly ajar."

"Do you think this is as far as it gœs?" Sara asked.

Shumuti progressed further into the darkness at the end of the chamber. She found herself wondering if Seaglen knew of this place. He had never mentioned anything of the sort, but then it seemed there was quite a lot he had not told her about. The chamber was empty, she was reasonably sure of that, and they were safe with this Magic in here. At the far end, there was a raised platform where a sweet smell was drifting towards her.

The meagre light from her candle illuminated a portion of the back wall of the room. Covering the wall, was the largest of the piece of artwork in here, but it was also different from the rest. Instead of more glass, a long, painted tapestry hung on the wall. It depicted an intense battle scene. At the back of the painting was a mass of dark cloud broiled with a red mist and large enough to cover the sky. The battle was taking place in the hollow between two hills and standing on the top of the mounds were six figures, three on each summit. Red, blue, silver and green light shone from the six and met in the sky, high above the battle to form a mist of gold that hung over the scene. Also in the air, though faint and distant, Shumuti thought she could make out a large, flying black shape, but it merged so effortlessly with the background of the painting that she was not sure.

Shumuti stepped up to the painting until she was right up against it and she could almost fall into the image. Two of the six figures shone with a red light, but there was no mistaking who was who. She reached out and almost touched the tiny image of her father as he stood minutely in his usual fighting stance, casting his Magic. She snatched her hand back as Sara appeared by her side and she spotted the image of Astrid, reflected in green light.

"This must be their battle, the one Seaglen told us about." She turned to Aurielle. "Why is something like this here?"

Aurielle joined them and brightened the scene a little further. She was staring at another of the figures, one surrounded by blue water, Lyria. But Aurielle was not staring at her mother wistfully, and Shumuti had no idea what she was thinking.

"Did one of them make this, do you think?" Sara nodded towards the six tiny, painted figures.

"Maybe," Shumuti said, "though it seems like a strange thing to do."

"This place feels like a memorial," Aurielle said, throwing candlelight around the room to check that there was nothing else of interest in there.

"Whatever it is, it's empty. Maybe the men got their information wrong," Shumuti said. Her arm gave a small shudder and felt a wave of dizziness. She needed to get out into the open air. "Shall we go back outside and decide what to do next?"

"Shumuti, are you all right?" Aurielle asked again.

"I think I need to get outside," Shumuti repeated.

With one final reluctant look at the painting, she turned and walked hurriedly back out of the chamber as the dizziness in her head grew, and headed up the steps to the glass entranceway. Her vision dimmed as she increased her pace, narrowing to a dark tunnel ahead of her.

Shumuti took a long breath when they got back outside. She put her foot on the first step of the stile and forced herself up and over the wall. But she had hardly swung her leg over the top when a deep, searing pain shot from her right shoulder towards her heart, and her legs collapsed. Shumuti cried out and fell, failing to clutch at the wall as she tumbled over and off the top, back down the slope. She was thrown to the ground with a sickening crack, and the momentum bounced her onward down the hill towards the city. Reaching out, she grasped for something to stop her fall and eventually landed in a hollow. The wound in her right arm reopened before her eyes, as blood began to dye the sleeve of her shirt an unsettling shade of red, and she clutched at it with her other hand, all the while hoping fiercely that Sara and Aurielle would not be far behind.

CHAPTER 22
THE HEALERS

Shumuti twisted and fell in slow motion as Sara and Aurielle watched. Sara froze in horror as she saw Shumuti bounce off the wall and disappear. She barely noticed Aurielle spring from her side to begin the sprint over the stile towards her friend.

Sara forced her legs into action and ran after Aurielle, catching up with her a few metres down the hill. As well as her arm, there was blood trickling from a nasty wound in Shumuti's head, giving her hair crimson highlights. She was not moving, and her face was a sickly pale shade of white. Her current state was beyond Sara's skills to heal.

"We need help," Aurielle said, thinking the same and desperately looking around.

"I don't remember seeing any medic centre in the city," Sara said.

"There must be somewhere!"

"We'll be able to carry Shumuti between us. Someone in the city will know. They have to."

"Quickly then."

Aurielle offered to take Shumuti first, so Sara helped her to hoist Shumuti over her shoulder so that she was steady.

"Knock on doors," Aurielle ordered, "get somebody to answer."

Sara ran ahead and raced back down the hill into the outer suburbs of the city. The first door she came to she hammered on, but there was no reply. The same happened with the next three and the four after that. Aurielle caught up with her as she ran further into Lyria.

"Nobody's answering!" Sara cried.

"Where are they?"

Sara and Aurielle hurried as fast as they could down into the main centre, but even here the streets were still deserted.

"HELP!" Aurielle shouted at the top of her voice.

There was no reply.

They swapped Shumuti over, and Aurielle ran ahead, back to the centre of Lyria where the Citadel was. Sara hobbled through the deserted streets after her until suddenly they heard a noise.

"This way!"

The voices were getting louder. Cheering, that was what it sounded like, a crowd celebrating. Sara's mind suddenly sprang back in time, back to the Carnival of Games that had arrived in Elmdale. They had come from Attaching, and there was a similar atmosphere here now.

"Sara, come on!"

Sara pushed her legs harder and seemingly came across the entire population of Lyria at once, a mass of red and gold. She staggered backwards, adjusting Shumuti's weight so that she did not fall.

A huge crowd had gathered around the Lyrian Citadel, decked out in their most elegant clothes, waving banners and flags of red and gold, cheering loudly. It almost seemed impossible to Sara that people could be celebrating when there was somebody so hurt close beside them. Next to her, Aurielle managed to find her voice.

"*Hey!* Help us! *Please!*"

Sara added her voice, but nobody seemed to listen or to care.

"*Help!*"

Sara spotted a guard, similar to the ones who had been at the Carnival. Without thinking, she started to hurry over but then stopped dead in her tracks. It was *him*. The same guard with the scar she had been so afraid of in Silverspring. Sara backed away from him in fear, as quickly as she could.

"Sara, what are you doing? We need help!"

"Not from them!" Sara cried, shaking her head feverishly, but Aurielle could not hear her over the noise of the crowd.

"Do you need a hand, my dear?" a voice asked in Sara's ear, making her jump.

Sara nearly dropped Shumuti. Turning, she saw a woman not dressed in red or gold, but deep, jade green. She had a kind and sharp face, and short hair that was sprinkled with grey.

"Yes! We need a medic. My cousin is hurt. Do you know where we can find one?"

The woman took one glance at Shumuti. "I can help you. I am a healer. Come with me."

Aurielle and Sara hurried after the woman without hesitation. She walked swiftly through the bottom end of the crowd and past the Sickle Inn. Sara rushed as fast as she could, frightened that she would lose the woman in the mass of people.

"In here!"

She turned to see the woman standing in the doorway of a surprisingly shabby-looking house. She vanished inside, and Sara hesitated for a fraction of a second before recklessly charging after her.

The inside was dark and gloomy. Candles provided the only source of light, and even that could hardly be called bright. Two more women sat at a small circular table.

"Your friend is hurt," one said, standing up. She was wearing a robe of deep, faded purple.

"Bring her through here," she said, gesturing to Sara.

Sara followed the purple-robed woman into another small room with a candlelit bed. With the woman's help, she lifted Shumuti off her shoulders and laid her on the mattress. The third woman, dressed in blue, entered the room.

"There," she said, "it's all right now. We'll take care of her. You go back to your other friend. We'll take it from here."

Sara nodded dumbly and reluctantly cast a final glance at Shumuti, and the occasional spots of blood that were still occasionally dripping onto the white sheets. The blue-robed woman ushered her out of the room and shut the door behind with a snap.

Sara wandered blindly back into the larger room. Aurielle now sat at the table with a steaming mug untouched in front of her. The green-robed woman handed Sara a second mug and gestured with a kind smile for her to sit down next to Aurielle. She took a seat and stared down at the table in shock. This situation felt all too similar to back in Merrywater when they had heard Seaglen was missing on patrol. But it had all been all right then, Seaglen had been safe.

Sara took a small gulp of the hot liquid in the mug which turned out to be tea. She felt a tiny bit better as the warmth began to spread through her body, and the shock reeled off a little. Aurielle's attention was fixed solely at the door to where Shumuti now was. Sara had never seen her expression so worried as it was now. She wanted to try to reassure Aurielle, but the words stuck in her mouth and she just gulped instead.

"Your friend will be fine," the green-robed woman said, returning with a third mug, "she's suffered quite a bit, but it's nothing we can't handle. She'll have to stay here tonight though and you may also if you wish, although I must say that you don't have the look of folk around here. Am I right in thinking that you three are travellers?"

Neither of them answered. Sara found herself unable to start up a conversation. Finally, she released a nod. The green-robed woman eyed them for a moment and set her mug down.

"You can sleep here," she said, "there are two beds."

She pointed towards the side of the room where two beds had been set out resting against the wall. Slowly, Sara got up and pulled Aurielle with her, neither of them felt as if they were functioning correctly.

"Finish your tea," the woman said.

Obediently they obeyed and drained the mugs. A drowsy sensation swept over Sara like a warm blanket, and she yawned.

"Get some sleep, and we can talk later."

Aurielle and Sara sunk onto the beds, fully clothed and dropped off immediately to sleep.

•••

Sara awoke to the strong smell of lavender. She was back at home, in her bed, high above the village of Silverspring. Her mother would be downstairs, waiting for her to make an appearance. Wait, that wasn't right.

Sara's eyes sprang open. She could hear Aurielle's steady breathing a few feet away, and she was lying on a small bed, facing the wall. Sara closed her eyes, rolled over and opened them again. She wasn't at home, she was in Attaching, in the house of three strangely dressed women.

They were there now, sitting together at the circular table - one in blue, the other in green and the last in purple. The blue-robed one seemed to be younger than the other two. None of them paid her any attention. The purple-robed one had her back to her, and the other two were sitting opposite each other, so Sara could only see half of their faces.

Spread out on the table in front of them were lots of small, rectangular stones. The three women appeared to be studying the rocks and turning them over, examining each different symbol engraved on the surface. Aurielle woke next to her with enough movement to alert the women that their guests were now conscious.

"Your friend is still resting," the woman in the green dress spoke, "she mustn't be disturbed. She still has lots of recovering to do."

"How is she?" Sara asked, sitting up.

"She'll live," the woman replied, "her head wound and a wound on her arm have been seen to, but she hasn't yet had time enough to recover."

"If you let her stay here for the next few days, she will be back to perfect health again, we promise," the purple-robed woman said.

"Sit down and tell us your names."

Sara and Aurielle moved uncertainly across to the circular table, before introducing themselves and giving Shumuti's name.

"My name is Gail," the woman in blue said, "my aunt," – she pointed out the woman in purple – "is called Wyn, and my other aunt," - she gestured to the woman in green - "gœs by the name of Isa."

"I'll get out some food," Wyn said, disappearing into another room with a swish of her purple cloak.

"We are healers," Isa said, "some of the best in the city, but I'll let you decide when your friend is better."

"What are those?" Aurielle said, referring to the stones.

"My aunts use them to make predictions of sorts," Gail answered, "they are called runestones. I don't fully understand how they work. I've only used them a couple of times."

"I recognise some of the symbols," Aurielle said.

"From yesterday." Sara realised she had seen identical ones in the chapel.

She looked around the shelves stocked with healing herbs and jars of mixtures and was surprised to note a lot of similarities between this house and her home in Silverspring, so much so that a thought crossed her mind.

"You say you're healers. Have you ever known another healer called Astrid?"

Both Gail and Isa looked amazed for a second and then Wyn opened her mouth.

"Yes," she replied, "she trained with us for a short time."

"She is my mother."

Wyn and Isa both looked astonished by the news

"Astrid? How is she? She is not with you, I assume?"

"No, she is in Merrywater."

"Well, this is a pleasant surprise," Wyn said, "I shall have to ask you more about her later on."

Sara touched one of the runes on the table.

"Are they linked to healing?" she asked, "I don't remember my mother using any."

"But she did," replied Isa, "these runes in fact. When your mother came to Attaching, years ago, she brought these with her and handed them over to us as a present.

We've kept them ever since. But there is no connection between them and healing."

"Your mother was very talented." Isa leaned closer in over the table. "Not just in healing. May I ask whether you have the same abilities?"

"When you say abilities...?" Sara began.

"I mean she was far more powerful than us." Wyn had a meaningful expression on her face, "if I remember right, she called it Magic. It was quite extraordinary what she could do."

Aurielle stiffened slightly beside her.

"Everywhere we go." She folded her arms. "We come across people with a connection to Magic. I am starting to wonder if it is not as secret as we were led to believe."

Gail glanced curiously between them, and Sara thought she knew what was coming next, "So then... can you use it too?"

Aurielle nodded and then glanced at Sara.

"Aurielle and Shumuti can. I can't."

"How is it that you know about this?" Aurielle asked.

"Astrid came to us with four others a long time ago, needing healing, just like you have," Wyn said, "they were all badly hurt and we were not sure we could help, but she told us what to do and combined our medicines with skills of her own. Together we managed to save the four of them and in return for our help, Astrid explained what she could do and taught us a few new things as well."

"How many of you are there this time?" Isa asked.

"What do you mean?" Aurielle asked.

"Well, there were six before, are there six again?"

"So far we know two."

"Two?"

"If you know Astrid, do you know Seaglen as well?" Aurielle added, "or either of the two others you helped?"

"Seaglen?" Wyn looked as though she definitely recognised the name.

"He's Shumuti's father," Sara added.

"Good grief," Isa said, "I had no idea he was still alive! Wyn, do you realise who we are treating?"

"We were friends to Seaglen and Astrid during their time in Attaching," Isa said.

"Seaglen led the group that came to us in Lyria," Wyn said, "I presume Shumuti leads you now?"

Sara could not help risking a glance in Aurielle's direction, who was sitting with her mouth open.

"Of course I could be wrong," Wyn added, seeing Aurielle's expression, "it's been known to happen."

"But you'd never admit it, would you?" Isa said.

"I'd better clear these away," Gail said. She scooped all the runes up into a small velvet pouch and locked them back away in a wooden box, placing them back on a shelf. The stones clinked as they moved, before she came to sit down again.

"We did not expect to have the daughters of Astrid and Seaglen as our guests," Isa said.

"We were told that that one of the others still might live in Lyria today," Aurielle said, "that's why we're here, to try to find them. Do you know of anyone living in the city, or around Attaching?"

"No," Wyn answered, "we knew that there was one of their friends had chosen to live in the city, but she married the captain of the guard in the Citadel, so she lived there. But that was a while ago. There is a new captain now."

"That must have been Annah," Aurielle said.

"Could she still be living in the Citadel?" Sara asked Aurielle.

Gail shook her head. "No, there is no one at the Lyrian Citadel named Annah. The current guard captain has no one he is close to."

"How can you be so sure?" Sara asked.

"Because I work there," Gail replied.

"You do?" Aurielle asked her, "then, do you know the King?"

"Oh no," Gail said, "I'm not that important. But rumours travel around fast and I'm close enough with several of the guards to know most of what gœs on inside."

Music rang out from a band outside and Sara turned her attention to the window, raising her eyebrows in surprise. The red and golden clad crowd were still gathered outside, the same as yesterday.

"What happening out there?" she asked.

"It's the five-day celebration," Isa answered, "to commemorate the days when the King first came into power and our days of peace. It happens every year, and there's a festival that spreads throughout the city. Today is the second day. The King himself should be coming out this afternoon. He appears today and on the final day of the celebrations."

"You like carnivals and festivals in Attaching don't you?" Sara said.

"Why?" Aurielle asked, "what others have I missed?"

"I meant the Carnival of Games," Sara replied, "the tournament always came from Attaching to Elmdale each year."

"That event was more than just a tournament this year," Gail said.

"What do you mean?" Sara asked.

"Gail," Wyn said, in a low voice, "perhaps we should close up if you're going to continue talking. We don't want to be interrupted while you are sharing information you probably ought not to know."

She obediently got up from her seat while Isa poured drinks for them and handed out a meal of cold ham, bread and apples. The blood-red curtains were suddenly drawn, plunging the room into near darkness. Then Isa brought out a tinderbox and set about lighting the several collections of candles dotted about the place. One gave out the same herbal scent as it burnt and soft pools of light from the flames lit the room with a cosy glow.

Isa sat back down again as Wyn took a drink from her mug. She set it down again and, satisfied that they were not going to be disturbed, opened her mouth to begin the tale. Neither Aurielle nor Sara moved as they both started to listen intently.

CHAPTER 23
THE TRUTH ABOUT THE CARNIVAL

~AURIELLE~

"King Pala has been worried for a while now about a threat to Attaching, and probably to Elmdale and Merrywater as well," Gail began, "over the summer, large, dark shapes were spotted in the skies above Lyria. So this year the King decided that a consort of guards should be sent with the Carnival members as they travelled to Elmdale. From the news that we heard back, I think they were lucky to reach Elmdale alive."

"The Carnival was attacked, wasn't it?" Sara said, "on their way to Silverspring. We saw ripped tents covered with patches and there was a large scrape down the side of somebody's cart."

"Yes," Gail replied, "they were. The guards never knew who the attackers were because they came in the dead of night. The guards did fight back but whœver it was, overpowered them. The strange thing was that when the attackers had the Carnival surrounded, they did not attack. One of the guards told of how he had a knife held to his throat and was ordered to show reveal the villagers. The guard replied how he hadn't got them yet."

"So the King was planning to bring Astrid back to Attaching?" Sara asked.

"He has been searching for people who can help him," Gail said, "or to unveil the identity of anybody working against him. I think he was getting a little desperate. The Carnival is meant to showcase talent from all over Meteorath and so far his soldiers have not been enough to fight against this threat that seems to attack straight out of the sky."

"When they questioned Astrid, she thought that they meant they were searching for Magic," Aurielle said.

"I don't know," Gail said, "I never heard that mentioned."

"So you haven't mentioned anything to the guards or the King?" Aurielle asked them.

"We did not share your secrets with anybody," Wyn answered, looking ever so slightly offended.

"So it's not the King who controls these flying creatures who have been attacking people?" Aurielle said.

"No, they are the enemy that he is worried about," Gail said, "he has not been very successful at bringing them down so far. He's lost a lot of men."

"Did you hear if anything happened in Silverspring after the Carnival?" Sara asked.

"No," Gail replied, "why?"

"I was just wanted to make sure the village was safe. One of my friends stayed behind there."

"I shouldn't worry, we have heard nothing since from there," Isa said.

"It was big news at the time though," Gail said, "the flight of you and your mother has become quite a tale through the Citadel, Sara, even though nobody really knows who you are."

"You...you're not going to turn me in, are you?" Sara asked suddenly, "to the Citadel guards I mean. If they're still looking for Astrid, if the King is..."

"Sara, we're all on the same side here," Wyn said, "I know we must still feel like strangers to you, but I promise you can trust us. Nobody here is going to hand you over to the guards."

"Besides," Aurielle said, "it's Astrid that they want, not you. Even if they don't know it, they're after anyone who can use Magic, aren't they? Oh, so I guess that means they'll want me..."

"And Shumuti," Gail added.

"Yes." Sara heard a hint of sarcasm in Wyn's voice. "It is probably better if you don't draw too much attention to yourselves. I don't suppose your plan was to get caught here and sent to the King to do who knows what."

Aurielle winced as she thought about the incident in the inn again.

"We knew it could be dangerous coming here," she said, "Gail, do you know anything about the King at all? What he's like? It sounds like he is looking for genuine help from us, but so far I don't like the methods he's using. Do you think he can be trusted?"

"He is a good King," Gail answered, "but he can be controlling. I don't know what he would want you to do, but he would leave you little choice in whatever it was."

"Seaglen warned us away from getting involved," Sara said, "I think we should listen to his advice. We need to find this person who can use Magic and get out before we become involved in something we don't want to be."

"One thing I don't get," Aurielle said, "is why the Carnival was attacked on the way there."

"There were a few theories amongst the guards," Gail answered, "the one that seemed most likely to me is that maybe the creatures were acting on confused orders and that they got the timing wrong by a week and attacked early."

"On orders from who?" Sara asked.

"I don't know," Gail said.

Aurielle sat back, thinking. There were two possibilities about the man they were looking for, and she was not sure which one she believed more. Either he was not in control of his Magic or he was using it willingly, and could be controlling these vultures. She wanted to believe that it was the first case, but somebody had to be behind what had been going on over the last few months and there was no doubt that it was somebody who could use Magic. She only wished they had not let him escape.

"Well, I'm glad you found us," Sara said. Aurielle nodded.

"Thanks a lot for helping us," she added.

"We are more than happy to help you any way we can," Wyn said.

The conversation was breached suddenly by a horn blast from outside, so loud that the vibration shook the windows.

"It's all right. It just signals that the King will be coming out soon," Isa said.

"I suppose it would be a bad idea to join in the celebrations," Gail said, peering out hopefully towards the window.

"Agreed," Wyn said firmly.

"I would like the opportunity to see the King for myself, though," Aurielle said.

"It would be a shame for you to come all this way and miss out on one of our best celebrations," Gail said, now by the window itself and slowly pulling the edge of the curtain open.

"Not a chance." Isa folded her arms.

"All they need to hide is the fact that Aurielle can do Magic," Gail pointed out, "I don't think she's planning on bringing attention to herself."

No, Aurielle thought, but there were some who might remember them from when the man in brown had blown apart the entire inn a few days ago. She had held back on mentioning him to Wyn, Isa and Gail and was glad Sara had not told them either. She found herself trusting the three of them, but there were a few things about which she remained uncertain. The main one was the fact that Gail worked so closely at the Citadel. Aurielle was not sure now whether they could trust the girl to keep their presence in the city a secret.

"Actually," Sara said, "some soldiers might recognise my face from Silverspring. It's probably not a very good idea."

"Well, that's perfect," Gail said, "it is a tradition at these festivals for the townspeople to dress in costume and masks. If you did want to go out there, we could dig up a disguise for both of you to wear. You would fit right in and be unrecognisable and get a chance to see the King in person."

"That could work," Sara said, "what do you think, Aurielle?"

Aurielle felt torn between not wanting to leave Shumuti and the intrigue of setting eyes on the King for the first time. It sounded like the King had the potential to end up complicating their time in Lyria, and it would be useful to see what they were up against in person.

"We'll go for a brief look," she said, "then we can run to Stannair and grab a few things for the next few days, at the same time."

Wyn finally relented and sighed in agreement. Gail got up, and they followed her into yet another room. Aurielle's eyes flickered over to Shumuti's doorway as she passed by. There was a large trunk at the back of the bedroom they entered, and Gail leant down and opened it with a creak. She then dragged out a pair of colourful red robes for Sara and Aurielle. They pulled the robes on over their shirts and plain leather surcoats. Aurielle made sure that her sword was still within easy reach, while Sara tucked the tip of her scabbard out of sight. Gail plucked out a golden mask and a jet black one from the very bottom of the trunk. Both were designed only to cover the top of a person's face, ornately embellished with feathers and ribbon that swirled out in spirals by the side of the wearer's head.

Aurielle dubiously took the golden mask and set it on her face. It matched perfectly with the red robes, and it did an excellent job of concealing who she was. Sara gave her a thumbs up of approval. Gail disappeared and reappeared in the doorway a moment later, unrecognisable in midnight blue, wearing a mask covered in feathers.

"Ready to go?"

"Be back before dusk," Isa called, as they prepared to leave, "otherwise, you'll miss dinner."

"We'll be back!" Gail promised.

Once they were out of the door, Gail began chatting merrily. She told them all the names of the different shops and the names of the people who were wandering around. A large number of stalls had been set up here and there to add to the number of items the people here could purchase. Even more tantalising smells wafted through the air than usual. The streets were crammed full of people. Aurielle looked around, knowing it would be hopeless to identify anybody in this sea of masked faces.

"Don't worry, Aurielle," Gail said, "my aunts want to do everything they can to help you. I've heard so much about Seaglen and Astrid that I feel as though I practically know them myself, and we want to do anything we can to help you. Nobody here is going to find out that you can use Magic."

Aurielle hoped that Gail was wrong. She wanted to believe that there would be at least one person here who knew all about Magic.

"Gail? Have you ever noticed a musician who plays on the streets around here? A young man."

"Hmm, not around here. It's too close to the Citadel for the guards to allow anything like that. Occasionally there is music coming from the market quarter, but I don't know the names of any musicians who street perform in Lyria."

Aurielle nodded and looked around once more. She kept her senses alert to any trace as they wandered, while her mind flashed back to when that strange young man in brown had fled the inn. Aurielle, Sara and Gail had almost completed the full circuit of the Lyrian Citadel, when several ear-splitting horn blasts rang out and echœd around the houses. Aurielle unconsciously reached for her sword as she heard Gail cry out next to her.

"It's the King. He's here!"

Her hands jerked away from her weapon and instead, she used them to shield her eyes, as she looked up to catch a glance of the famous King. All was silent for a second and then an enormous cheer rang out as a tall man in a scarlet red and silver surcoat and white cloak emerged out from under the castle gate with a golden wrought crown set high upon his grey-black head. King Pala raised a hand to the crowd from atop of an inky black horse. His guards rode on his right and left, with banners fluttering from long pikes that they carried. The riders set out from the Citadel walls and down into the enchanted crowd.

As King Pala rode, Aurielle was reminded forcefully of Seaglen in the King's posture and stature. The two even looked something alike, if you imagined the King without a crown. Perhaps King Pala had felt Aurielle scrutinising him because, at that very moment, his gaze turned from the rest of the crowd and his eyes locked onto her own. She wavered under his fierce, almost hawk-like stare and cast her eyes to the floor. When she looked up again, the King had descended into the main body of the crowd.

Gail was keen to follow with the rest of the townspeople, as the King would do a round of the outskirts of the city and it was a tradition that everybody would follow, singing, dancing and cheering. Aurielle feared they had chanced their luck too much for one day and was reluctant to fall under the gaze of the King once more. Thankfully Sara felt the same, so the two of them managed to dissuade Gail and instead they took a trip to Stannair to fetch extra belongings of food and clothes.

Their companion quickly forgot about the King's parade as she clapped her eyes on Stannair. The river harbour looked deserted, as everybody was at the festival. So there was an unnatural stillness everywhere, and the water was the calmest Aurielle had ever seen it. Sara offered to take Gail on a tour of their boat, so they spent the next half an hour explaining how all the bits worked and recounting the adventures up the river. She asked lots of questions, so it was getting late by the time Gail leapt up and remembered that they needed to go.

Sara and Aurielle grabbed the extra gear, and they retraced their steps back the way they had come to the centre of the city, and then round to Gail's house. For the first time, Aurielle noticed a cracked and faded sign resting above the door which read 'Remarkably Witchy Remedies'. She winced internally at the name and resolved that the three of them should move on as soon as possible after Shumuti was awake. It hardly seemed like a safe place for them to linger.

"About time!" Isa exclaimed, as they all stood by the door and took their boots off, "where have you been?"

"We've brought some food from our boat that you can use," Sara said.

"Oh, lovely," Wyn said, "I'll go and put it away."

"How's Shumuti?" Aurielle asked.

"Still resting," Isa said, "I checked on her earlier, and she was sound asleep. Don't you be worrying about her, she'll be fine, you'll see."

They all sat down and ate. It was the first proper meal Aurielle had had all day and realised she felt a lot better for it.

"Was there anything interesting out there?" Isa asked.

"The usual," Gail replied, "we didn't follow the parade, though. Those two didn't want to," she added sourly.

"It's a good thing you didn't," Wyn said, "they haven't returned yet."

"Really?" Aurielle said, "does the parade normally take so long?"

"Not usually but I think they are taking a different route this year. We spotted the crowd earlier, and it was heading past the east gate. It will take another few hours to return here."

Gail huffed quietly, and they finished eating in silence. Aurielle climbed into bed that night with the small disappointment of there not being a trace of Magic during the parade. As soon as Shumuti recovered, she considered bringing up the idea to revisit the chapel, but wondered if when the man had fled the inn, he had fled the city as well. It sounded like the residents of the inn had known where he lived. If it had been her, she would have known she was no longer safe there. She willed Shumuti to get better quickly so that they could get back on the hunt and track down the man in brown before it was too late.

CHAPTER 24
RUNES

Shumuti's sleep was laced with nightmares. She felt trapped in an endless dream, composed of dark creatures with milky white eyes. An eternal, distraught scream ran ceaselessly through her head, echoing inside her mind. Unable to escape the dream, she felt her unconscious mind writhe frantically in desperation to be free until tiredness finally overcame it and she passed out for a time until the cycle of nightmares triggered again. Dimly, Shumuti was also aware of other pains that were affecting her physical body, although, she was not sure whether the pain was outside or inside her skull and eventually concluded that it was quite likely to be both.

In her hazy grip on reality, Shumuti occasionally thought or dreamed that she could hear voices. This feeling was also probably not a good sign, but whœver it was seemed to call her name over and over again for a few minutes before there was silence once more. She was sure she did not recognise the voice of whœver it was, but still, she looked forward to when they would return and call her name once more. Each time she tried to respond, but it was beyond her to answer them. Hearing voices, the first sign of madness, but Shumuti didn't care.

She could remember nothing of how she got into this state and fear gnawed at her as voices in her mind suggested that perhaps she had simply always been this way. Now and again, panic would sweep across, and her body would jerk as if it was attempting to shake off a persistent fly. All she could honestly remember clearly was her name. It was her one firm connection to a reality that she fully intended to return to. She feared that the longer she remained in this state, the harder it would be ever to escape, but there was nothing she could do to wake up. She was a prisoner inside her mind.

Then, instantly, or perhaps an age later, at last everything changed. Shumuti was ensnared in the grip of the nightmare once more when suddenly a different voice called out to her. This time Shumuti recognised the speaker. She desperately tried to answer back and make her mouth form words, but it refused to obey her, and only an odd gurgle came out. She sounded like an idiot, Shumuti found herself thinking. That was strange, though. She couldn't remember thinking actual words before. Then the voice spoke again.

"Shumuti, what was that meant to be?" the voice asked, sounding half-exasperated and half-amused.

Hey! Shumuti thought indignantly, delighting at words that were forming in her head. She managed to twitch her eyebrows, but that was all she could do to respond.

"Well, at least you can hear me."

Shumuti found that by listening to the voice, she could focus on it and maybe bring herself out of this state. She willed the voice to speak again.

"Shumuti, can you open your eyes?"

Open her...? In all of her time here, it had never once occurred to her to try, but then Shumuti wasn't sure if she remembered how.

"Shumuti?"

Urged on by the voice and her newfound determination, she concentrated her mind on working the set of muscles that would open her eyes. Painstakingly slowly, the dark, grim world that she had known for what seemed an eternity began to dissolve, like a cloud fading under a bright day. Blurred colours sprang back into her vision before they sank and intermingled again with each other. Hazy shapes began to form in front of Shumuti's eyes, but each was fogged and undefined around the edges.

A large shape was close to her and Shumuti focused everything onto it. Inch by inch, the outline drifted into sharp focus. Shumuti blinked and recognised Aurielle smiling down at her. Feeling a rush of energy, Shumuti pushed herself up and tried to get into a sitting position. The eager movement caused her eyesight to black over for a second. Then the world began to swim again. She was falling, over and over, tumbling down the hill slope. She could hear Aurielle calling from so far away.

"No! Shumuti! Stay awake! Wyn! Isa! Stay awake, Shumuti, stay..."

Darkness again, but there was something odd about this darkness, something different. It wasn't as complete and dark as the darkness Shumuti had become used to. It didn't press down on her, but instead, it just existed.

She realised with a jolt that her eyes were open again. Slowly, hardly daring to believe it, she looked around. The room was just as she had seen it before, but this time she was alone, and there was no Aurielle beside her. There was a faint light in the room. Turning her head slightly, she realised it was the moon shining in from the open window across the room.

Gently, she pushed herself up on her pillows. She remembered what had happened before and completed the motion much slower this time. Once she was sat up, Shumuti waited for a minute, but no wave of sickness or dizziness came over her this time, and she relaxed a little.

Beside her, on a table next to the bed was a jug of water. That was good, Shumuti thought, just what she needed. She attempted to pour some water into a cup, but her hands kept shaking, so instead, she lifted the jug and poured the water directly into her mouth, slopping some down her front in the process. Then she used some more water to splash her face.

Feeling much more refreshed, Shumuti wondered if she was strong enough yet to stand up. The door was quite close to her and propped up against it was a long walking stick. She realised that there was quite a chilly wind whistling through the room from the open window. On the back of the door, there was a long white woolly coat; its sleeves buffeted slightly by the breeze.

Using her foot, Shumuti managed to reach the stick and hook her foot around it to pull it closer. The top end of it slid slowly down the wall until eventually the bottom end was by the side of the bed. She leant over to pick it up, but a surge of nausea overcame her, and she had to lie down again for a minute.

When Shumuti had recovered, she didn't attempt to bend down again but instead managed to hook her feet around the pole and steadily lifted it. When it was high enough, she grabbed it with one hand and moved it through her fingers so that it rested straight up from the floor again.

Then she threw off her blankets and gently hoisted herself up with the pole. It took three attempts to get into a standing position, and from there, she shuffled over to the back of the door and took down the white coat. Shumuti didn't bother with the sleeves as she guessed they would prove beyond her, and instead draped the blanket over her shoulders, over the top of the simple, white cotton dress she found she was already wearing.

A mirror hung on the wall by the door, and Shumuti turned to look in it. Keen blue eyes stared back, and her reflection revealed a slowly healing mark on her head that had not been there previously, half covered by her hair. Shumuti was not used to seeing her hair not tied away from her face. The ends were slightly damp, and so was her face, from the wash. Her skin itself had become shockingly pale, where it was usually quite brown and in the moonlight, she looked almost transparent. In the white clothes and leaning on the stick, Shumuti's overall appearance was one of either a crippled ghost or a beardless wizard. Neither was particularly promising, she thought glumly.

It then sunk in that she was no longer on Stannair. It also occurred to her that she had no idea where she was, geographically, at all. The window seemed to be the obvious solution, so she shuffled over to it, using the pole as a walking stick and looked out. The Lyrian Citadel was spread out high on its hill in front of her, clarifying that she was defiantly still in Attaching. She was also in a house, which felt strange after spending all that time on the boat.

Shumuti had to get back to Aurielle and Sara. She shouldn't be here, and they had a job to do. But Aurielle had been here, Shumuti realised, she had come to visit her. That meant she might still be somewhere nearby. Filled with a sense of purpose, Shumuti hobbled back past the mirror the way she had come and stealthily unhooked the latch. Thankfully, the door swung open silently, and she staggered drunkenly out, all the while trying to get used to walking again.

She was in a larger room now with a round table as the centrepiece. Lit candles defined the edges of the room and steadily flickered on shelves, set into the walls. In between these lit spotlights, the rest of the room was cast into shadow. For a second, Shumuti thought that she heard a noise, but all was quiet, and Shumuti brushed it from her head. She crept to the door and prayed that it wasn't locked. A thought flashed through her mind of what would happen if she met somebody outside. It would be a bizarre situation, but at the very worst, at least she had her sword. Wait, there was a problem there. She didn't have her sword.

In fact, she did not have any of the clothes or belongings that she remembered wearing. She had no idea what had happened to them after she had fallen down the hill. Suddenly, a snore cut through the silence and Shumuti yelped in panic, facing back towards the room.

As she spun around, she lost her already precarious balance. Her hands scrabbled out and clutched hold of one side of the table. Shumuti yanked herself upright once more and stood still while the world stopped spinning. Small noises were coming from one corner of the room. She edged her way over to them, gripping her walking stick firmly to try to see who was there. Her heart leapt as she discovered the two sleeping figures of Aurielle and Sara. Both of them were here! They could escape back to Stannair together, get out of here and then everything would be back to normal.

Thoughtless of Aurielle's feelings, Shumuti lifted the stick and jabbed her side with it to wake her up. Perhaps she did it a little too forcefully, Shumuti couldn't tell, because Aurielle's eyes shot open and she yelled in what Shumuti could only imagine being a combination of fear, at the sight of her, and pain inflicted by her walking stick.

"Aarrgghh!" Aurielle screamed.

This, of course, woke Sara up.

"Shumuti, what the hell are you doing?" Aurielle hissed, rubbing her arm.

"Shumuti?" Sara asked, "is that you?"

"Well, I think so," she replied, checking herself.

"She's gone mad," Sara whispered to Aurielle.

"I know she has."

True, Shumuti thought, it was unusual to be walking around with a walking stick and prodding people, but that was because they had to get out of here!

"We need to go."

"Go?" Sara asked, "go where?"

"Back to Stannair!" What was wrong with them? "Away from here, it's not safe!"

"Shumuti, you're not making any sense." Aurielle spoke in an annoyingly rational tone. "We are safe here. You've been ill for four days now. We're in a house with the three women who have been looking after you. They're called Wyn, Isa and Gail, and they're not going to hurt us or keep us locked up as Xeylia did. We're safe in this house. Trust me."

Shumuti had been solely concentrated on getting back to Stannair, that it took her a moment to consider the fact that she might not be completely feeling herself. Then the sound of footsteps interrupted her scattered thoughts.

"Are you all right down here?" a voice asked.

Shumuti turned using her staff and saw a woman dressed in purple standing by the side of another open door. The woman's eyes registered shock as she noticed Shumuti for the first time.

"You're awake! You're Shumuti, am I right?"

"You are."

"My name is Wyn," she said, coming forward.

"I heard your voice before," Shumuti said, "you talked to me when I was sick. You called my name."

Wyn nodded. "I'd hoped you might have heard me. But what was the yell about?"

"Oh, that was my fault," Shumuti said, "sorry, Aurielle, I didn't think. And I'm sorry for waking you up as well."

"I was already awake," Wyn replied, "my sister and niece sleep a lot heavier than I do and are less troubled by worries at night."

"I must have slept for days." Shumuti realised.

"Yes, quite a bit has happened since you have been out," Wyn said.

"Like what? Oh, but perhaps I should wait until the morning."

"I am happy to stay up and update you," Wyn offered, "if Sara and Aurielle wish to sleep."

"I'm not tired," Sara said.

"Not anymore," Aurielle said.

Out of the corner of her eye, Shumuti glanced apologetically at Aurielle as she sat down at the table and listened to Wyn and the other two run her through the events of the previous few days. As she listened, she was surprised to learn about the vultures attacking this far north and knew that Seaglen would want to learn this information if the word had not already reached Merrywater by now. The coincidence also struck her that Sara and Aurielle had managed to run into Wyn, of all people in Attaching and her connection to Seaglen and Astrid. She was surprised Seaglen had not mentioned Wyn to her before, but maybe it seemed like they shared a closer friendship to Astrid than to him.

"Since you all are awake, perhaps I can offer you some guidance that may prove useful in your task?" Wyn offered, once they had finished filling Shumuti in.

"What sort of guidance?" Shumuti asked.

They heard a clink at her hip as Wyn drew out a small velvet pouch and placed it on the table in front of her. The three of them stared at it uncertainly.

"You want to read our futures?" Sara asked.

Wyn shook her head. "That is not these runes do. If you agree, what will happen is you will reach into the bag and draw out the runestone that feels correct, to you. Each one is individually named and has its unique meaning, even dependent on which way up the rune is facing. They can offer you an idea of your character. Some hint at events that may play a part in your future but there are many interpretations. I know there is no direct link to the Magic that you use, but they are distant cousins, so to speak. You may be able to learn something useful."

Shumuti stared curiously down at the bag. She knew some of the types of runes, as she remembered playing games with them with Seaglen when she had been younger. There were twenty-five different stones, each with a different symbol carved onto the surface, save for the one that was blank. She had heard of other people who used the runes for other purposes but had never much trusted in the reliability of the information.

The set that Seaglen had owned had been nothing special, but Shumuti knew instinctively that this collection of runes was something different. She had felt the Magic there as soon as she heard the stones move and it was something she had never encountered before. She had never seen Magic become fused within an object in this way. Wyn herself, had certainly not done it, but then who?

Wyn drew open the velvet pouch. Knowing that there was Magic on the table, Shumuti was suddenly unsure about what this rune-telling might mean. Could these stones contain something valuable for them? Casting a furtive glance over at Aurielle, she saw the same hesitant, untrusting expression etched on her friend's face. A part of Shumuti could not help but deny that she could use some advice.

Before Shumuti could speak, Sara spoke up at the table. "I'd like to," she said.

Shumuti wondered for a brief moment if Seaglen or Astrid had been the ones who had set the Magic in these stones. Sara was not a Guardian, so Shumuti wondered whether there was any chance that Wyn would be able to tell her anything meaningful. There seemed no danger in it at least, and Shumuti was curious. It would be interesting to see what happened here, so she slowly sat back to watch, trying to force her weakened self to concentrate on what Wyn was about to do. Wyn deliberately pushed the velvet bag to the centre of the table, and unconsciously, every person found their eye drawn to it.

"Sara," Wyn said, "I am going to give you the pouch, and I would like you then to draw out one rune from it. You will know when you have found the right one, let it fall into your hand."

"Right," Sara said, "what kind of information can you tell from these runes?"

"Well let's find out, shall we?"

Sara carefully placed her hand inside the bag, as though it were the fangs of a snake. Shumuti could hear the jingling of the runes as her fingers passed over them and after a few seconds, her hand rose back up out of the bag with a white, oval-shaped stone clutched inside her fingers.

"Lay it on the table," Wyn said.

Sara gently laid the small stone on the wooden tabletop, face-up, with the black shape of the symbol showing for them all to see.

The symbol on the rune was this:

"What does it mean?" Aurielle asked.

"The rune you have drawn is named Perth. The rune has the sign of a bird of fire, and it is associated with hidden matters or secrets."

"A bird?" Sara said.

"Yes," Wyn continued, "the connection of this rune to flight means that the drawer, Sara, will be lifted high above the normality of everyday life and she will acquire a wider perspective. Perth is the rune of questing."

"Well, that kind of fits," Sara said.

"There is one other thing," Wyn said, suddenly seeming unwilling to continue. It was so faint that Shumuti was unsure she had felt it, but there seemed to be a hum that echoed through the air around them. A slight wave of faintness washed over Shumuti, but at the same time, she saw Aurielle twitch her arm as if she had felt it too. The rune sat enigmatically silent on the table before them.

"Another thing?" Sara asked.

"A more unfortunate side to you drawing the rune of questing is that it can also mean undergoing a form of death..."

Her words hung in the air forebodingly.

"Are you telling me I'm going to die?" Sara asked.

"Well, one day you obviously are," Wyn replied, "but the rune doesn't necessarily mean you in particular or even death in its most obvious form. Death associates itself with change, so this can be interpreted as a change in yourself. Like I said earlier, the runes have many interpretations and often coincide with what you least expect. However, there is a possibility that somewhere down the line that death, in whatever sense, will play a part."

Sara's face now resembled a similar colour to what her own had been in the mirror. Shumuti frowned at Aurielle, her brain trying to quickly run through the possibility of Wyn's statement holding any bearing. This was not any

Magic she knew, and yet she could not forget the uncomfortable niggle she had felt before Wyn had translated the second part of the rune.

"What you read from the runes," Shumuti began, "have you seen events come true?"

"Like I said, usually not in the way I expected," Wyn answered, "but yes, I have. I am sorry Sara, I did not know they would reveal something like this."

"It dœsn't matter," Sara said, in a falsely calm voice, "as you said, it could mean anything."

"Shumuti?" Wyn continued, "Aurielle?"

She offered them the pouch each. Aurielle drew back instinctively in her chair. After a reading like Sara's, Shumuti was hardly enthusiastic to hear her own. It didn't seem like these stones would be able to help them in their current situation. A more substantial part of her though, still doubted that these runes were the genuine articles. She wondered if she would feel any Magic reaction with the runes placed in front of her, and she knew the only way to find out would be to accept Wyn's offer.

"I'll do it."

She saw Aurielle try to catch her eye and warn against it, but Shumuti ignored her friend. Wyn slid the pouch over towards her.

Shumuti felt the runes shift as she placed her hand inside the bag. She did not look down at what she was choosing, but stared straight ahead at Wyn, until her fingers felt their way over a few different stones. Her finger landed on one and a strange vibration shot through the tip of it. The rune fell into her hand, and she drew it out of the bag, placing it symbol side up on the table in front of her:

"You have drawn Mannaz," Wyn said, "it is about the self. You. The meaning of this one is that you must have a good relationship with yourself before you can with others."

"Yeah, Shumuti," Aurielle said, "it means don't poke people while they're asleep."

Wyn silenced her with a swift look. She cleared her throat and continued.

"The main advice related to this rune is to remain modest and not to seek praise or judge anybody else. Only by remaining unassuming can you follow your true purpose in life. Do not judge quickly, seek credit for your deeds and accomplishments or become complacent. If you get to know yourself truly, you can accomplish this. Be aware of the past and future, but always ensure you remain living in the present."

"Is that all?" Shumuti asked.

"Aurielle?" Wyn turned to her as she scooped up the rune from Shumuti's hand and replaced it in the bag.

Aurielle took a minute and finally nodded. Shumuti sat back in her chair with her arms folded and pondered on what she had learnt, if anything. Very little specific information lay in either the stone or the words. Know yourself? In contrast to Sara's reading, her own seemed rather vague. She had also felt no kind of connection to Magic at all in her reading and was starting to wonder if she had imagined it in Sara's.

The small white stone with the engraved symbol lay silently on the table next to Sara's. Aurielle dipped her hand into the bag, and Shumuti sat up, waiting for what she was going to draw out of the small velvet pouch.

Chapter 25
The Plans of a Journey

The rune that Aurielle drew out of Wyn's bag was called Uruz:

ᚢ

"Uruz," Wyn said, "means strength, manhood and womanhood."

An odd combination, Aurielle thought.

"It is an initiation rune and part of a cycle of change. This cycle includes a passage into darkness, where a loss can disguise an opportunity. You will have to find a new strength then, to continue the cycle back to the light once more."

Wyn's gaze flickered towards Sara, but she was staring fixedly at the rune. There it was again, loss and darkness. How could something terrible become an opportunity? Were all the runes similar to this? Aurielle looked suspiciously at Wyn. How did they know she was not making this up on the spot? She certainly could feel no Magic in what was happening, and only when she had touched the rune with her finger had she thought there was some connection.

"There," Wyn said, "you now all know what your runes are. Keep in the back of your mind what I have told you. The information may help you at a moment when you need it the most. But do not spend time dwelling on what they mean because it will do you no good. Ah, look, the sun is rising. The day is almost here..."

"I need to go for a walk," Sara said. She stood up.

"Me too." Shumuti stood up as well and Aurielle followed suit.

"Oh, all right," Wyn said, slightly taken aback, "breakfast will be ready when you get back. Nobody should be about this early, but keep an eye out for anybody who might have seen you at the inn. I won't mention the rune readings to either Isa or Gail. It is not my knowledge to share."

They nodded, and Shumuti hurried off to change out of the unfamiliar white robe she was wearing. She rejoined the others soon after, fastening her dark coat up to her neck. Aurielle slung her own across her shoulders, and they stepped out into the stillness of the dawn.

The three scurried through Lyria's streets as quickly as they could and towards the walls behind the Citadel. The first streaks of a pale pink light splashed onto the sides of buildings through the dark shades of the night. There was a blissful calm in the air that felt so good and warmed Aurielle's heart. She looked across at Shumuti and felt the weight of worrying about her friend lift from her shoulders, being more grateful than she wanted to admit that Shumuti was on her feet again and all three of them were back together.

They walked quickly through the northern quarter of Lyria and up on to the wall that circled the whole of Attaching. They were further west than the glass chapel was located and they were also now on the side nearest to the volcano.

It stood out now, in such contrast to its level surroundings. There was a definitive line of where vegetation cover ended, and rocks took over. The Ember Mountain brooded intimidatingly above where they stood.

"What are we going to do now?" Sara asked.

"Have you found out anything new about the man we met in the inn since I was out?" Shumuti asked.

"He's vanished," Aurielle said, "I think he might have left the city entirely. But there is something else I haven't told you though, that I think might be linked to him."

"What?" Shumuti asked immediately.

"The night before last, I was woken up by something that felt like an explosion," Aurielle continued.

"I didn't hear anything," Sara said.

"That's because there was no sound. It was a magical explosion, a huge release of energy, just like Seaglen said that he originally felt from Attaching."

"Do you know where it came from?" Shumuti asked.

Aurielle cast another uncertain glance up at the volcano.

"I'm not sure, but I think it came from up there."

"Wouldn't that be the perfect place to find a Guardian who could wield fire?" Sara said, staring up at the volcano.

"Yes," Shumuti agreed, "but unfortunately from the display we saw at the inn, it's clear the man we're looking for uses earth Magic."

"Earth and fire aren't too dissimilar," Sara said.

"In a sense."

"I think it could be the man we've been looking for," Aurielle said.

"You can't tell if he is up there now?" Sara asked.

"The distance is too far," Aurielle said, "only if they use Magic again would we be able to tell."

"In that case," Shumuti said, from her side, "I think we're going to have to go up there."

"I think we should hurry," Aurielle added, "the amount of Magic I felt up there was huge. Whœver is up there could also be a threat."

"You think they're using lots of Magic on purpose?" Sara suggested.

"I hope not," Aurielle answered.

"We should go carefully," Shumuti said, "when we saw the man in the inn, I thought he was friendly, but perhaps there is a reason the other men were so hostile towards him."

"It won't take us too long to get up there," Sara said.

"You will have to wait for me to recover a little though," Shumuti said, "I'm in no fit state to be bounding up mountain slopes. Unless of course, you went without me."

"No," Aurielle said, "we're not separating again and leaving you. We'll wait and then go together."

"Just a day or so," said Shumuti, "I don't want to waste any more time than that."

"We can plan the route with Wyn and the others," Aurielle said.

Sara's quiet voice interrupted their decision-making. "I don't want to go back in there just yet."

Aurielle realised she had been caught up in the moment had almost forgotten what had just happened.

"I wouldn't take Wyn's words about the runes too strongly," Shumuti said, "we should never have agreed to that. I just thought the runes were a game to play as a child, but somebody has infused her set with Magic. I don't know what it means, but it is not a Magic I am familiar with, and I don't see how what she said could have any true meaning. Listen. Nothing is going to happen to you, Sara, not while we're here."

"I don't believe a word of it," Aurielle added, "I am grateful to Wyn and everything she has done for us, but it does not mean I believe in what she said."

Sara laughed.

"What?" Aurielle asked.

"Nothing," Sara said, "it's just funny that I am standing here with the two of you and you are both trying to tell me you deny that you believe in Magic."

"The irony isn't lost on me," Shumuti replied, "we only have one more day there, and then we can be back out on the road again. Come on, we should get back before the sun rises properly and people start moving about."

They skirted around the houses by using the darker streets that were still in shadow and managed to make it safely back to the healers' house undetected. Wyn, Isa and Gail welcomed them with breakfast. The runes now gone, left the table looking strangely empty, but once the six of them were sat around it celebrating Shumuti's return to consciousness, the atmosphere that had been in the room earlier that morning vanished and they all cheerfully joined in the celebrations.

It was only later that night it struck Aurielle how nice it had been to be living in a house, even if it was just for a short time. It had been a while since she had felt at home anywhere and she had arguably felt more welcome here than she felt at home in Thayll. She loved travelling more than almost anything else, but there was a certain sense of isolation that it brought with it sometimes, and she realised with surprise that she would be slightly sad when they came to leave this place.

"So," Wyn said to Shumuti, Aurielle and Sara, "this task of yours. Do you know what you are going to do next?"

All eyes turned to them.

"Well," Shumuti said, "we had thought maybe the volcano."

"Why the volcano?" Wyn asked, "nobody could live up there, surely?"

"I think I detected some Magic being used up there," Aurielle said, "a lot of Magic, which matches the description of the person we're looking for."

"We're not sure if we'll meet a friend or an enemy on the top of there," Shumuti said, "there's a chance whœver it is has lost control of their Magic, or it could be that they are using it wildly, on purpose."

"What could they be doing intentionally?" Isa asked.

"The only explanation that would make sense to me would be something linked to the vultures," Shumuti answered, "maybe we can finally get to the bottom of who they are and what they want. If that is the case then I can finish what I started on the banks of the Winterburn River."

"In that case," Wyn said, "we will show you the best way to get up there."

After a minute or two of searching, an enormous musty and cobweb-ridden scroll thudded heavily down onto the hastily cleared tabletop. Four weighty candlestick holders were securely fastened down at the four corners of the parchment to ensure that it was incapable of shooting closed again. Once the dust had cleared from the repressed scroll, it became clear that it was, in fact, a faded old map, a map that appeared to show the whole of Meteorath.

"The volcano." Wyn pointed at the significant mass that covered a vast quantity of the northern section of the parchment.

"Wait, my mother made this map!" Sara said, "I recognise her handwriting!"

Wyn nodded. "She did. Along with five others."

"Look," Gail said, "they each signed this corner."

Eagerly, the three of them craned their heads over to see clearly. There at the bottom-left corner of the large chart were six names, written one after the other; Seaglen, Astrid, Dagaz, Annah, Lyria, Jemina. Aurielle did a slight double-take at Astrid's handwriting; it was not dissimilar to her own.

"They made a map of Meteorath?" Shumuti asked.

"The five of them came from all over," Wyn said, "so they combined what they knew about each region and added sections of where they travelled together."

"What do these symbols indicate?" Shumuti asked, pointing to several scratches, scattered across the map.

"I don't know," Wyn answered, "you will have to ask Seaglen or Astrid. You can keep this map."

"Now then," Isa said, and they all sat back down, "how are we going to get you up this mountain?"

"Five routes will lead you to the summit of the volcano," Wyn said, pushing the map back to the centre of the table, "these three wind up from the eastern side, closest to the city, while the other two come at it from a southern or westerly direction. The north face is not traversable. Now, if whœver it is living in the mountain is keeping a watch, they should expect travellers to appear from the east because the land to the south and west is uninhabited and wild. There is also a much clearer pathway from the eastern three trails than the other two. I think, therefore, that if you wish to travel undetected, then you must journey from either the west or from the south."

Next to Aurielle, Sara shifted gently in her seat.

"Would this person live at the very summit of the volcano, do you think?" Sara asked.

"It's difficult to say..." Isa replied, "but I doubt that they would be at the foot. You will have to climb to find them, I'm afraid."

"They were high up," Aurielle confirmed.

"When are you going to go?" Gail asked.

"Tomorrow night," Shumuti said.

She took one long look at the route stretched out on the parchment in front of her, before lifting the candlesticks and allowing the map to spring back into a scroll.

"Then we ought to get you some supplies ready," Isa said.

CHAPTER 26
UNDER THE COVER OF TWILIGHT

So the preparations began. Efficient would be the only way to describe the speed at which the three women worked to prepare Sara, Shumuti and Aurielle for their journey. Shumuti and Aurielle departed during the middle of the next morning back to Stannair to collect their armour and a few extra supplies, leaving Sara to pack the bags.

Despite the uncertainty that lay ahead of them, excitement was surging through Sara like she had not felt for weeks, and she knew that the others felt the same. She had missed being on the road and were eager to get travelling again. Sara's thoughts ran back to her mother and speculated about what she was doing now. She wondered how long it would be before their journey took them back towards Merrywater.

A crow soared past the open window to set off on a journey of its own, a voyage that could be destined to Elmdale, Merrywater, Boctor or even Nimaz. Or equally, to the rooftops of the house a little way further down the street. The front door creaked gently, and Sara quickly stepped away from the window to see who it was.

"It's us!" Shumuti called, "we're back!"

They stepped in and closed the door after them. Sara walked forward and took a bag from Aurielle.

"Thanks." She removed her cloak and hung it up. "We weren't sure what to take, so we brought everything we thought useful, and we can sort it here."

"Start with this one." Shumuti dropped a large leather pack onto the table which they unfastened and tipped out the contents. It contained blankets and spare clothes.

"We'll need some of this," Sara said.

"Take one blanket each and two or three spare shirts," Isa said from the doorway, drying a mug in her hands.

"We shouldn't be more than a few days, should we?" Shumuti said, checking the supplies.

They each selected a blanket and clothes before Aurielle crammed the rest of the gear back into the emptier pack. The second was full of pots, pans and cutlery which they mostly discarded, but the third contained food, so they chose some of it and saved the rest for the journey home.

The other bags were smaller and held various items that they either took or left behind until they were satisfied with their selection of supplies and what remained was not too much that the packs overflowed their brims. The blankets were added last, rolled and secured on the top of the bags. They were ready to go, packed light for what they hoped would be only a short trip away.

Their final meal with Wyn, Isa and Gail felt quiet and subdued. It was decided that they would set off at dusk up the volcano. Their three packs were set ready by the door, and their cloaks hung, waiting on the pegs above, swords looped over the top by their belts. They were already wearing their freshly washed sets of travelling gear.

It had also been agreed that Gail would accompany the three of them to the outskirts of the city, as she knew of the most secretive ways and could guide them safely through the watched gates without being questioned, or getting lost. Gail had heard news from the palace that the King had indeed ordered an investigation into the 'inexplicable' events at the Sickle Inn and commanded that witnesses found and questioned. Somebody had also passed detailed enough descriptions of their likenesses on to the King's guard so that if any guard saw them, they would likely get called into the Citadel for questioning.

They finished eating later than usual, and Wyn cleared the plates in silence. Finally, evening fell, and the time came to leave. Shumuti, Aurielle and Sara gathered by the doorway and slowly strapped on each of their swords before reaching up to their cloaks and wrapping them around their shoulders, hoods tight against their faces. Sara looked back at Wyn, Isa and Gail stood by the table and felt an odd pang of regret to leave. The time spent here had been easy, fun and peaceful, but it had also been normal for the most part, which Sara knew was something she should never forget to appreciate.

"Thank you so much for letting us stay with you," she said.

"You are welcome any time," Wyn said.

"Thank you for your help. For everything you have done," Shumuti added.

"We are glad that your paths led past our door," Isa said.

Wyn and Isa stepped forward and gave them each a farewell hug. Then Gail strode forward to join them, fastening up her coat with an eager look in her eye, ready to head out.

"Return here once more before you leave Attaching, if you can," Isa said.

Gail led them from the warm cosiness of the house and into the crispness of the evening. Twilight had settled all around, and the four were no more than shadows, slipping off one by one into the darkness, indistinguishable against the night.

They followed Gail for a little over a mile, through the twisting alleys and darkened streets, until the buildings thinned and the eastern border wall of the city loomed before them in the distance. As they prowled through the streets, Sara could not help feeling as though they were being followed. Once, she turned back and could have sworn to see a black shape vanish into a street a good distance behind them on her left, along with the faint tiptœ-ing of boots on stone. Sara hoped she was simply imagin-ing things, as after that she neither saw nor heard any sign of a follower again. Soon they arrived at the outer wall of Lyria. They halted in the shadows and ran over the plan to slip past the guard at the gate.

"You must be quick," Gail whispered back to them, "there will be only a few minutes. I'll distract the guards, and you'll have to run. Go as soon as I say and get to the gate over there. Then slip out, and you're free from the city. All right?"

They nodded.

"Thank you, Gail," Aurielle muttered.

"Don't mention it."

"Yeah-" Sara began.

"Shh!" she hissed, "get ready to go."

Gail turned and winked at Sara. "Now!"

The three of them shot out like silent cannons and fled to the outer wall as the back of the guard was turned. They pressed themselves flat against the wall and prayed the guard would not turn back early. If he did, it would be a curious situation to try to talk themselves out of. Sara held her breath as the guard reached the end of his walk.

Just as he began to spin on his heel, Gail called out. The guard jumped, flashed out his sword and peered intently into the gloom. All was still. Then Gail screamed.

Forgetting that Gail was meant to have shouted and not screamed, the three took their chance and ran across the city border as the guard left his post and ran to the direction of the cry. They broke out into the sharp wind of the moors beyond and picked up speed in relief as they ran over the grass and the heather, thrilled to be in the free air once more.

They stopped running when they became aware of the weight of their packs and stopped for a break. The walled city stood out on the landscape before them, and the Lyrian Citadel shimmered in the moonlight, turning black as a trail of silver cloud drifted across the face of the thickening band of the crescent moon.

There was little chance of finding anywhere to sleep for the night that offered them cover out on the plains. They carried on for a few hours and by this time the moon was high in the sky and surrounded by winking stars, as the clouds had drifted away elsewhere. Uncovering a small hollow in the heather that would be deep enough to provide them with a little bit of protection, they ate a little and then slept deeply, taking the risk of not leaving anybody on guard so close to Lyria. The gamble paid off, and they awoke the next morning with all their possessions and limbs intact.

The three travellers continued over the plains and eventually hit a wide, well-ridden road that led back the way they had come, towards the city. Deciding not to risk meeting any of the King's soldiers, they crossed over the road and picked a more direct route towards the mountain ahead. As the position of the sun in the sky tipped over the apex and began its descent, the volcano started to tower menacingly high above them, cast in a warm afternoon glow. The wind had picked up, so they chose a spot to huddle down in and eat a small meal. While they ate, the three of them stared up at the mountain before them, their minds pondering each possible outcome of the journey and what may lie at the top. Finally, Shumuti broke through the musing.

"There's nothing else for it, is there?" she said, "and no point in delaying it any further. We're going up, that's for certain, and this path seems to be the best to choose..."

"I think we should wait for night," Aurielle interrupted, "I mean, if there is somebody up there watching then we'll evade them more easily under the shadow of the moon than the sun."

"If it is our man in the brown robe who's up there, that doesn't matter," Sara said.

"We don't know that," Shumuti said, "he might not be a friend to us."

"It could be someone else entirely," Aurielle said, "we still don't know for certain what happened to Annah. The events in Attaching could well tie to her."

"If it is Annah, I am more worried," Shumuti said, "because she should know not to use so much Magic."

"There's no point in speculating," Aurielle said.

Shumuti nodded. "You're right. Do you agree to the plan, Sara?"

"I daresay it will do," Sara answered, "but if we are setting off at night, why not use those hours to get some rest? I think we are going to need it."

The plan was agreed to and settled by them all, and though none of them managed to sleep much, they at least felt rested by the time darkness was creeping up around them once more. As they gathered up their packs, a mournful howl cut through the air, sounding close to where they had camped.

"Did you hear that?" Sara whispered.

"We should move," Shumuti muttered.

Hurriedly, they broke camp and ran towards the slope to reach the volcano's foot. A crudely carved path ran under their feet, and in the pale evening glow, a cairn loomed out against the bare landscape, marking the start of their route up the mountain. Not hesitating, they picked up speed, moving further on, blindly into the dark.

"Stop!" shouted Shumuti after a minute, "Sara, Aurielle. Stop!"

Surprised by the sudden noise, Sara juddered to a halt, spraying up a small cloud of gravel and dust as she did so. Aurielle came to a standstill just as swiftly, and they turned back to where Shumuti had stopped a few paces behind.

"What is it?" asked Aurielle.

"Listen..."

Sara froze and listened as hard as she could, and her hand gripped the hilt of her sword. There was something in the quiet darkness with them. They had come quite far up the track already, and the visibility was failing. Then slowly, slate-coloured clouds drifted away like a veil and the moon shone through the gap.

Grey shapes moved not only across the sky, Sara noted, but across the earth as well. With the moonlight now overhead, she could see several forms below them, patrolling the base of the mountain.

"Wolves," Shumuti whispered.

"Keep moving," Aurielle hissed, pulling the others further up the track.

"Would they attack, do you think?" Sara whispered to Shumuti as they hurried on.

"This must be their territory, or perhaps a hunting ground."

"They will still be able to smell us from here."

"Maybe we should have waited until day to do the climb," Aurielle said, "back there down the path, I thought we passed a marker. How many more things like that will we miss, stumbling around in the dark?"

"We can't stop," Shumuti argued, "we agreed to put this night to good use. We need to cover as much distance as we can before light, while we remain hidden from whœver lives up the volcano. Besides, we should put some distance between the wolves and us, in case they decide to follow."

"What if they have alerted something else further up the volcano?" Sara stared upwards, nervously.

"Then let's get up there while it is still dark and we have cover," Shumuti said.

"I can't see the wolves anymore," Sara reported, after a minute or two.

They continued up the path under the silent, watchful eye of the stars, glancing back every minute or two. Now visible underneath the veil of the cloud, thousands of these tiny pinpricks displayed themselves in twinkling constellations and patterns sketched out across the sky. The path they were following ran up the left side of the volcano. Shumuti led the way, and Sara brought up the rear, all the while listening out for any sign of followers. The night had become silent again and clear, but no owl hooted, and no animals seemed present at all, so they walked on unhindered until dawn.

CHAPTER 27
ROCKS AND ASH

~AURIELLE~

They had not slept at all that night, but as dawn found its way to the eastern slopes of the volcano, the trio found themselves standing at the uppermost section of the mountain that was accessible without leaving the path. The crumbling track only led around the volcano from here. Shumuti looked down at the distance they had hiked and was impressed. The view from up here at dawn was stunning. The whole of Meteorath spread out before her, coloured orange and pink by the soft morning light.

Closer to home though, nothing surrounded them but the desolate rock and dirt of the mountain slope. Next to her, Sara was perched on an uncomfortable-looking boulder, also admiring the view. The events of last night and the wolves seemed almost fictitious now, like imaginations from a bizarre dream. The moon had gone, and a dawn chorus had replaced all nightly sounds, made up of the whistles of small, darting birds. A slight breeze had picked up and with it came a sensation Shumuti had not been aware of since the day they had encountered that mysterious man in the inn in Lyria. Aurielle turned to Shumuti.

"Did you feel that too?"

"I do," Shumuti replied, all of a sudden attentive.

It was unmistakable, the feeling that came with the wind. Aurielle had been right about this place. Somewhere close to them had recently been the location for Magic use. Now that she thought about it, Shumuti realised, looking around, the ground here resembled an enhanced version of the destruction she had created on the banks of the Winterburn River. A flicker of caution ran through her, somebody seemed to be casting Magic here on a fairly regular basis, but why?

"You mean you were right?" Sara asked, "there is somebody here?"

"It seems so," Shumuti answered, "where exactly, I can't say yet but whœver it is was here recently."

"Look!" Aurielle called them over to where she was standing.

She nudged some stones away with her boot and pointed down at the ground, "Paw prints. Do you think they belong to the same wolves we saw last night?"

The path had a covering of sandy dust for a short way, and the large tracks could be seen imprinted into the ground before the trail turned to bedrock once more.

"Where do we go from here?" Sara asked.

"The path leads around to the other side," Shumuti answered, "we can't go any higher without actually climbing, so this is the only way left for us. Wherever that magical scent came from, it seems to originate from this direction. I say we head around and see what we find, but go slowly. We don't know what we might find up here."

Shumuti took the lead on the trail. The track was treacherously narrow and wound close to the edge on more than one occasion. The rocks were sharp and dug into the soles of her heavily worn boots. The worn tread caused her to slip occasionally on the loose shale of the path, so Shumuti slowed their pace. They were already tired and she could not afford to be distracted by the uneven surface beneath her feet.

She was so focused on what lay ahead that Shumuti was taken by surprise when the first incident occurred from behind her. A loud crash had her almost stumble herself, as she twisted to see what had happened. It was Aurielle who had lost concentration. Shumuti saw her come crashing to her knees and almost off the side of the mountain. She yelped in pain, clutching her ankle as Shumuti and Sara rushed to her aid. They sat her down against a long slab of rock and assessed the injury.

"I think I just twisted it," Aurielle grimaced.

Shumuti slid off Aurielle's dust-covered boot and gingerly laid her foot out against another smooth rock. Aurielle stifled another cry of pain and Sara, and Shumuti exchanged a worried glance.

"I'm not sure it's a good idea to go on with your foot like this," Sara said.

"We can't go back either," Aurielle said, "don't worry about me, I'll be fine..."

"No, you won't," Sara said, "you can't go further. It will only make your foot worse."

"Then what do we do now?" Aurielle asked.

"Well," Sara said, "if we can get you to a wider part of the path, you can at least sit down without risking falling off the mountain."

"Ah, I'm so stupid," Aurielle said, "I heard a few rocks come loose on the mountain above me. I was distracted, so I stood on a broken section, and it gave way under me."

"We can support you for the next section," Shumuti said, studying the way ahead, "the path widens for a little way, and once we get to the boulders over there, we can rest properly and decide what to do."

Shumuti stood over Aurielle and offered her left arm. She leaned on her gratefully, and Sara appeared at her right. Together they slowly trudged their way over the strewn rubble and picked the gentlest path through the broken shale and sharp rock to a place where they could rest properly.

The sun was high in the sky when they arrived and supported Aurielle to the rocks. Aurielle pushed herself into a sitting position and groaned, her leg trembling slightly.

"S...sorry, you two."

"It's not your fault," Sara replied.

"I'm just going to take a look at what's ahead," Shumuti said, "I won't go far, I promise. I only want to see what the road looks like from here onward and make sure we are safe to stop here."

"Don't be long," Sara said.

Shumuti cursed their luck. They were vulnerable now, out on the mountain, and possibly stuck here. If whœver's trail they had followed up here was a friend, then they might be able to get help for Aurielle, but Shumuti knew there was an equal chance of their luck falling the other way once more.

Leaving her pack behind, she jumped lightly over the rocks and headed around the corner. As she feared, the path narrowed once again and became steeper. There was no way they could walk abreast with Aurielle beyond here. Scrambling her way up, Shumuti peered over the next rise and saw a slightly more open platform after that, and with a jolt she also saw a dark opening in the rock face. There was a cave here.

Traces of Magic were emanating from the cave, leaving Shumuti in no doubt that this was the source of the trail they had been following. She also realised in that instant how powerful the source of Magic was that she was detecting. It wasn't just the presence of one person, but it was also the volcano itself. This place was almost if not as equally enriched as the underground waterfall in Thayll.

For a second, she considered going inside the cave, but she had been away for too long and instead retreated from her viewpoint back towards the others. Sara stood up, and half drew her sword as Shumuti skidded back into view, before sitting back down with a sigh of relief.

"Anything?" Sara called over.

"Yes, quite a lot," she replied, regaining her breath.

Shumuti adjusted her sword belt as she examined the best way to scramble back over the rocks towards the other two. Just as she leapt up to grab a hold, something reached out and tugged on the end of her coat, strangling her slightly and whipping her over onto her back. The force of it winded her, and she lay there with the sun directly blinding her eyes before Shumuti felt cold steel placed against her exposed throat.

"Lie still," a soft voice ordered, "or I may accidentally hurt you."

Shumuti slowly twisted her muddied and weather-beaten face towards the source of the voice, preparing herself for the sight of the man from the inn, or of Annah. Her eyes widened in astonishment, as it was neither. Her gaze met the face of a tall, handsome, black-haired man who was staring down at her, holding his exposed sword to her neck. On the shoulder of his coat, she noted with surprise that there was the same crest she had seen on the banners at the Lyrian Citadel. His eyes sparkled as he smirked down at her. He was not at all what she had expected they might find here. Sara muttered something inaudible from across the other side of the rocks.

Chapter 28
In the Lair of Fire

~AURIELLE~

"Now, what should I do with you?" the darkly clad man spoke as he towered over them in the dirt, "three attractive girls trespassing at the entrance to my home?"

If it had not been for the blade he still held to Shumuti's throat, Aurielle would have answered back in an instant. As it was, she remained quiet and tried to figure out who this man could be. He was not the same person they had seen before in Lyria, but Magic ran through him so strongly it almost shone like a light.

"Who are you?" Sara asked.

The man grinned again. "Shouldn't visitors declare themselves first? Tell me, who are you? What are your names, and why have you made it your business to travel all the way up here?"

"We've come from the city to see you," Shumuti replied, from the ground, "and to find out who you were."

The confidence on the man's face slipped as he flashed another, less convincing smile across at them. "That is quite an effort you have made. I'm honoured, truly that you have come all this way. I must be important..."

"Maybe you are," Aurielle answered, "or maybe you mean nothing. Now let my friend go and tell us who you are so that we can decide."

"You are weak and in no position to relay orders to me," he said to Aurielle, "I'll bet you can't even stand up."

Aurielle's eyes flared up at him, but she did not move, and he smirked again.

"How about I carry you into my cave, and you can carry on trying to order me around inside?"

Aurielle stared resolutely back and said nothing. She was fairly convinced that this man was no immediate threat to them, but she had no desire to follow him anywhere. Then again, she realised that with her leg in this state, she had not left the group in much of a position to refuse him.

"Deal," Shumuti said finally, holding out an arm.

The man lifted his sword away from Shumuti and sheathed it before helping her up. He then leapt the rocks and bent down over Aurielle, before scooping her up in both arms and hoisting her onto his back, before she could even try to object. Reluctantly, she clung on around his neck, her grip tightening as he climbed the rocks over towards Shumuti. Close against his neck, her nose wrinkled, and she was surprised to discover that he smelt faintly of smoke and fire. Aurielle exchanged a glance with Shumuti as they passed her, one of concern but also mingled with curiosity. Sara brought up the rear, carrying the bags.

"My name is Gabriel, by the way," he said over his shoulder to her, as he led the way along the path towards a small cave entrance. His dark eyes glimmered back at her as he waited for a response.

"I'm Aurielle," she responded finally, "my friend you attacked is Shumuti, and the other is Sara."

"Nice to meet you then, Aurielle," he said, looking away from her and ducking down inside the entrance of the cave.

"You live here?" she asked him.

"You don't like it?" he replied.

"No."

She was carried further down into this volcanic lair that Gabriel called home and descended slowly down a long passageway that felt as though it led directly towards the heart of the volcano. When the tunnel opened out into an open cavern, Gabriel halted and lowered Aurielle down onto a makeshift camp bed against the curved wall.

"You can rest here." He turned to her with a trace of genuine concern in her eyes. "You're hurt. Let me look at your injury."

"No," she said at once, "I'm fine, thank you. Sara can do it."

"Aurielle, you're not fine." Shumuti sighed, "Let him help."

"Sara is our healer," Aurielle said, "I'd rather have her take care of me, thank you very much."

"Actually," Sara admitted, "I've never been all that good at this type of injury, sprains and muscle strains and such."

Gabriel turned back to Aurielle expectantly.

"Fine," she grumbled.

Gabriel leapt up and disappeared around a passage to get some supplies. Shumuti and Sara burst into quiet laughter once he was gone. Aurielle rounded on them indignantly.

"What's so funny?" she asked.

"You," Shumuti smiled.

"I don't trust him," Aurielle said, "I can hardly stand to be around him, he's so arrogant!"

"Says you!" Shumuti laughed, "you're acting just as bad. Besides with your leg the way it is, we can't get off this mountain. You've gotten us stuck with this man."

Aurielle huffed, realising the pain in her leg was making her even more irritable.

"Who is he?" she asked, "this is not who we were meant to find up here."

"I don't know," Shumuti answered, "but did you notice he wears the emblem of the King on his clothes?"

"What?" Aurielle said.

"Can he use Magic?" Sara asked.

"Yes," Shumuti answered, "I think he is the cause of the Magic disturbances here in Attaching. The one that Seaglen detected and that you did the other night, Aurielle."

"But what about the man in the inn?" Sara asked.

Shumuti looked at Aurielle, as though she could hardly believe what she was about to say herself. "There must be two Magic users in Attaching."

"I can't believe he is who we've been searching for from the beginning," she said, crossing her arms.

"Well, he is." Shumuti grimaced. "Friend or enemy, he is who we set out to find. But he has a lot of explaining to do."

"Not talking about me are you?" Gabriel's voice echœd down the passage. "You, the wounded one. Aurielle, wasn't it? Lie still now and let me ease the pain."

Shumuti and Sara went to sit at a close distance away. Out of the corner of her eye, Aurielle could see them, watching half in concern and the other half in amusement as she refused to express to Gabriel how much pain she was in. Reluctantly, she allowed him to take off her boot and ease her leg into a straight position. He reached over to a bowl of cold water and pulled a clean rag from it before taking a closer look at her injury.

"This might take a little while," Gabriel said, over his shoulder, "feel free to have a wander around, if you like."

"Thanks for the offer," Shumuti answered, "but I'm not sure we should leave our friend alone in the care of a man we've just met."

"Ah, you don't trust me?"

"Why would we? We know nothing about you," Aurielle said.

"You do owe us some answers," Shumuti said.

"And you owe some to me," he said, "I know what the two of you are."

He glanced between Shumuti and Aurielle and they stared uneasily back.

"Have you ever met anyone like us before?" Shumuti asked.

"Once, I thought I came across someone in the streets of Lyria," he answered, "but other than that, just my mother."

Gabriel paused in consideration. "How about I make you another deal? Trust me now to take care of your friend and later, we will talk about everything."

Shumuti thought over his words for a minute and turned to Sara. "We'll just be outside, Aurielle."

Don't you dare leave, she tried to shout mentally across to them.

Aurielle heard their footsteps slowly retreating until she was alone with Gabriel. She refused to meet his eyes.

"So," he said, "now we're alone."

Aurielle spotted the King's crest on his clothes that Shumuti had mentioned before and glanced at the rest of him, searching for more clues, but there was nothing. The uniform that he wore looked old, as well as being a different colour to any that she had seen on the soldiers in Lyria. Everything else he wore was plain black, and even his sword was ordinary.

He took hold of her ankle with his hand, and under the warmth of his fingers, she suddenly felt a rush of Magic that made her gasp out loud. It was the strength of the energy he had that shocked her. It was wild and almost uncontrollable. The reasons behind the scars and excessive Magic use on the land around the volcano suddenly became clear to Aurielle. Gabriel was not in control of how much Magic he was using. She met his eyes finally and saw curiosity and excitement staring back, contrasting her shock and fear.

"I'm sorry," he said, "sometimes that just happens."

"Who do you fight for?" she found herself asking him, still reeling from the experience.

"Fight?" he repeated, "I fight for no one. Why do you think I am up here? I sit here high above in this volcano, watching the world at my feet. I have decided not to take part in any of it. I think it's safer that way."

He wrapped the cloth around Aurielle's ankle, the coolness of it calming the injury slightly before he rested her leg on top of the packs.

"Keep it elevated," he instructed, "I wish I had something colder to apply to it, but here on the volcano, cold is hard to come by. Except in our first greeting, there it was found in abundance."

He gave her a small wink, and Aurielle found herself disliking him again.

"Can I ask you a question?" Gabriel asked, apparently these were questions he had wanted answering for a long time.

"Wait until Shumuti returns," she found herself saying, unwilling to talk anymore to him, "she will explain whatever you want to know. But thank you, my leg feels a little better."

Gabriel said nothing for once and stood up, leaving Aurielle alone with her sore injury.

Shumuti and Sara returned soon after, with Gabriel behind them. They sat down beside Aurielle and Gabriel chose a place opposite them and waited expectantly for the chance to begin talking.

"We're going first," Shumuti said.

Gabriel nodded, his attention fixed on Shumuti. "You ask one question, then it is my turn."

"Who are you?" she asked, "from your clothes, I'm guessing you have not always lived in this cave."

"No," Gabriel answered, "not until quite recently. Before then, I was a member of the King's guard in the Lyrian Citadel."

"Then, what happened to you?" Aurielle asked.

"A mixture of things," Gabriel replied, "firstly, I disagreed with the King and the methods he was using, so I left. But also, my Magic was getting a little out of my control. I nearly caused quite a large fire in the Citadel. Thankfully, I handled it before anyone was hurt, but I knew after that, I had to get out."

"That's why we're here," Shumuti said, "to stop you losing control of your Magic again."

"Shumuti's father felt the effects of your Magic from halfway across Meteorath," Aurielle said.

"What?" Gabriel gasped.

"Don't worry," Shumuti said, "he's exceptionally good at picking up signs of Magic. We only knew you were nearby when Aurielle detected you from Lyria, a few nights back."

"Oh," Gabriel said, "things did get a bit out of hand a few days ago. Luckily there's no one else around up here."

"Weren't you ever taught?" Aurielle asked him, "you mentioned your mother could use Magic?"

"My mother's name was Annah," Gabriel said.

"Ah, that makes sense," Shumuti said, "is she still in Attaching?"

"Do you know her?"

"We know of her."

"Yes, she did teach me a little. But both my mother and father disappeared on a patrol for the old King when I was young, and my Magic has grown considerably since then. My father was the Captain of the royal guard, and I followed in his footsteps. It was the present King who took care of me after they had both gone."

"What did you mean that you disagreed with what the King was doing?" Shumuti asked.

"It all started a while ago. You see, there was this carnival. A Carnival of Games, it was called." That got Sara's attention. Gabriel saw Shumuti's head shoot round to her and faltered in his tale.

"Do you know about this?" he asked.

"Yes," Sara explained quickly, "we found out in Lyria that the reason behind it was to search for people who could help the King."

"Not just that," Gabriel said, "he was specifically searching for people who could use Magic. I didn't like the way the King was trying to recruit people like us and I refused to be a part of it. That and the fact that these incidents with my Magic were becoming more violent meant I left the guard and Lyria altogether, retreating up here where nobody was trying to control me, and I couldn't hurt anyone either."

"Wait." Sara spoke up. "Shumuti, you told me that the existence of Magic has always been kept secret. How does the King know of its existence?"

Aurielle realised that Sara was right. There was no way the King should know. She turned on Gabriel.

"Did you tell the King?" she accused him, in shock.

Gabriel sat up defensively, his mouth open.

"I was never informed about this need for secrecy."

"Then you did tell him?" Aurielle repeated.

"My parents had gone," Gabriel answered, "I was a child, I had no one else left. He helped me."

Aurielle looked over at Shumuti in stunned astonishment.

"Who else knows?" Shumuti asked him quietly.

"Nobody," Gabriel assured them, "the King has kept my secret for years. Only now that he believes people like us are the answer to his problem has he had any interest in it."

"This is worse than I thought," Shumuti said in a hollow, "can the King be trusted, Gabriel?"

"I would always have said yes," Gabriel answered, "he was always confident, and I would have followed him, unquestionably. But recently, I can see him becoming uncertain. He is doing things that he would never normally do to try to face this threat. He wanted me to go with the Carnival to Elmdale to find others like me. It didn't sound too bad until I heard the word 'prisoners' spoken several times by the guards. In the end, I refused to go."

"So, the King wasn't just searching for Astrid," Aurielle said, "he was searching for all of us."

"Why?" Shumuti asked Gabriel, "what dœs he want with us?"

"The King is concerned about a threat from Nimaz," Gabriel answered.

"Nimaz?" Shumuti's eyes widened.

"He has sent several patrols across the Winterburn River, into Nimaz over the last year and none of them returned, at least not alive. But things from Nimaz have made it across the river and into Attaching."

"Can you be any more specific?" Aurielle asked.

"Not really. What the creatures remain a mystery to me. They were not human, that was certain. They flew."

"The vultures," Aurielle said.

"Yes," agreed Gabriel, "that is how the scouts described them."

"They're not human because they've been altered using Magic," Aurielle told him, "we met them on the road up here from Merrywater."

"You've fought them? None of the King's men stood a chance. That is why he is so unnerved. He has never faced a threat he could not defeat before. Maybe he was right to think we can beat them."

They fell silent as the three of them took in everything Gabriel had told them.

"We thought the vultures might have come from Attaching," Shumuti told him, "that's why we were wary of you. We were worried you might be controlling them."

"No," Gabriel shook his head, "the King is most definitely fighting against these creatures. He believes they come from over the Winterburn River."

Aurielle said nothing, still looking at Gabriel in disbelief at the fact that he had told the King about Magic.

"Something larger is happening here than we first realised," Shumuti said.

"Wait a minute," Gabriel said, "I'm the one who is meant to be asking you questions as well here, and you've turned it on its head! What's your story? I demand now you tell me in exchange. Women! How do you do this?"

Shumuti took a deep breath and honoured her promise to Gabriel. She launched into their tale, and Gabriel listened transfixed without speaking a word. Sara reminded Shumuti of rare things she had forgotten, but Aurielle remained silent throughout.

When Shumuti finished, Gabriel stood up and paced around the cave, his footsteps echoing on the rocky surface.

"So you want to bring me with you to Merrywater," Gabriel said, "so your father can teach me how to control my Magic?"

"That was our original plan," Shumuti said, "you can't keep overusing it like this. Aurielle and I can teach you pieces on the road, but Seaglen is by far the better teacher. He can show you more than either of us ever could."

"You want me to join you," Gabriel said, "well, nearly all of you do."

"We all do," Shumuti said firmly, "right, Aurielle?"

Aurielle gave a non-committal grunt.

"You see?" Shumuti insisted.

"Hmm...What about you, Sara? What's your part in all this?"

"I'm just here as a friend, to do what I can to support you all," Sara said.

"So will you come back with us?" Shumuti asked.

Gabriel fell silent. Aurielle watched him from under her eyebrows, and Shumuti sat upright, eyeing him intently and waiting for a reply.

"I will," Gabriel answered finally, "yes."

Shumuti's breath came whooshing out like a gust of wind. "Great! Yes!"

"Glad you're joining us." Aurielle said with sarcasm.

"It's a pleasure," Gabriel answered in a similar tone.

"Well if that's it, I'm going to bed," Aurielle said.

"Sweet dreams," Gabriel called.

"All right, see you tomorrow," Shumuti said, getting up and looking pleased with herself.

Sara and Shumuti followed Aurielle's lead, and they left Gabriel sitting cross-legged on the cave floor, alone, with a frown under the shadows of his eyes and an expression of heavy thought resting on his face.

"Try not to think about it too much," Aurielle said down to him as she left.

It took no effort to fall asleep instantly. Aurielle fell into a dreamless sleep and woke up the next morning with a jolt, forgetting where she was for a second. She was the first of the company to rise; Shumuti and Sara were still sleeping peacefully next to each other. Aurielle hastily remembered the evening before and glanced over at where Gabriel had slept.

He was no longer there.

She sat up straighter and scanned around the cavern to search for signs of him, but he was no longer here. Her ankle throbbed now with a dull pain, but it had not been too severe an injury and she found her relief that she could walk, taking care not to place too much weight on her injured leg. The shadow of something flashed by the entrance to the cave. Suspicion aroused, Aurielle gently gathered up her longsword from the floor as well and carefully hobbled out of the cave towards the dawn on the mountainside.

There was no sign of any other life, but a faint trail of boot prints padded into the dust, heading further around the peak. The tracks confirmed that somebody had been here just a moment ago. Aurielle began to stalk onward slowly, her ankle causing her to wince now and then.

Before Aurielle had time to think more about anything, she stumbled onto a broader plateau, as the ground abruptly levelled off and she let out a whistle. She was almost at the summit of the volcano and resting just above her was a giant crater, with an unfathomable depth. She was taken aback at the heat emanating from the ground up here. It had managed to alter the temperature from the chill of the winter morning to the level of a midsummer afternoon.

The view from the top was unlike anything that Aurielle had ever seen, but she wasn't the only one enjoying the scene. Somebody else had arrived here before her.

Gabriel was dressed in his long, black coat, from head to foot. He looked tall and grim set against the skyline, and Aurielle noticed one hand rested on the hilt of his sword by his side. She eyed it uneasily before looking up at his face and finding that he had noticed her arrival. There was no surprise at all in his eyes that she had followed him. He had a grim expression on his face, no trace of the smile that before had been permanently affixed there.

"I don't think you should stay up here with me," he said, with an effort.

"What do you mean?" Aurielle asked.

"That burst of Magic you felt in the city, I'm due for another. I don't think I'm safe to be around when that happens."

"Why have you brought your sword?" she asked.

"Why have you brought yours?" he retorted.

"Because I'm not certain yet if I can trust you," she answered.

"Likewise," he replied.

Aurielle shifted her foot to make herself steadier and ease the pain in her ankle. The Magic traces all over the volcano had intensified, and the air almost seemed to buzz before her. It was like static electricity. She had never encountered anything like this before. Perhaps this time she could help Gabriel to control it before he destroyed more of the mountainside.

"There was me thinking that you followed me because you missed my company," he said, with a trace of the Gabriel she remembered from yesterday.

"How often does this happen?" Aurielle asked.

"It's getting more frequent," he said through gritted teeth, "I think it will happen soon, you should get back to safety in the cave."

Aurielle noticed his forehead contort with pain as he tried to fight back against the Magic that was welling up inside him. Her mind began to race through the techniques Seaglen had taught her in the beginning when he was trying to help her control her Magic. She hobbled closer to him determinedly, sheathing her sword as she went.

"No, I can help," she said, "keep talking to me, distract yourself from it. You have to believe you can take hold of it. I can help you control this."

"You can't." His eyes widened slightly. "Not now, I've almost lost my grip on it."

"You won't hurt me," Aurielle said, "focus on the energy. You have to concentrate. Then you'll be able to do what you want with it."

"It's no use," he said, "I have tried many different ways to prevent this from happening, believe me. But there is always too much. Please Aurielle, it's too late. Get back down now before I injure you."

Smoke was beginning to curl from the soles of his boots Aurielle noticed as Gabriel held what looked like a stitch in his side and grimaced in pain. She could physically see the air before them shimmering with heat that was not from the volcano, a concentration of Magic that was swelling inside Gabriel, getting stronger and stronger as he let his will slip and gave in to it.

It was then that Aurielle confirmed that Gabriel's element was fire. The heat emanating from the volcano was nothing compared to what she felt from him at that moment. Her eyes found his once again, and they were unrecognisable. Heat radiated from his skin, and his eyes were black as two hot coals.

"Gabriel, can you hear me?"

"Please, get away," she thought she heard him whisper.

"Gabriel!" Aurielle found her voice rise in panic.

She faltered as flames erupted around him.

"Gabriel! Stop! Listen to me! Look at me! Gabriel! Don't use it..."

Dimly, she noted Gabriel's expression twist to fear. There was a mælstrom churning up inside him, a violent torrent of Magic that he couldn't control. He would release that Magic on whatever stood in his path, which happened to be her.

Aurielle tried to run, but her ankle failed her, and she fell to the ground, vaguely trying to remember anything that Seaglen had taught her for a predicament like this she watched as Gabriel fell to his knees as well beside her, contorted in pain. Fire surrounded him now, running from head to tœ until she almost could no longer see him.

In what seemed like incredibly slow motion, Aurielle saw Gabriel lose control over his flood of Magic. The air grew intensely hot around them. Flames erupted out from his body and multiplied, catching fire even with the air. They headed for Aurielle, and she prepared to do the only thing she knew that could save her life. Suddenly she doubted herself that she had the strength.

Gabriel's fire incinerated everything as it flared towards Aurielle. Somewhere in the background, strange voices were calling out. Then suddenly, a clear sound rang out. It screamed in her head.

"Act! NOW!"

She reached out and grabbed Gabriel's leg. Amidst the fire, she heard him scream.

CHAPTER 29
THREE BECOMES FOUR

Shumuti woke Sara abruptly up from the middle of a dream about Silverspring and nudged her to get up.

"Aurielle and Gabriel are missing."

"Really?"

"Something outside that feels badly wrong."

Sara's face fell. Spurred on by Shumuti's sense of urgency, she got up quickly, buckling on her sword as they ran out of the cave. Once outside, they turned to look up the volcano. The flames were the apparent draw that led Sara and Shumuti to the top of the mountain. They began to half run, half scramble up the slope and Sara recoiled as the rocks she reached out to grab began to grow painfully hot under her fingers.

As they got nearer, they felt a harsh scalding heat, accompanied by thick smoke that entered their noses, making it hard to breathe. Sara faltered, as a heart-rending cry hit her ears. Shumuti broke over the summit and Sara crashed into her, gripping her shoulder at the sight that reached her eyes. There were flames everywhere, and it was as if the volcano was erupting, but the source was Gabriel. A wall of blistering heat reared up from around him and crashed through the air into Aurielle. She screamed out and was devoured in an instant. Dread rocketed through Sara's bones, and she heard Shumuti dimly shouting.

"Aurielle! Act! NOW!"

She had no hope. She was gone.

"Aurielle!"

She heard Gabriel crying out in pain as well, and both were encircled entirely by fire. Sara and Shumuti stood at the edge of the flames, unable to go forward any further.

"Shumuti!" Sara froze. "What do we do? We have to get to her!"

She moved to dash forward, but Shumuti held her back with a hand.

"Do something!" Sara cried.

"I can't," Shumuti said, "wait. Look there."

Sara felt her cheeks burn from the heat. She squinted towards the whirl of fire where Aurielle had been.

In amongst the unrelenting blaze, gradually Sara began to see tinges of another colour flickering beside the red, and glowing progressively brighter. A whirl of blue water emerged as Sara watched, fighting off the flames that hounded it. The orb of blue was slowly building in size. The mass of water faltered as the fire raged against it from all sides, before gaining momentum once more. There was a yell heard from within the water as, like a breaking wave, it crashed outwards and repelled the fire. A second and a third wave followed before finally, the hunched silhouette of Aurielle emerged and a thick cloud of steam billowed over from the scene.

Everything was drenched, including Aurielle and Gabriel. Both had collapsed on the ground, and Aurielle had one hand on Gabriel's foot. Pools of water lay on the ground about the volcano, and a thin mist of rain hung in the air. Rocks scattered about the ground hissed with steam as the water on them boiled. The spray hit Sara and Shumuti where they stood, and steadily, they felt their faces cool. The scene around them gently smoked as everything became still once more.

Beside her, Shumuti slowly moved and ran over to where Aurielle lay. Sara picked herself up and sprinted after her. Aurielle was on her side with her eyes closed. Was she alive? In a second of fear, the rune reading from Wyn sprung into her mind, as she lay lifeless in Shumuti's arms.

Sara jumped, as a fit of coughing erupted from Aurielle. She was drenched in water and coughed a substantial amount more up. With the help of Shumuti, she managed to sit up and lean against the volcano crater, gasping for breath. Shumuti sighed in relief, and Aurielle managed a weak smile back. Suddenly she started coughing again and stopped.

"Where is Gabriel?" she whispered, "I'm going to kill him."

"No, you're not." Shumuti prevented her from rising. "You're in no fit state to murder anybody."

"Is he still alive?"

"We haven't checked yet. You were the priority."

Aurielle coughed again and joked. "Surely this ought to cancel his membership as a Guardian? He can't even protect himself from Magic."

"He lost control," Shumuti said, "we knew he did this. What happened?"

"I tried to stop him," Aurielle said, struggling again to sit up, "I thought I might be able to help."

Sara looked at the ground. Around the crater summit everywhere was burnt and the heat had even partially melted the rocks. Sara could smell the incinerating tang in the air around them. What she could see around her was a far greater display of destruction than at the Winterburn River. A few feet away, Gabriel had visible steam smouldering from his immobile body.

"I'm sorry, Shumuti," Aurielle said, "I know what I did was wrong. There was nothing else I could think of."

"You did the only thing you could," Shumuti answered.

"What did you do?" Sara asked.

"Instead of using the Magic that is everywhere around us, I used the energy that was in Gabriel to overpower his fire."

"Why is that bad?" Sara asked, "isn't it the same thing?"

"No," Shumuti said, "two properly trained Guardians can combine their Magic to increase its power. But if one is untrained, you are putting them in grave danger by drawing Magic from them."

"And Gabriel is about as far from trained as it is possible to be," Aurielle said, "I could have killed him."

"I think he's still alive," Sara said.

"We should probably check," Aurielle said.

"Can you walk?" Shumuti asked.

"With help."

"Sara, get on her left side and help her down, I'll take a look at Gabriel."

Together they hoisted Aurielle upright, and Shumuti detached herself from the pair.

"He's still alive," she confirmed, "but barely."

"We need to get you both back into the cave," Sara said.

Aurielle managed a nod. Shumuti stood over Gabriel's limp body and hauled him up, grimacing at the weight.

"Are you all right?" Sara asked.

"If we hurry," Shumuti panted.

Aurielle and Sara led the hobble back down the volcano slope. They travelled at a cautious pace, and it took a while to get back safely inside Gabriel's cave. Once inside,

Sara laid Aurielle down and ran back to help Shumuti with Gabriel. Aurielle then drifted off almost instantly.

Sara tried her best to tend to Aurielle and Gabriel, using her notes of what Astrid had taught her about healing. Eventually, when she was satisfied that both would live out the day, they both set to making some food and reviving themselves. It had been a strenuous morning, and the sun was not nearly high in the sky yet.

"They'll both survive, then?" Shumuti asked.

"They'll be fine now, I think," Sara answered, "physically. But I'm not sure that this will have improved their chance of friendship."

"No," Shumuti agreed, "this trip to the volcano has not been what I expected at all, Sara. Gabriel's Magic is so free and wild. In Aurielle's case, and mine, we knew how to control our Magic from the start. Seaglen trained us to do more than we ever would on our own, but we had that initial, intuitive knowledge of how to wield it. Gabriel has none of that, and this complicates matters. We need to get him back to Seaglen before something like this happens again."

"At least Aurielle defeated him," Sara said.

"Only because her element was water," Shumuti replied, "if it had been me up there against Gabriel, I'm not sure that I would have survived."

Shumuti ran a hand through her, unsettled.

"So now there are three of you," Sara said.

"Three Guardians of Magic," Shumuti said, "but four of us to fight our way back to Merrywater."

Sara gave a small smile at her words.

"Do you think he is a friend to us then?"

"I'm fairly confident," Shumuti replied, "despite everything."

Gabriel suddenly let out a soft moan and jerked awake. He stared around wildly, unseeing, and Sara went to his side to calm him back down again.

"Wh...where am I? What happened?"

"You're safe," she said.

"But I went too far this time." Gabriel's eyes were wild. "What did I do?"

"Nothing," Sara said, "everything is fine. You're just hurt. Relax and get some more rest. You'll feel better soon, I promise."

"What happened to Aurielle?" Gabriel asked, paying no attention.

"She's here," Sara reassured him.

"You two almost tore each other apart," Shumuti informed him, ignoring Sara's tactic of trying to calm Gabriel down.

Gabriel turned his head to the other side and saw Aurielle sleeping gently near to him. His eyes took in her face, scattered with burn marks and a singed trail of her hair.

"Oh, no," he groaned.

"She'll recover," Shumuti answered.

"You saw what happened?"

"She took on your fire with her own Magic and defeated it, just about."

"I warned her to run. It's never been that bad before."

"Don't worry," Shumuti said, "when we get to Merrywater, Seaglen will teach you how to stop this from happening."

"It's not possible," Gabriel insisted, "it's too powerful for me ever to control."

"My father uses fire, just like you do," Shumuti continued, "there is no one better out there to train you how to wield it properly."

"He does?"

"He can help you," Shumuti repeated.

"I know so little about this skill I have." Gabriel hid his head in his hands.

"We've got lots of time to explain everything to you," Shumuti reassured him, "but for now, Sara's right, you should sleep and regain your strength."

Shumuti looked at Sara out of the corner of her eye and nodded. Sara opened up a pouch of sweet-smelling herbs.

"Wait!"

"Later," Sara said, wafting the smell over to him, "we'll talk later."

Gabriel slowly gave in to the fragrance of herbs and fell back into his dreams. Sara quickly pulled the cord on the pouch and shut off the scent. With a smirk of satisfaction, she stifled a yawn and got up to go over to the entrance of Gabriel's cave, where Shumuti stood, looking out with her arms folded.

CHAPTER 30
A VISITOR IN THE NIGHT

Over the next few days, Shumuti and Sara looked after Aurielle and Gabriel. Both of them awoke now and then for a little while before falling back into sleep. They ate occasionally but drank more, and four dawns had broken over the volcano by the time that Aurielle had returned to some form of her old self.

Gabriel took longer to make a recovery. Sara had been right about Aurielle. She had seemingly not warmed to Gabriel ever since he had almost singed the flesh off her bones. Half of Shumuti was relieved on the day that Gabriel woke, but the other half of her had been dreading it.

"Oh, you're awake," Aurielle had grunted, and she did not acknowledge him for the rest of the evening. Shumuti and Sara agreed that it had been a fairly disastrous start to their friendship.

The weather grew cold and frosty. The time spent inside the volcano was bearable because they had heating from the core of the mountain, but outside there was a bitter chill in the air that froze their bones and dug deep past any cloak or lined coat that person happened to be wearing.

Shumuti naturally ended up spending more time with Sara than with Aurielle in the volcano. She had become moodier ever since Gabriel had joined them, and so Sara and Shumuti seemed to find they wanted to escape the volcanic cave for long periods and ended up spending the days outside, exploring the mountain.

Shumuti and Sara had planned to let the tension between Aurielle and Gabriel settle down a little before they attempted to begin the journey down the volcano. But when a cold evening storm forced them all together in the warmth of the cave and the weather showed no signs of abating any time soon, they plucked up their courage and spoke up.

"Gabriel, Aurielle," Shumuti began, "Sara and I have been thinking, and we should get down from this mountain before the weather gets any worse here."

"You didn't ask me what I thought," Aurielle objected.

"That's because you've been impossible to talk to for the last few days," Shumuti said.

"Sorry." She appeared genuinely apologetic. "So, what about the other Guardian we found in Lyria?"

"His trail has gone cold by now," Shumuti answered.

"I don't know," Aurielle said, "Seaglen wanted whœver couldn't control their Magic to go back to Thayll. While Gabriel definitely wins the prize for least control over what they're doing, this other stranger still comes quite a close second. Let's try to find him if we can."

"If he is in the city, I know some people who might be able to help gather information about him," Gabriel offered.

"Won't the King be too happy to see you again after you left?" Aurielle asked.

"I am prepared to face him," Gabriel said.

"Well, we're not," Aurielle said, "not if you're going to drag us into a bigger mess if we go down into the city together, searching for a man who might not even be there."

"Then why don't you offer up a better suggestion?" Gabriel said.

A chill wind had gathered around the volcano, and it whistled into the cave. But underneath it, Shumuti swore that she could hear another noise. A series of slow crunches echœd faintly out and she looked up from the fire with her senses alert. All was still, and for a moment, she doubted her ears. Crunch. Slow footsteps in the dark. Shumuti stood up silently to face the entrance, and the blanket around her shoulders slithered down her back and onto the floor.

"Shumuti?" Sara spoke up.

She lifted one hand for silence and listened.

"There's somebody here."

Immediately, Gabriel sprung into action. He stood up and stalked over to the cave opening, pausing to draw his sword as he went. Sara and Aurielle also stood up, a little slower and they joined Gabriel at the entrance.

"What should we do?" Shumuti asked him in a hushed voice.

Gabriel paused in slight surprise that she was letting him take the lead, before opening his mouth. "We need to cut them off. Stop them escaping until we know who they are and why they've come up here. Two of us should take the way over the top of the volcano around the other side and the other two move out and confront them from here. Shumuti, Sara you're the two smallest so you'll get through the tunnel to the top quicker."

"Oh no," Aurielle said, "no way am I going with you!"

"Aurielle, now isn't the time!" Shumuti said.

Aurielle glared at both of them but fell silent.

"Right," Gabriel continued like nothing had happened, "don't let them escape."

Shumuti and Sara nodded and ran back the other way along the tunnel Gabriel had shown them, that led to the top of the volcano, as Aurielle and Gabriel disappeared into the darkness outside. Sara and Shumuti plunged into the passage, one after the other, as the way narrowed. They broke out of the mountainside and abruptly felt the bitter chill of the evening cut into their bones. Shumuti shivered once and began to run.

Gravel skidded about underneath their feet, and they soon shuddered to a halt. Below, the cave entrance was visible from the light of their burning fire. Someone was indeed there, ascending the volcano, so, as silently as they could, Sara and Shumuti shuffled along above the figure, tracking their progress. Shumuti could hardly see a thing in the darkness and nearly jumped enough to reveal their position when the person called out on the path below them.

"Hello?"

Layers of a thick cloak muffled the voice, but Shumuti realised they did not sound entirely unfamiliar. Momentarily distracted, she strained her eyes forward, trying to catch a better glimpse of whœver was down below her. Unable to see anything, Shumuti called back.

"Who are you?"

The figure turned their face upward, striving equally hard to identify whœver called to them. In the dim moonlight, Shumuti noticed a faint hue of purple to their cloak.

"Shumuti?"

"Aaaarrrghhhh!" A battle cry rang out from above as Gabriel and Aurielle sprang out of nowhere each, swords drawn and ready.

"What is your business here?" Gabriel challenged the figure, "declare yourself!"

"Stop!" Shumuti cried out, "I think I know-!"

"Speak!"

"Gabriel, wait!"

"Shumuti, what do you mean?"

"Wyn?" Aurielle questioned in disbelief.

"What's happening?" Gabriel asked in confusion.

"Gabriel, it's all right!" Shumuti laughed. "We know her."

"Shumuti, it is you," Wyn said, "thank heavens, and Sara and Aurielle as well. I need to talk to you."

"We should get back inside first, shouldn't we?" Aurielle said.

"Yes," Shumuti agreed.

Gabriel led the way back into the warmth of the cave, and they swathed themselves in blankets, huddling as close to the fire as it was possible to, without actually catching alight. He turned to his newest guest in be-musement.

"So, not meaning to be rude but, who are you?"

"Her name is Wyn," Aurielle answered, "one of the women we stayed with in Lyria."

"Right," Gabriel said, "but you didn't come all this way up here for a chat, I am guessing?"

"No," Wyn said, "that's true, I didn't."

"Has something happened?" Shumuti turned to her with concern.

"Yes." Wyn swallowed.

"What is it?" Sara asked.

"It's Gail." Wyn wrung her hands. "She's been...taken."

"What do you mean?" Shumuti asked, "taken where?"

"To the Citadel."

"Why?" Aurielle asked, aghast.

"Oh, Aurielle," Wyn replied, with tears in her eyes, "they think she can use Magic."

"No!" Shumuti cried, "what happened? Why would they think that?"

"Because after you left, there was a green light and a disturbance in the alleyway where she was standing. The guards at the wall-gate knew something was out of the ordinary, and they took her away."

"But she can't use Magic," Aurielle said.

"A man was found with her. They were both taken."

"A man?" The hairs on Shumuti's neck prickled. "Who?"

"I have no idea," Wyn answered, "but Shumuti, they will never let her go now. The King has become quite intent on finding you. Lyria is being searched for any others who can use Magic. I don't know what will happen to her."

Shumuti saw the fear in her eyes and looked up at the others apprehensively. She knew that they were all thinking the same thing.

"Well then," Shumuti said, "we'll just have to go and get her out of there."

"Shumuti, it's not that easy," Aurielle said, "this is the King's Citadel. We won't be able to march in and demand they free her."

"We can if we have something he wants in exchange," Shumuti said, "the King is searching for us after all, not Gail. Perhaps it's time that we let him find us."

"Your captured friend may have already told him about you," Gabriel said, "I assume she also knew you were coming up here."

Shumuti nodded.

"Then your choices are either to go to the King before he comes to find us here, or flee Attaching," Gabriel said.

Shumuti looked at Wyn. "We can't do that."

"What if this man they caught with her is the same one from the inn?" Sara spoke up.

"The King will not let him go," Gabriel warned them.

"It looks like we're getting involved with the King whether we want to or not," Aurielle said.

"Then we'll go?" Sara said.

"First, we need to think up a plan," Gabriel said.

"We'll get Gail out of there, I promise," Shumuti said to Wyn.

Wyn sighed in relief. "I knew the journey would be worth it."

"Let me think this over." Gabriel stood up and walked slowly out, with his head bowed.

"Shumuti?" Wyn turned to her. "Would you mind if I took up a bed for a while? I think the journey has drained me a little."

"Of course."

Quickly they arranged a makeshift bed for Wyn, and gratefully she lay down, falling asleep almost immediately. They left the cave to let her rest and wandered outside. It was deep night outside, and the wind had now died down. Gail was out there in the Citadel, possibly held with the robed man they were trying to find. Alone once more, Shumuti, Sara and Aurielle paused for a moment and sat down on the rocks.

"Shumuti, what are we going to do?" Aurielle asked.

"Seaglen warned us to stay away from the Lyrian Citadel," Shumuti said, "he dœsn't trust the King and getting involved with royal politics is the last thing we want to do. But at the same time, there is more going on here than I realised. These vultures are related to Magic after all and therefore, it's our job to deal with them. If the King is trying to do the same, maybe we should offer our help to him."

"Either way, it's our fault that Gail got captured," Aurielle said, "she was trying to help us. We need to rescue her."

Shumuti nodded. "I know. We owe it to Wyn and Isa as well. It's just such a risky idea."

"Do you suppose the man found with her is the same one we were searching for?" Aurielle asked.

"I hope so," Shumuti said, "it seems he might have been trying to track us down, at the same time as we were searching for him."

"I just hope the King can be trusted," Aurielle said.

"His intentions do seem good, despite his actions," Shumuti said, "but I just don't see how he is going to let anyone with the skills that we have go about our business freely after this."

"I don't know if we'll end up regretting it," Aurielle said, "but at least for the moment our intentions are aligned."

"I thought the journey back would be smoother," Shumuti admitted.

"Whatever happens, we'll face it together," Aurielle said, "so far, we've been successful every time, even if it wasn't in the way we expected."

"You're staying with us you know, Sara." Shumuti caught her eye. "Right up to the end."

She met Shumuti's gaze and held it. "I know. I'm not going anywhere."

"Good."

Out beyond Lyria and the volcano, they saw the faintest band of light blue begin to sweep across the eastern horizon. Shumuti had a sinking feeling that things would only get more complicated from here. They had still not discovered who was misusing Magic and attacking the regions east of the Winterburn River, but they had begun to piece things together and perhaps the King was the ally they needed to understand what was happening and deal with this threat. Down in the Citadel below, Gail and this stranger needed their help, and Shumuti had a responsibility not to let them down.

Acknowledgements

I've been writing bits and pieces with these characters and this world for a while now. First, as hand-written stories in notebooks when I was little and then on a computer, given to me by my Uncle Frank, and recently I've written this story as it is now, so I want to thank everyone who's given me support, even if it was a long time ago.

Thanks to all my family and friends, for inspiring bits of the story and for helping me get some of the details right. To my Mum, Granma, Jemma, Sheila, Christine, Barbara, Vicky and Heather for being willing to read parts of many drafts of this book and helping me decide on various ideas.

To Vicky, my original writing buddy. Thanks for keeping me excited to write and read new books that you had discovered. I'd say we should publish the story we wrote together but I don't think the world is ready for it.

Also, thank you to Liam, who kept asking me when I was going to publish my book, until I finally felt like I had no excuse not to give it a go. You helped inspire me to want to follow what I'd always dreamed of doing. To Mark from Sulis International Press for all your help with the editing and for agreeing to publish my book in the first place.

Lastly, I want to thank you for picking up a copy of my book. I hope you enjoy reading it as much as I did writing it.

About the Author

Melissa Nash was born in South Africa, grew up in Yorkshire and studied Geography at Aberystwyth University in Wales. She has spent the last few years travelling and working as a freelancer and musician, all the while gathering ideas to combine her interest in the natural environment and fantasy into her first novel, Autumn.

If you enjoyed this book, please consider leaving an online review. The author would appreciate reading your thoughts.

You can follow the author on social media
Instagram: *@melnash*
Twitter: *@melnash*

About the Publisher

Sulis International Press publishes fine fiction and non-fiction in a variety of genres.

For more, visit the website at
https://sulisinternational.com

Subscribe to the newsletter at
https://sulisinternational.com/subscribe/

Follow on social media
https://www.facebook.com/SulisInternational
https://twitter.com/Sulis_Intl
https://www.pinterest.com/Sulis_Intl/
https://www.instagram.com/sulis_international/

9 781946 849649